Death Taker

BOOKS BY J. C. MCKENZIE

The Lark Morgan Series

Death Stealer (prequel)

Death Maker

Death Raiser

Death Taker

Isle and Eyrie Series

Cormorant Run

Heir of the Eyrie

House of Moon and Stars

The Night House

House of Chaos

Crawford Investigations

Conspiracy of Ravens

Nevermore

Queen of Corvids

The Call of Corvids

From the Shadows

Into the Fire

Dark Legacy

Embrace the Flame

The Carus Series

Shift Happens

Beast Coast

Carpe Demon

Shift Work

Beast of All

Obsidian Flame

Dangerous Dreams

Dangerous Liaisons

Dangerous Decisions

That Old Black Magic

The Good Griffin

Standalones

Immortal Throne (with Harper A. Brooks)

Call of the Deep (The Shucker's Booktique)

Stormbound (Be My Love)

DEATH TAKER

J. C. McKenzie

COPYRIGHT INFORMATION

Death Taker

Contact Information: jcmckenzie@jcmckenzie.ca

Cover Art: Tricia Beninato

Character Art: Kalynne_Art

Publishing History:

First JCM Publications Edition, 2023

ISBN: 978-1-990143-28-1 (print)

ISBN: 978-1-990143-29-8 (ebook)

To all the dreamers who look at the shadows and wonder, "what if?"

Thank you.

You're entering the creative domain of a Canadian author. There will be a combination of British and American spellings, a combination of measurement systems, and maybe even a little French thrown in to spice things up. You've been warned...

This book contains explicit language, open-door sex scenes (yes, finally), ghosts, spirits, souls, skeletons, bones, violence, blood magic, necromancy, and animal sacrifices. This book also contains death, grief, and loss.

Please read with care.

"A gift from the sea of the dead is the key to the door of the living."

~ The Book of Life

Lark Morgan's
Rules to Necromancy

1. ~~Never use your own blood~~
2. Never meet the Lord of the Veil
3. Never run into a barghest
4. Never reveal your lineage
5. Never take more than you need

CHAPTER ONE

"Where do you think you're going?" My brother's booming voice stopped me at the door leading out of our two-bedroom apartment.

The noise from the traffic outside filtered through the weak seals around our apartment's windows, and the news reporter on the television in the other room dutifully announced a story about another werewolf sighting, but what I fixated on was the mixture of judgement and worry in my twin's voice.

With my hand grasping the metal doorknob, I hesitated. "We talked about this."

"The fuck we did. Get your ass back here."

I sighed and turned around, my leather outfit creaking with the movement. Logan's pained expression stabbed at my heart. "It's been a week, Logan. It's time for me to venture outside. You can't keep me in bubble wrap forever."

Logan crossed his arms over his chest, the thin, cotton shirt stretching over his muscles. At six foot three, my twin was a taller, stronger, masculine version of myself. He had the same black-brown hair, piercing blue eyes, fair skin, and attitude problem. "You were stalked by an unknown rose-giving weirdo, abducted and shot by a sadistic murderer, and nearly magically coerced into a deal with the Lord of the Veil."

"And I survived," I pointed out. "Steve is dead, and the Lord of the Veil kept his oath and let me go. And I no longer owe him a favour. Win, win."

"You were *shot*." His expression darkened, the shadows around the room clinging to his features. "And the roses?"

"Stopped," I said. "I received a grand total of two—one outside our apartment door and one inside my room. I know Steve said he wasn't responsible, but as you pointed out, he was a fucked up serial killer. He probably lied." While I could detect when the dead lied, or at least tried to lie, from the flare of death energy, I had no such ability with drabs.

"And if it wasn't him?"

"You probably scared them off with all your safety precautions, but I have no less than three knives strapped to me just in case some random person tries to approach me with flowers. I refuse to live the rest of my life closeted away in my apartment and supervised by my overprotective twin with stab first, ask questions later tendencies."

Logan vibrated, his gaze darting to the door as if calculating whether he could beat me to it and lock me in. He took a deep breath and rolled his shoulders back. "How's the arm?"

I moved my arm up and down, kind of like I performed half a chicken dance. That wasn't the vibe I was going for. I dropped my arm. "All good."

Logan narrowed his gaze.

"Okay, it aches. And the skin is still healing. But I'm cleared for duty, sir." I mock saluted, probably getting the form horrifically wrong.

Logan glowered, but he didn't tackle me to the ground. And when I reached for the door handle for the second time, he didn't move to stop me.

"You just want to see your cop boyfriend." His scowl turned into a smirk.

"He's not my boyfriend." Sucking his face half off after I survived a murder attempt suggested otherwise, but I hadn't seen Kang since he brought me home.

"He's something."

I flipped up my middle finger at Logan and opened the door. Instinctively, I checked the floor in the hallway. No roses. Had something happened to the person behind it? Like maybe he got ripped to shreds by a barghest on his personal Murder Island? Or, if the roses hadn't been from Steve, did the unknown person just give up? Take a hint? Or were they biding their time so they could also take a shot at abducting me? Did psychos take a number to see who was next in line?

I shivered and my arm ached at the reminder of what happened a week ago.

"You should stay home," Logan shouted as I closed the door.

I ignored him and the ice clinging to my spine. Logan was probably right—I should stay home. But I just couldn't stand staring at the walls, leafing through my copy of Dad's missing persons case, or mindlessly scrolling through social media with all the fake smiles anymore. The online therapy sessions—compliments of victim services—had helped a little, but I itched for everything to return to normal.

With a deep sigh, I hiked my purse on my shoulder and walked down the hall to the stairs to make my way outside. The fresh air hitting my face brushed away some of my worries and fears. The weather was in that sweet spot between summer and fall, where the days were still nice and clear, but the nights cooled off completely. Soon the rain would start and it wouldn't stop for months, so I had to enjoy this weather while it lasted.

The sky had that striking shade of dark blue that faded into inky black. The moon shone down on me, while the crickets and katydids made their final songs of the season. They'd disappear once the temperatures dropped, and I'd miss their music during the night.

Some people hated the persistent noise they made, but to me they heralded late summer nights and memories of good times.

At least until recently.

I turned the corner and skidded to a stop.

A tall man with striking golden eyes and long brown hair that gently fell to his shoulders stepped back into the shadows of the alleyway, but it was too late. I'd spotted him.

"Pierre?" I called out.

The young vampire stepped out of the alley, his head bent, his back hunched. He looked like a kid who knew he'd been naughty and was about to get yelled at.

Geez. I wasn't his mom, and he wasn't in trouble.

Pierre wore dark jeans and a black hoodie, but he didn't suit the contemporary outfit. With his long hair, pale face, and the stoic way he carried himself with a stiff back, he'd be better suited wearing the elaborately embroidered coats with large cuffs, long waistcoats with intricate woven patterns made with variously coloured silk threads, and matching breeches reminiscent of the French Rococo era.

"What are you doing here?" I asked. Pierre was the first baby vampire I'd raised for the Master Vampire of Victoria as a part of a deal we'd brokered. In return, Gregor healed Mom's blood from sanguimort, the illness that plagued her. What Gregor didn't realize was I could control vampires with my death magic. If he ever found out, he'd either kill me or find some way to irrevocably bind me to him for all eternity.

No, thank you.

I liked my freedom.

Pierre walked over to me and took my hand to press a chaste kiss on my knuckles. "You've caught me, Ms. Morgan," he said, his voice a rich purr. His golden gaze met mine. "I was spying on you."

"For Gregor?"

He shook his head and gently dropped my hand. "For myself."

I frowned, not sure why Pierre would want or need to spy on me at all.

"I'm worried about you."

Oh.

Well.

Given my recent track record, that was a legitimate concern. I worried about myself, too. "Any particular reason why?"

He shook his head with a small smile. "Do I need to specify? You're still indebted to Gregor. You were recently abducted by a serial killer, and you're constantly placing yourself in unnecessary danger. I have lots of cause to worry."

I'd ask how he knew about the abduction, but if he'd spied on me, he probably overheard Logan losing his shit on more than one occasion. My twin had demanded I raise Steve, my would-be killer so he could beat the crap out of his corpse, but I'd refused. Steve's remains were on Murder Island, and I never wanted to return to that place.

"Do you know of some looming threat to my personal safety?" I asked instead. "Or is this a general warning?"

Pierre sighed dramatically and briefly glanced up at the moon as if to ask for help. "Please, Ms. Morgan. Be careful."

"Did my brother put you up to this?"

Pierre frowned. "I'm not in contact with your brother, though I know of him."

I snapped my mouth shut, not sure what to say to that. Logan was an assassin who did a lot of work for the underground glamy community, but he wasn't supposed to be well-known by anyone. When people discovered his identity, it usually followed with their deaths. Gregor knew the name of my brother, obviously, and had even met him once. But did he know more than that and shared the information with Pierre? Was I overthinking Pierre's comment?

"I can hear the gears turning in that mind of yours," Pierre said, mischief flashing in his gaze and a smile tugging at his lips. "You should never play poker."

I scowled. "What *exactly* do you know about my brother?"

"More than Gregor, and I'll do everything to keep it that way," Pierre said.

"Why?" I asked. "Why would you go against your master like that?"

"You led me out of the veil, *ma belle*," Pierre whispered. He'd said something similar to me before. "You have nothing to fear from me."

"But I should fear Gregor?" I asked.

I always had a healthy dose of respect and fear for Gregor, he was the Master Vampire of Victoria, after all, and ruled by blood, but Pierre's words seemed to imply something else had shifted to place me in more danger.

"He doesn't trust you," Pierre said.

Well, the feeling was mutual.

CHAPTER TWO

I stepped under the police tape blocking off the familiar busy Victoria intersection and swore. After parting ways with Pierre, I had made my way to the crime scene. Kang had texted with the location over an hour ago, asking me to consult on the case, and after my confrontation with my brother and chatting with Pierre, I was late.

The night air was thick with the power of death and the pulsing red and blue lights from police vehicles cast an eerie glow over the active scene. In the middle of the intersection, a white tarp covered what was presumably a body.

"About fucking time, Morgan." Detective Kang, wearing plain clothes and a sour expression, stomped over to me. Tall, with broad shoulders, chiselled features, smooth skin, black hair, and dark brown eyes,

Connor Kang was a sight to behold during any of his emotional states.

Right now, he wore anger really well.

"Good to see you, too, Detective." I might've used a sarcastic tone, but I meant every word. God, he looked good. Though he had different ancestry, he always reminded me of a younger Keanu Reeves.

My mind flashed back to our kiss last week. He'd stamped his claim on me with his tongue as we stood over the bloody remains of my would-be killer. I would've gladly done more with him, but he'd dropped an absolute truth bomb on me, and my brain had short-circuited. The trip home had been quiet. I'd sat in the passenger seat of Kang's car, shaking from shock while he drove. He'd held my hand the entire time until he delivered me to my apartment and my over-protective brother.

Logan had shouted at Kang, but the detective calmly stood in the face of my twin's rage and quietly explained the events and provided information on how to get in touch with a good therapist.

I'd taken the week off work and Logan only allowed me out of the house—under his supervision—to go into the precinct to make a formal statement. Kang hadn't been there, but I didn't need to talk to him to know it was best to leave out the part where Steve got ripped to shreds by a glamy when I made my statement.

Drabs—or non-magical humans—might accept the

existence of supernatural beings, but they sure as heck didn't like it. We still missed out on job opportunities and security, but at least we had the better nickname. Referred to as glamies for our ability to cast glamour, even though most of us didn't have the skill —myself included—magical beings had been out of the supernatural closet since the Awakening forty years ago. Society still had a long way to go toward acceptance and empathy, but even with all the crap flung my way, I'd rather be a glamy than a drab any day.

"How are you?" Kang's rumbling voice interrupted my thoughts. He'd dropped his voice and his expression softened.

I tightened my hands into fists and straightened my back. "I'm fine."

"Fine?" Something dark flashed in Kang's gaze and he pressed his lips together while he studied me for a tense moment. "Okay. Let's pretend I believe that. Do you want to explain why the victim of that search you asked me to do last week just showed up in my crime scene?"

I rocked back on my heels. "What are you talking about?"

"Lily Zheng." He waved his hand and stepped back to provide me with an unobstructed view of the tarp-covered body in the middle of the intersection. "Also known as Zheng Mei Hua."

According to police records, Lily and her unborn

child had died at this intersection four years ago in a hit and run while waiting for her boyfriend to pick her up.

A resident nearby had noticed the appearance of Lily's ghost and had hired me to investigate. I got as far as identifying the ghost but met a dead end—pun not intended—when I discovered Lily's remains had been stolen from her gravesite.

"There's no way that's Lily." I nodded at the fresh corpse. "I spoke to her ghost. Embalmers are good, but not that good."

"It's her. Fingerprints match. We'll get dental records to confirm."

"But...how?" My gaze drifted to the apartment building where Cathy lived. She had been an odd client and her interest in Lily's ghost even odder. After I finished with the victim, I was going to ask Cathy some pointed questions.

"No one knows and it's a mess," Kang said. "My guess is it's some freaky death magic glamy shit at play."

"Is that why you got called in?" I asked. "To provide helpful expert evaluations like that?"

Kang narrowed his eyes. "I got called in because I opened a case to pull those records for you."

I flinched. Right. I was the reason this case was dumped on his already full plate of work. "Sorry."

"I don't fucking care about that," he said. "I'd just like something to make sense."

"When and how was she discovered?" I asked.

"We're still pulling local security footage," Kang answered. "But as far as we can tell, the body just showed up. There are no wounds, Lark. None. Not even the ones she sustained in the motor vehicle accident."

"Is it possible Lily wasn't actually involved in an accident four years ago? Mistaken identity?"

Kang frowned. "We're pulling the coroner's report, but with a hit and run, I'm assuming they did their due diligence to identify the victim."

"Well, someone fucked up."

He blinked at me.

I held up my hands. "Hey. It's not me this time."

He shook his head and walked over to the body.

I followed. "Hopefully, she can provide some clarification."

Kang kept shaking his head and crouched to pull back the tarp to reveal Lily's unmarred face. The victim had long straight hair and features consistent with East Asian ancestry. With high cheekbones and Cupid's bow lips, she was a striking young woman.

I sucked in a breath. That certainly looked like the ghost I'd met. Only as a ghost she'd had a more hollowed-out, haunted appearance with a large gash down one side of her face, and the hazy outline of her clothes had shown rips and blood stains.

The woman lying on the ground in front of me looked like she was sleeping—no visible signs of trauma, her face and clothes unmarred.

"What is it you're not telling me?" I whispered to Kang.

He glanced up and took in the scene, tracking the movement of the forensics analysts and uniformed officers, before standing. He stepped closer to me. "She doesn't feel right. Something is off."

I leaned in and whispered back, "Is that your detective skills tingling, or your...other skills?"

He crossed his arms, his shirt tightening over his muscles.

I winced. I wasn't sure how to phrase that last part. I'd found out two world-shattering things about Kang a week ago—he was a phenomenal kisser, and he was also a barghest—one of the biggest, baddest, supernatural beings featured in the cautionary bedtime stories told to necromancers since infancy.

Myths and legends portrayed barghests as demonic dogs or goblin canines who heralded the death of drabs and fed on the souls of necromancers. At least that was what the legends said.

Kang hadn't attempted to eat my soul yet, but when he released his tight control over his magic, his death energy made my blood sing. Instead of being scared of him, I just wanted to strip him down and do very naughty things.

Though Kang had texted me a couple of times over the last week to check in and ask me how I was doing and whether I needed anything, I hadn't seen or spoken to him in person. But I'd thought about him.

I'd thought about him a lot.

"How's your arm?" His gaze dropped to where my jacket covered the still-healing wound. Levi, the Lord of the Veil, had healed the majority of the damage, but it still ached.

"Much better. I—"

"If you two are done whispering sweet nothings to each other..." Detective Jacobs interjected. "I'd really like to hand over this chicken."

Kang's partner stood a few feet away holding a healthy white hen in his arms. Tall, with blond hair, blue eyes and fair skin, Jacobs gave off serious golden retriever vibes.

If Kang was salacious nights full of dark promises that made my blood trill, Jacobs was gloriously bright summer days full of sunflowers and laughter. The two detectives played off each other in that bad cop good cop kind of way all the time. Jacobs was also one of the few people who knew Kang's true glamy identity.

And he'd keep his partner's secret. The Victoria Police Department was one of those agencies that still needed to work on acceptance. The most progressive thing they did, at least on the books, was hire me as a consultant.

I held out my arm toward Jacobs and flapped my hand. "You're relieved of your chicken duties, Farmer Joe."

Jacobs sighed and held out the chicken for me to take. I hated this part of the job the most. Death raising did not occur without a sacrifice. Blood for blood, death had to occur in order to bring life—even if it was temporary. I could either sacrifice another living thing, or use my blood, and given that my blood would send me to the veil where I'd have to face the Lord of the Veil who wanted to use me, I planned to stick to Option A.

The chickens were all ethically sourced and their deaths were not made without deep consideration—they were either laying hens at the end of their life and riddled with cancer where a quick death was an act of mercy, or they were poultry hens that would go to feed families. After I used this chicken's lifeblood to recall Lily's soul from the veil, the poultry chicken would be placed in a sealed bag and taken to a local butcher.

I still felt like shit every time, though.

With a deep breath, I pulled out my knife and went through the motions of calling Lily's spirit.

Nobody came.

Or rather, Lily's soul did not answer my call.

I tried again.

Still nothing.

My heartbeat thudded in my ears as my focus narrowed and I pumped more magic into the incantation.

Nothing.

My magic snapped back, and I stumbled to the side with a loud curse.

"Is the spirit attacking her?" Jacobs asked. "Should we do something?"

As a drab, Jacob couldn't see or hear spirits. Kang could but there was no spirit dancing around for him to spot.

"What's going on, Morgan?" Kang asked.

"The spirit isn't answering."

"Like the summoning slaughter stuff?" Kang asked.

A shiver wracked my body. Kang had called me to a bloody scene where a summoning had gone wrong. All that remained of the victims were enough blood to indicate at least five people died, a severed finger and a lot of questions. When I'd tried to raise the owner of the finger, the spirit had appeared but something, or someone prevented him from answering my questions, and the crime remained unsolved.

"No. The summoning slaughter was different," I answered Kang's question. "That spirit answered my call but wouldn't or couldn't respond to anything I asked."

"And this is different?" Jacobs asked.

"There's nothing. No tug, no attempt to respond to me at all." My stomach twisted and fell.

"How is that possible? You always call the spirit," Jacobs said.

And he was right. While other necromancers might struggle to recall a powerful spirit, I never faced any such difficulties. Until now. Was this what it felt like to other necromancers when their magic failed?

Had my magic failed me? I gathered my power around me. It thrummed in the air.

Kang sucked in a breath.

No. My power hadn't failed me at all.

I wiped the thin sheen of sweat that had begun to form on my forehead.

"What does this mean?" Kang asked. He clenched his teeth together hard enough to make the muscles along his jawline ripple. Unleashing more of my magic had visibly affected him. Maybe I should douse him with it again to see what happened.

But not right now.

We had a crime to solve and Kang had asked what the lack of response from Lily's soul meant.

"I don't know," I answered.

CHAPTER
THREE

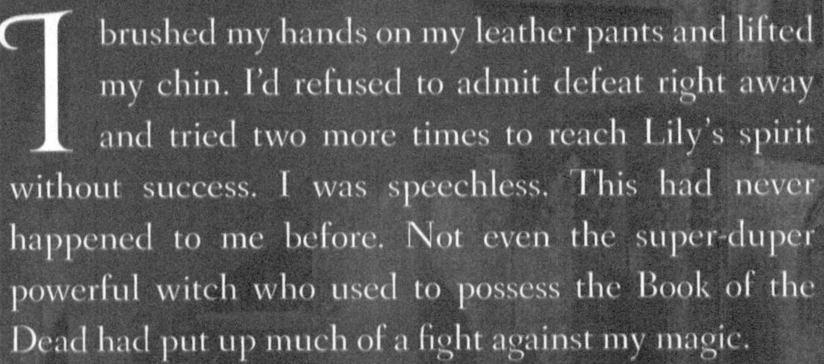

I brushed my hands on my leather pants and lifted my chin. I'd refused to admit defeat right away and tried two more times to reach Lily's spirit without success. I was speechless. This had never happened to me before. Not even the super-duper powerful witch who used to possess the Book of the Dead had put up much of a fight against my magic.

"Is there a record of Lily being a glamy of some sort?"

"No, and I would've told you if there was anything in her file," Kang answered.

If the deceased was a glamy, they could potentially resist the call of a necromancer if they had a strong enough spirit or the necromancer was weak. I had encountered a bit of a fight before but had always prevailed.

This was different though. This hadn't been a battle between two powerful beings.

"There was nothing," I mumbled. "No response at all. Not even a tingle of recognition."

"A tingle?" Jacobs asked.

I shrugged. When he said it like that, it sounded a little silly, but it really was the best description for how it felt when a spirit first recognized my call.

"I don't know what's going on." I pointed at the apartment building overlooking the intersection. "But I know who might."

Kang followed me as I walked out of the crime scene and made my way to the front entrance of Cathy's apartment building. Cathy had hired me over two weeks ago to find out who Lily was and help her finally rest instead of haunting the streets and causing car accidents.

An older man with a labradoodle walked out of the complex as we arrived, and I quickly reached out before the front door closed and locked behind him.

"Hey!" The man with the dog stopped long enough for Kang to flash his badge. With a grumble, the stranger carried on and the door closed with us standing in the lobby.

Kang shoved his badge back into his pocket. "You've been avoiding me."

I stiffened. "Not true."

Kang folded his arms over his chest. "I called."

"You texted."

He smirked. "I texted and all I got in response were thumbs up reactions and a gif of someone walking into a door."

"That was a funny gif."

His lips quirked up at the corners. "It was, but I wanted to know you were okay."

And I wanted him to think I was strong.

"I do," he said.

"What?" Crap. I'd said that last part out loud.

"I do think you're strong, Lark. You're one of the fiercest people I know. It's not a weakness to ask for help or to admit you're having a hard time. What you went through..." He clamped his mouth shut and sharply inhaled before continuing. "You never should have gone through that. It's okay to not be okay. But if I'm being completely honest, I don't think that is why you were avoiding me."

I sighed and tried to shrug away the tension knotting my shoulders. "I wasn't avoiding you."

He waited.

"Okay, maybe a little. But not because of what you think."

"So you're not avoiding me because you're scared of what I am?" He raised an eyebrow.

"Okay. Maybe it's a little of what you think, but not really."

"Are you going to start making sense?"

"Probably not." My heart thundered in my chest. I'd mentally prepared to see Kang tonight, but I hadn't prepared for this conversation.

He narrowed his eyes.

"We should probably place this conversation on hold and go speak to Cathy." I pointed at the hallway we needed to walk down.

"She's not going anywhere," he said. From his body language, neither was he.

"Look. I grew up with stories about barghests. They're supposed to be monstrous demon dogs that herald a person's death."

"Mmhmm." He nodded. "Sounds scary."

I scowled. "They're omens of impending doom, full of potent death magic and ready to consume the souls of their enemies—specifically necromancers."

"Terrifying."

I frowned. "Are you mocking me?"

"A little." He stepped forward, gaze flashing. "Is this your way of telling me I scare you?"

"You do scare me."

He froze.

"Tremendously."

He nodded slowly to himself and stepped back to give me more space.

"But not because of what you are," I finished, not liking the hurt expression on his face one bit. He'd ripped Steve apart because he thought Steve had killed me. Hell, he probably still would've torn him to shreds for abducting me in the first place even if he knew I was safe. But I wasn't scared of Kang in that way. I didn't care that he was a barghest. He'd never hurt me. He'd always looked out for me, protected me. Always.

Obviously, the bedtime stories got some things wrong, and I added this to my list of things to grill Mom about when I finally worked up the courage to confront her. Kang wasn't the only one I'd avoided this past week.

Kang frowned again.

Right. I had to explain my last comment.

"I'm not scared of what you are. I'm scared of you because of how you make me feel," I said. Without waiting for a response, I spun on my heel and stalked toward Cathy's apartment. My cheeks burned but at least I'd been honest.

"Lark!" Kang growled. "Get back here."

"No." I shot over my shoulder. We were not having this conversation in some random apartment building lobby.

Kang grumbled some more but ended up following me. When we stopped in front of Cathy's door, I risked glancing up at him.

His gaze flashed brown and black as he lost control of his death magic and a little leaked out. "This conversation isn't over."

"Of course not." I knocked on the door to

announce our arrival. The intensity in Kang's gaze threatened to melt me on the spot. "Just placed on hold."

Kang barred his teeth and a deep rumble rattled in his chest.

Cathy chose that moment to open the door to her apartment. Her eyes widened and she hesitated as if she thought about closing the door in my face.

"Good evening, Cathy, I apologize for the late call. Do you remember me? My name is Lark Morgan and you hired me a few weeks ago to find the identity of the ghost that haunted the intersection outside your home."

"Of course, I remember you. You're hard to forget." Cathy glanced over at Kang.

"This is Detective Connor Kang. He doesn't talk much."

I felt Kang's glare burning a hole into the side of my face but refused to look over at him.

"May we come in?" I asked.

"Uh..." Cathy glanced over her shoulder. "Now isn't a good time."

"Oh, I'm sorry. Do you have company?" Really, it was none of my business. I hadn't anticipated her turning me away and blurted the first question that came to mind in order to stall.

Silly, really.

I should've thought this through better.

Cathy bit her lip. "If I have cops dropping in to

visit, they'll think I'm involved with whatever is going on outside."

"What's going on outside is a dead body. There's an active crime scene outside your apartment," Kang said. "Hardly unexpected to have a cop stop by to ask if you saw anything."

I squinted at him.

Kang gave me a one-shoulder shrug. He may have received the message to stay quiet, but apparently, he wasn't listening to it.

Cathy might be my former client, but this was his crime scene.

"I guess." Cathy bit her lip. "This really is a bad time."

"Did you know the body out front is Lily?"

Cathy's eyes somehow widened even more. "The ghost?"

I nodded.

"How is that possible?" she asked.

"I'm not sure," I admitted. "Did you see or hear anything suspicious earlier tonight?"

"Like what?"

"Like a coven of witches chanting or a demon bellowing its rage to the world?" Really, I had no idea. None of this made sense.

"I think I'd remember that," Cathy said.

"I would hope so," I said.

Cathy shook her head and stepped back to close the door some more so only a strip of her body remained visible while the rest of her was hidden by the door.

"If you think of anything or something new comes up, please give me a call." I held out my card.

Cathy waved her hand. "I already have your contact information. I'll call." She stepped back and shut the door in my face.

I stiffened and exchanged a glance with Kang. He nodded toward the hallway, and I followed him to the front of the building.

"That was odd," I remarked.

Kang nodded and pointed at the security camera scanning the lobby of the apartment building. "Not here. Follow me."

He pushed open the door to the building and held it for me. Once I stepped through, he released the door and headed down the street away from the crime scene and the whir of flashing lights.

Instead of saying more to me, he pulled out his phone, hit a contact number and held it to his ear. "It's me. I need you to get a warrant to pull the security footage for a building."

He paused.

"Please."

I smirked. Kang could use a couple of lessons on manners.

He listened to the other person before rattling off the address of Cathy's building and citing the grounds for the warrant. He ended the call without a goodbye.

Looking up, he surveyed the sidewalk and surrounding buildings. His black hair shone under the streetlights and the wind tussled the ends. He'd let it grow out a little longer than he normally kept it.

I balled my hands into fists to stop myself from reaching out to touch his hair. "You need to work on your phone etiquette."

He grabbed my arm and pulled me into the alley between the next two buildings.

"Hey!"

He invaded my space, pushed me against the wall and pressed his body into mine. He braced himself on the wall with one hand and let go of my arm to use his other hand to cup my face. He inhaled deeply while he stroked my jaw with his thumb. "Let's resume our previous conversation."

"Kang..." I tried to straighten my mouth into a stern frown. Very stern. I tried and failed. "You can't just haul me into an alley and manhandle me."

He raised an eyebrow and turned so I had room to shimmy out from my current position. The absence of his body pressing into mine left me cold and irritable.

Dammit.

He called my bluff.

I scowled and remained where I was.

Kang grinned and shifted back, warming my body. He leaned down and whispered into my ear, his breath fanning the sensitive skin of my neck. "I didn't think so."

Well, he definitely had my number, and I wasn't sure if I was upset about it. What was there to be upset about? Besides the whole barghest thing and years of being conditioned to fear him.

"You can't just say what you said and walk away from me, Lark." His chest rumbled, sending vibrations down my body to the tips of my toes. This man could just smother me and rumble and I'd beg him for more.

"I can't remember what I said," I admitted. I'd be surprised if I remembered my own name right now.

"Let me help you out. You said I scared you because of how I make you feel." He leaned in more, pressing his leg between mine so his powerful thigh rubbed against me. "I want to investigate that statement."

"We should be investigating Cathy. She slammed the door in my face and acted shady as fuck."

Kang shook his head and tsked. "Your avoidance skills are no match for my determination, Lark."

I sighed and titled my head back so I could meet his piercing gaze. "I'm not sure what else you want me to say. I kind of already left it out there and now I'm just waiting to see what you'll do with the information."

His gaze flashed and his hand stilled on my jaw. Whatever shield he used to hide his death magic slipped, and power cascaded from him to flow over my skin. The magic fused with my own, sending trills of energy through my body. I closed my eyes and moaned. My whole body hummed with power, the sheer potency shook me to my core. Heat and warmth exploded from within. If I died right now, I'd go with a smile on my face.

"God, that feels so good." I finally opened my eyes to find Kang drinking in my expression with a wild gaze.

Without saying anything, he kissed me.

His magic wrapped around me and made me forget everything else in the world. All that existed was his delicious mouth on mine and I kissed him back as if my entire world depended on it.

Leviathan had once told me I'd never find someone who could make me feel the way he did with his death magic and with a single kiss, Connor had already proven the Lord of the Veil wrong.

Too soon, Kang pulled away. Gaze intense, his chest heaved against mine. He rumbled without speaking as if the beast inside him fought to escape.

"If you had any idea what you did to me," he said. "I've craved you all week and it's been torture staying away."

If I were capable of speech, I'd make some sassy comment, like I hadn't done anything yet, or how I could feel what I did to him pressing into my hip. Or I might ask if that was his beast coming out or if he was just happy to see me.

But nope.

That kiss made speech beyond me, so I mentally ran through the comments and licked my lips.

"You smell delicious." Kang swore and pushed off the wall, raking a hand through his thick black hair.

"I'd really like to point out that I was diligently attempting to focus on the case." I finally found my words and that was what I chose to do with them?

Kang chuckled and shook his head. "I'll let you change the topic this time, Lark, but only because we *do* have a case and Cathy *was* shady as fuck."

"And she shut the door in my face." I pointed at my nose.

"I saw," Kang said.

"I didn't sense any death in her apartment though. Did you get anything? With your...senses."

Kang shook his head and glanced up at the night sky.

"I'm sorry. Was that offensive?"

"No," he said. "Just weird, but I've come to realize something."

"What's that?"

"It's how you deal with awkward and uncomfortable situations and topics." He shrugged. "It's kind of cute."

"Excuse me?" I rested my hand against my heart.

Kang followed my movement, his gaze snagging on my chest.

"That is...entirely too accurate and perceptive for this time of day."

Kang looked up from my breasts. "It's ten in the fucking evening, Lark."

I waved my hand in the air.

"Her house smelled like bleach," he said. "I'm not some sort of bloodhound. My nose is more attuned to present and recently present scents and anything involving souls and the dead. If something or someone had been in her apartment earlier today, I'm not going to catch it. Not unless that something or someone is a spirit from the veil." He opened his mouth to say more but must've thought better of it and shut his mouth.

I straightened. "Cathy has to be hiding something. We should go back."

"*We* should go on a date," he said. "But *we*..." He pointed between us. "Aren't going back. She might be involved or she might've just cleaned. I need to get a search warrant for her apartment and for that, I need probable cause. The body outside her building gave us grounds for a warrant for the security feed from the building. We'll have to watch the footage and see whether or not it will give us enough to get another warrant for Cathy's apartment. Currently, we don't have enough to connect her to the crime."

"We already have a connection. She had me investigate the ghost."

"That's not enough for a warrant and you know it. The ghost haunted this corner so her body showing up here doesn't make Cathy look any more or less suspicious."

I sighed. He was right, of course. But I couldn't bring myself to say it.

Old habits.

"Do you really eat souls?" I asked.

Kang laughed and headed back toward the street. "Let me take you out on another date, and I'll show you what I eat."

CHAPTER FOUR

I stepped into the clearing on Gregor's estate and shivered. The master vampire had called me soon after I left the crime scene and I decided to come straight over instead of delaying. I hadn't seen Gregor for weeks, but I owed him a vampire raising after he provided an additional blood-cleaning session for Mom.

She had an incurable blood disease known as sanguimort and had been on her deathbed when Gregor and I struck a deal. I helped him raise his baby vampires and he cleaned Mom's blood with his own. It worked very similar to making a vampire, the difference being he didn't fully drain Mom of her own blood before providing her with his own. If Mom died with his blood in her system, she could still be raised as a vampire.

She wouldn't want that.

I hadn't avoided Gregor because I owed him a payment. Not only had I been banished to my room to heal after my ordeal and gunshot wound, I was also hiding from Gregor because of what happened when I was last in the veil. One of his vampires had somehow travelled to the veil and infiltrated Levi's castle. He'd attacked me and I'd stopped the vampire from stealing the Book of the Dead.

By controlling him.

Gregor could never find out.

"Good evening, Ms. Morgan." Gregor turned from the group of vampires standing with him in the clearing. Their death energy pinged off me, teasing and tantalizing. Their souls called to me, tempting me to pull the power from their bodies.

Gregor's manicured yard surrounding his multimillion-dollar home in one of the most affluent areas of Victoria, B.C., was a wonder to behold, whether at day or night. Even the moon, with its weaker light, illuminated the emerald green lawn, trimmed to perfection. A tall, thick hedge surrounded the clearing and protected the orderly patches of exposed dirt that marked the graves of unborn baby vampires.

Gregor Fissore looked exactly like what you'd expect of an Italian master vampire. He wore expensive clothing and had his hair fastidiously styled. Despite his avoidance of the sun for centuries, he had a rich olive skin tone. With piercing dark brown eyes, and shockingly white teeth that gleamed in the dark, I sometimes just wanted to stare at him and appreciate his beauty. Sometimes I wanted to make a joke about seeing him on a billionaire romance book cover. I did neither because I valued my life.

Four guards waited patiently behind him. I didn't recognise them with the exception of Esmonde, Gregor's right-hand man. Pierre and Antonia, who usually accompanied Estelle when we went out, were nowhere in sight.

"Hello, Gregor. Where's Estelle?" I asked.

Estelle was his mistress, girlfriend, or whatever vampires called their significant others that spanned lifetimes. She was also his human servant and more recently, my friend.

Usually, Estelle greeted me when I arrived at the mansion, but tonight the front steps had been notably empty.

"She doesn't attend raisings," Gregor said.

And he was right. Estelle never stayed in the clearing, always opting to leave before the magic happened, but I already knew that. And Gregor already knew that I knew that. Why was he being purposefully obtuse?

I narrowed my eyes. "She better be okay."

Gregor rolled his eyes. "Estelle is fine. She's otherwise occupied." He waved at the ground. "Let's start, shall we?"

I stepped forward and Gregor waited patiently.

"We need to renew the blood bond," I said.

"Is that so?" He raised an eyebrow. "Bonds usually last a lot longer than that."

They usually lasted as long as the lifespan of human blood, roughly a hundred and ten to a hundred and twenty days. "I can't feel the bond anymore."

"Have you been to the veil recently?"

I needed to tread carefully. My heartbeat quickened, but it did that every time I thought of the veil. "I got stuck there over a week ago. It's a long story."

"I bet it is," Gregor said.

Sweat pebbled on my nose.

"You smell of fear."

All the vampires watched me now, a predatory gleam in their gazes.

"Yeah..." I licked my lips. "I almost died. A couple of times. I'm...I'm still not over it."

"Does this have anything to do with the injury to your arm?" He leaned forward as though his vision could penetrate my shirt sleeve.

Of course, he'd detect the gunshot wound, even if it was mostly healed. "Yes."

Gregor rocked back on his heels and blinked. His body posture relaxed. "That is understandable."

As if receiving an unspoken message, the other vampires stepped away.

"Did you see the Book of the Dead while you were there?" Gregor asked.

"Yes," I said. "Leviathan was reading it in the library."

"Did you see where he stores it?"

"No," I answered truthfully, though I knew roughly where it was when I was in the freaky death castle, I hadn't technically witnessed Leviathan moving it to that location, nor did I know for certain that's where he stored it. I wasn't lying. Wording was everything.

"Did you see a vampire while you were there?" Gregor asked.

Technically I could lie, but I wouldn't get away with it. Vampires were like walking lie detectors.

"I saw a vampire." Even though only powerful necromancers and barghests had the ability to travel to the veil. I hadn't really thought about it before, but now my brain stuttered on the past events. "How'd he get there?"

"We have our ways," Gregor said, tone clipped. "What happened to him?"

"Leviathan killed him."

One of the guards swore and stalked off.

Gregor continued to watch me, probably taking in every twitch and tick of my expression and change in heart rate. "Did you not think to inform me of this once you returned?"

Fuck. I couldn't claim ignorance. I'd known the vampire was one of Gregor's. I also couldn't let the conversation lead to how I stopped the vampire.

Gregor would kill me.

Or try to enslave me, which was pretty much the same thing, and in some ways, worse.

"Do you want to know about every vampire death?" I asked.

"Do you see that many?"

"Well...no." I looked away. "I'm sorry, Gregor. I was dealing with my own crap and didn't consider how it would feel to be on your side and not knowing. I should've reached out."

Gregor frowned.

Silence descended on the clearing, the vampires more still than the leaves on the surrounding hedge.

"Apology accepted." He held his arm out and waved me forward. "Let's renew the bond and get this vampire out of the soil."

I never thought I'd be glad to hear those words.

CHAPTER
FIVE

A misty, ethereal fog shimmered with an otherworldly glow and sifted over the uneven, barren ground. Spirits floated around me, caressing my skin. My nails tingled and grew into long talons and my hair lifted from my shoulders as if I held on to one of those static machines high school teachers hauled out of a dusty back room for a lesson or two. The veil always had this effect on me.

I'd successfully pulled the new vampire's soul into her slumbering body to rise from the ground and then I blinked to find myself back in the veil.

Not good.

I'd only just left the place. When I was last here, I discovered Levi wanted to use me to form a portal he could travel through to the living realm. He didn't struggle to form portals for me to use, but as the Lord of the Veil, he was trapped in the land of souls. Apparently, he desperately wanted a way out, and my blood was the ticket.

I shivered.

The spirits lurked around me, pulling at my essence and magic as if beckoning me to stay.

Yeah, no.

I didn't know a lot of facts about Levi. My knowledge stemmed from those cautionary tales that had obviously gotten a few things wrong, if barghests were any indication. But there had to be a very good reason Leviathan was trapped in the veil.

One of the legends said the fae created the veil to imprison Leviathan before he destroyed our world. Out of all the theories I'd heard over the years, that one seemed the most plausible.

Helping him seemed like a very bad idea.

Luckily, Leviathan couldn't force me to give him blood. According to the Book of the Dead, he needed my willing participation.

Grasping my magic, I reached inside to find my bond with Gregor. The magical tether acted as an anchor to the living realm, and I planned to haul ass back there.

"Leaving so soon?" Levi's deep voice broke my concentration.

I sighed and released the bond. Levi wouldn't harm me, but I still needed to be careful.

"I didn't want to impose." I batted my eyelashes.

Levi stood by the front gates to his castle, wearing

all leather and an amused grin. He had the kind of beauty that hurt to look at. A muscle-bound giant, with features that appeared etched in stone, Levi had black eyes that tracked every movement and power that tried to lure mine out to play.

"I was surprised to feel your magic in the veil again so soon."

"Vampire raising. I had to pay a debt."

"Ah..." Levi nodded. "Is this for the same vampire who sent one of his minions to steal from me?"

"Yes, and no I won't take a message to him." Getting between the Master Vampire of Victoria and the Lord of the Veil? No, thank you. I might surround myself with death, but I didn't have a death wish.

Levi snapped his fingers theatrically.

I snorted and studied the spirits floating by. They seemed calmer today. They usually whipped by me, fast and feral, causing my hair to float as though I were submerged in water. My hair was still lifted, and my nails elongated, but the souls were gentle today. They whispered along my skin like a soft caress.

"Does the vampire master know of your involvement with his minion's death?" Levi asked.

"Involvement? I didn't do anything."

"Gregor won't see it that way."

His spirit spies kept him well-informed. Maybe I told him Gregor's name before. Maybe I didn't. "Are you threatening me?"

"Of course not. Seems rather counterintuitive to

harass the one person I'm trying to win over. I'm concerned for your safety."

I swallowed. "He doesn't know."

Levi studied me for another long second. "You are not allowed to be harmed. When he finds out and tries to exact his revenge on you, remind him of that."

When, not if.

I didn't like his word choice.

I shivered.

More spirits floated by, creating a moving cocoon around me. Were they trying to keep me warm?

A thought pinged in my mind. "What would cause a spirit to ignore my call?"

Levi frowned. "Your call? They would've had to be exceptionally strong in life to fight your power in death."

I shook my head. "There was no fight. There was nothing at all. Not even a ping of awareness."

"An old soul? They'd have to be ancient, but they might've been reborn."

"No. Four years dead."

"Ah, well." He shrugged. "That probably means the spirit was destroyed."

I hesitated. Though Kang had warned me I might destroy the spirit from the summoning slaughter if I kept trying to force it to speak, I'd thought at the time he was exaggerating or speaking figuratively. I'd never heard of a soul actually being destroyed by anyone other than Leviathan or barghests. "How does that happen?"

"Someone destroys it."

"Who?" Me? Could I have accomplished the task had I kept going?

"You do not wish to meet those capable of destroying souls," Levi said. "I suggest you drop it."

"Can you?"

"Destroy souls?" He cocked his head, amusement tugged at his lips. "Yes, I can."

"Have you destroyed one recently? Like in the last two weeks?"

Levi smiled slowly, flashing his long white fangs. "As a matter of fact, I have."

"Was her name Lily Zheng?"

Levi's smile faltered. "Am I supposed to know who that is?"

"Maybe?"

We stared at each other, neither of us blinking.

"Who the fuck is Lily Zheng?" Levi snapped.

"New case. Who the fuck did you destroy?"

"Steve. I crushed his soul after you left. He touched you, hurt you. He planned to kill you and he needed to pay for that. Permanently."

Oh.

I scratched my head. If I were a good person, I'd feel remorseful for the loss of an eternal soul, but Steve had hunted women like deer and killed them. He'd tried to do the same with me, and I still saw him in my nightmares with that stupid rifle every fucking night.

Fuck Steve.

He deserved his soul getting crushed.

"Thank you," I whispered.

Levi nodded. "Now, follow me and let me take you to your room."

"I'm not staying." I reached for my bond with Gregor. I highly suspected Levi could block me somehow, at least when my bond with Gregor was weak, but hopefully, he wouldn't try to trap me here.

"How am I to turn you to my cause if you don't provide the opportunity for me to do so?" He flashed me a charming smile.

"I'm not going to help you."

"You will see things my way."

I shook my head. "There's nothing you can say or do and there's nothing you have that will convince me to willingly help you."

I pulled on the anchor to Gregor, blood thrumming in my veins. The master vampire's awareness on the other side of the bond pinged to life. My body grew weightless as the portal opened.

"I wouldn't be so sure of that." He turned and walked away as the bond pulled me back to the living.

CHAPTER SIX

I stared at the gruesome scene laid out before me and swallowed down the stomach acid threatening to bubble up my throat. I'd managed one night of normal work after seeing Gregor before Kang texted me another address.

Thankfully, I was alone with Kang in the small living room of a house on a quiet side street. I took deep breaths and waited for the nausea to pass. Kang had asked the technicians to leave so we had privacy to discuss the massacre without anyone overhearing, but I was thankful no one besides Kang would witness me violently throwing up if I couldn't tame the turmoil in my gut.

"You really know how to charm a lady," I hissed through my clenched teeth.

"I wanted to see you again," Kang said with a straight face.

"You don't need a gruesome murder scene to call me, you know." I waved at the blood-soaked carpet a foot away.

"I know." His gaze raked my body. "But I went a whole week without seeing you, Morgan. Humour me."

I sighed and turned to the scene again, the morbid view feeling eerily familiar. The living room was dimly lit with an outdated 70s style chandelier hanging from the ceiling. The flickering light cast shadows on the faded floral wallpaper that had stained rectangles marring its pattern from where pictures used to be mounted. The furniture was a mixture of old and worn-out pieces with the exception of a gamer chair tucked into a large desk in the corner of the room. On top of the desk sat a wide screen monitor and computer.

Opposite of the gaming station, an old stone fireplace dominated the far side of the room, its red and brown bricks decorated with thinly spun cobwebs and dust. The air in here should've smelled like burning wood or smoke, but all I smelled was death.

The chandelier, wallpaper, furniture, and fireplace weren't the things that made this room feel familiar.

It was the blood.

Large blood stains pooled in five places, all of which were arranged in a circle. The small sections of the carpet not covered in blood showed the remains of a salt circle.

"Another summoning slaughter?" I asked, though I didn't need the answer. Kang had called me to one of these before, but I couldn't get the soul to speak. Someone or something had controlled it from the other side, and I'd nearly ripped the soul in half trying to force it to answer my questions.

"Looks like it."

I glanced up at his angry tone. "No hunches this time? Your glamy senses aren't helping you connect the dots?"

"It's been cleaned."

I raised my eyebrows and waved my hand at the blood spatter on the walls.

"It's like last time. Aside from the blood, salt circle and the one bone we found, there's little to no evidence —no hair, flesh, bones, bodies... Not even a sign of struggle."

A chill swept through my body. What had happened to these people? "I thought maybe the first scene was the consequences of summoners making bad choices..."

Kang nodded. "But a second scene implies someone else is pulling the strings. I agree. I think the five bodies were sacrifices, and once the person got what they wanted, they used magic to cleanse all traces of their involvement."

"You said you planned to bring in an occult specialist?"

He grunted. "They confirmed what Jacobs and I

already figured out—magically cleaned. They couldn't identify the source of the magic, either. That's part of the spell, apparently. Forensics confirmed the previous scene involved five bodies based on the amount of blood and blood types. The DNA analysis will take a little longer. They also confirmed the white powder is salt."

So many questions remained unanswered, including the glaring one about the purpose of these circles. Were the summoners bringing something in or sending something away? Only one way to find out.

"You said you found a bone?" I asked.

Kang hesitated.

"Kang?"

He pulled an evidence bag out of a bin sitting on the nearby counter and held it out. "Promise me you won't push yourself."

I snatched the bag from his hand. "I'm not some fragile piece of glass, Kang."

"Lark..." His voice dropped, the single word both a warning and a plea.

I sighed and dropped the arm holding the bag to my side. With my free hand, I reached out and placed the flat of my palm on his strong chest. Kang stilled, his gaze narrowing on my hand before flicking up to focus on my face and drink in every detail.

"I promise," I said.

Kang kept his lips clamped together but nodded

and stepped back. He waved at the open space in the living room. "I'll get the chicken."

I opened the evidence bag and reached in to pluck out the bloody molar. The smell of blood and a tingling sense of déjà vu surrounded me. I closed my eyes and reached for my magic. It curled around the scene, needy with anticipation.

Kang walked back into the room, holding an old laying hen. She snuggled contently in the crook of his arm. A familiar pain knotted my stomach as I reached out and gently took her, still clutching the tooth in the hand that held her. With a silent apology, I sacrificed the hen and used the power in her blood to coat the tooth and call the spirit.

Kang removed the hen from my hands, bagging her somewhere behind me as the death magic swirled around me. I repeated the incantation and pulled. Awareness pinged on the other side of my call.

But the soul didn't appear.

I called again, sinking more power into my incantation. The soul tugged on my magic, like a fish taking the bait, but when I tried to pull it to me, the soul refused to budge. I sank more power in. My body vibrated, magic thrumming in my veins, my power demanding a soul answer.

Yet the soul remained stuck. I felt its need to answer my call, its pain of being torn between two places.

"Lark..." Kang spoke behind me.

I let the soul go and the call slipped away. I squeezed my eyes shut and slowly placed the tooth back in the sealed bag. My magic still coiled around me. Energy vibrated my limbs. At the last summoning circle, I'd managed to get the spirit to appear but couldn't get it to answer any of my questions. The magical whiplash had been minimal, but I'd stomped over to the nearby cemetery to call another spirit anyway as an outlet. The grave had ended up being empty, but the fresh air and time helped relieve the magical buildup.

This time...

I turned to Kang. His eyes had darkened, the surrounding skin turning gray.

"I need..." I hissed. My power was retrieving souls from the veil. It had found one but failed. And now, my magic wanted release.

Kang stepped forward, pulled me into his arms and his mouth crashed down on mine. He released his magic, letting it flood my senses and I gasped into his mouth. He stroked my tongue with his and deepened the kiss while our magic coiled together. I groaned and he spun us around to pin me on the wall, hopefully one of the only ones not covered in blood spatter. His lips moved from my mouth and travelled down my neck while one hand slid up to palm my breast. My head snapped back as the strain on my power eased, feeding a different need and purpose.

My phone vibrated in my back pocket, but I

ignored it, threading my fingers through Kang's silky black hair. I'd let him take me right here, in the middle of his crime scene and wouldn't regret a thing.

He would though. He was his job.

As if sensing the direction of my thoughts, Kang groaned and eased away from me. I dropped my hands to my sides, curling them into fists to prevent them from reaching out to haul him back.

His gaze cleared, his eyes returning to dark brown, his skin fair. Need and desire still flashed across his expression as he called his magic back and secured it behind his protective walls. He swallowed and his gaze dipped down to my heaving chest.

Either he just wanted to look at my breasts or he worried I'd have a heart attack from the way I panted.

"Both," he said.

"Did I say that out loud?"

"You did." His lips quirked up at the corner and I imagined what they'd look like clamped onto my breast.

I groaned and shut my eyes.

"I'm beginning to think your mind is even dirtier than mine, Lark." His amused tone had me opening my eyes again, only to find he'd taken several steps away, as if distance would somehow prevent him from trying to touch me again.

I looked down to find his pants had tightened considerably and licked my lips. "I don't know about that."

"Eyes up here, Morgan."

"You were literally checking out my boobs two seconds ago," I pointed out.

"I was and they're magnificent," he said.

"Connor."

"Lark."

"Please talk about the case. This is torture and I don't want to mess up your crime scene. You'll never forgive me," I said.

His gaze darkened and he hesitated, swaying forward as if planning to scoop me up but thought better of it. He cleared his throat. "I'm assuming from the lack of soul and your pent up...magic...that you weren't able to retrieve the soul."

"That's correct."

"Is this like Lily? You didn't try to jump me at the last crime scene."

"First of all, I didn't try to jump you. If I recall correctly, you were unable to resist my considerable charms. And second, no. With Lily there was nothing. Absolutely no tug or awareness, so it didn't trigger my magic like this. Even though I couldn't get this soul to appear, I felt it, my magic touched it. I could tug on it. This soul is stuck somewhere, most likely still anchored to his or her body."

"Still alive?"

"Maybe? But I don't think so. The magic felt like the veil."

Kang pressed his lips together as he thought for a moment. "They are, you know."

"What?"

"Your charms. They're considerable."

"Connor."

"Lark." He smirked and leaned in. "I'm going to let you escape this crime scene, but you're going to let me take you out tomorrow."

"If you play your cards right, I might let you do a little more than that."

He growled, barring his teeth at me. "Don't tease."

"I'm not."

CHAPTER SEVEN

Navigating my vehicle onto a side street, I found the pinned address and parked. Denise had texted me again as I left Kang's crime scene, asking for me to come to this location and help her with a case. In the middle of an industrial area, with the sun setting, shadows clung to the corners of the alleyway, shrouding everything in darkness.

I checked my phone. This was the address. And it was creepy as fuck. I'd met Denise in a lot of sketchy areas in the past and she'd definitely owe me some coffee and a sushi date for the callout, but this wasn't even the worst place she'd asked me to travel to for a necromancer job.

Stepping out of the car, I closed the door behind me and walked down the alley. "Denise?"

The buildings loomed tall and imposing above me, their windows dark or boarded up, their backdoors locked and chained. An ambulance raced down a nearby street, the blaring sound of its sirens growing louder until it passed my location and faded. A gentle wind rustled debris and garbage littering the cracked pavement, and the alley smelled faintly of urine, dirt and rust.

"She's right here." A man spoke and stepped out from behind a large dumpster, hauling Denise with him. Her arms were tied behind her back and mascara-streaked tears ran down her face. He'd wrapped one beefy arm around her to hold her in place, while his free hand held a gun to her head.

"Denise!" I stepped forward.

"Uh-uh." He tapped the side of Denise's head with the gun.

My friend whimpered. She wore a sequined mini skirt, low-cut top and high heels. They must've grabbed her while she was out clubbing last night. That meant they'd had her for almost twenty-four hours.

I froze in place and focused on the man. He looked vaguely familiar, but I couldn't place his face. "What the fuck is going on?"

"We've gone to a lot of trouble to find you, Lark," the man said.

We?

I glanced around the alleyway searching for others but saw only shadows. Did he have an accomplice? A group of friends? Who on earth would associate with a slime...

The face clicked.

Denise had been with this guy and another man at a club when I'd run into her over a week or so ago—before my abduction and subsequent jaunt to Murder Island. I'd mentally referred to them as the slimy twins—they both had their hair gelled back with too much product, hollow cheekbones, and lingering stares. They might've been handsome in a classical starving male model sense, but even in our brief interaction, they gave off a bad vibe.

What were their names again?

Had Denise even told me?

Where was the other one?

I flicked my gaze to my friend. "I told you to stop hanging out with losers."

Her eyes widened.

Someone tsked behind me and I spun in time to watch the other man walk out of a shadowy corner in the alleyway near my car. "We might be losers, but we still found you."

"Well, technically I found you..."

The man holding Denise narrowed his eyes. "Because we texted you. But we found you a long time ago. It just took time to get things in place."

"Okay..." I stepped to the side so I could turn and see both men a little better, though they were still too far away, and I had to whip my head back and forth to keep track of them. "Why don't you tell me what is going on here?"

"Stanley and I have been tracking you for a while," the man holding the gun to Denise's head spoke. Cooper. His name popped into my head. Denise had introduced them as Stanley and Cooper in the club.

"Well, that's not quite right," Stanley said. "We found you fairly quickly. Did you think you could mosey into the master vampire's lair without anyone noticing? Did you think you could then hang out with his human servant and not raise suspicion? Death raisers like you are the reason we have this infestation problem."

Mosey? Who the fuck said mosey? "Did you ever pause to think I went to Gregor's house to see Estelle? She's my friend."

Cooper smirked and his grip on the gun tightened. Denise quivered in his arms, tears continuing to streak down her face.

"You tell such pretty lies," Cooper said. "We've seen Gregor at your apartment and at your mother's house. Once we pulled her medical records, it didn't take much to put two and two together."

Pulled her medical records? Who were these two? "That Gregor cares about his human servant and therefore her friend?" I lied through my teeth and pulled on my magic, pooling it around me. "You're making a big deal about something not that complicated."

"Stop lying." Cooper tapped the gun barrel on Denise's head.

She squeezed her eyes shut and whimpered.

My magic spread out, flowing over the pavement to create a pool of power around the four of us. The drabs wouldn't sense it, but Denise did. She stilled and opened her eyes to focus on me.

"We know what you do for him," Cooper said. "We know what your grandfather did for him. We've been watching the master vampire for generations."

Well, shit... "Generations? But you're drabs."

"Not us, personally," Stanley said. "Our organization."

That sounded ominous. An organization watched Gregor's house, saw me visit, pulled my information and Mom's medical records and put it all together. They knew I was raising baby vampires. My only option here was to deny and sow seeds of doubt, because that was all I had going for me.

"Like Cooper said," Stanley added. "We know what you're up to."

"And?" I flung my hands up. "Let's say you're right, which you're not. What's your play here? What do you intend to do? Kill me? Kill Denise? Do you think that won't go unnoticed? Do you think you'll escape unscathed or that the fate of two necromancers will somehow greatly impact Gregor's life?"

"Ah, well..." Stanley had walked closer. Now only a few feet separated us, but I had no way to stop him from coming closer. My magic lapped at his legs, begging for me to use it. But how? I had no bones and these two were living drabs.

"We stopped your grandfather," Cooper said. "And we'll stop you as well."

Stopped my grandfather? What did they mean by that? Did whatever group these two belong to harm him? Kill him?

Anger simmered in my blood. My magic pulsed with the need to attack, to make them hurt like I now hurt.

"We plan to use you to track Gregor and lure him into a trap," Stanley continued.

I clamped my mouth shut.

"As for Denise..." Stanley looked over at my friend.

Cooper leaned in and whispered something into Denise's ear. Her eyes widened and she trembled.

Everything happened so slowly.

Cooper pulled back, keeping his arm out to create some distance between himself and the gun. His finger slid to the trigger.

I lashed out with my magic and gripped his soul. The power wrapped around the vile, inky darkness of his spirit and without thinking, I yanked. I ripped his soul from his body, hauling it to me.

Cooper didn't make a sound. He didn't gasp or scream. He crumpled to the ground with a sickening thud. Denise remained standing, quivering exactly where Cooper had left her.

His soul thrashed in my hold and I let it go, watching it shriek and zip away to the veil.

What in the preternatural science did I just do?

My heart hammered in my chest. My scalp prickled. I'd just killed someone. I'd ripped a soul from a body and murdered a human being. I didn't even know I could do that.

Fuck, that would've been handy to fucking know when I was stuck on Murder Island with that psycho Steve.

"What the hell did you do?" Stanley stomped toward me, quickly closing the distance.

Before he reached me, a dark shadow dropped out of nowhere and landed in between us. Tall, lean and wearing dark jeans and a simple black T-shirt, I'd recognize this vampire even from behind.

"You'll never touch her," Pierre said. The French vampire struck with quick efficiency, latching onto the man's neck and ripping away a chunk of flesh. Stanley gurgled as he fell to the ground, blood spurting from his neck wound. Eyes wide, he twitched on his back and then lay still.

My heart thudded in my chest, threatening to punch free of my ribs.

Pierre turned to me, and I stepped back.

"I would never hurt you, *ma belle*." Blood ran down his face and soaked the neckline of his black T-shirt.

I opened and shut my mouth a couple of times. "Wha...?"

"Lark?" Denise stammered behind me. I turned to find my friend shaking so hard, she barely stood.

I rushed over to her and gathered her in my arms. She sagged against me. The smell of her perfume and sweat tickled my nose. She clung to me and continued to shake.

"I'm so sorry," she said. "I didn't know. I didn't know. They asked about you, but I just thought Cooper had a crush and was trying to figure out if you were single, you know?"

She kept apologizing as if I chastised her, but I didn't and I never planned to. My mind had already filled in the gaps. Cooper and Stanley had latched onto Denise and used her to get access, and probably information, on me.

As someone who'd recently been used to get a book and access to the veil, I understood the pain and anger all too well.

"Shhh." I ran my hand down her hair. "It's okay. We're going to be okay."

While I'd run over to Denise, Pierre remained where I'd left him by Stanley's body. Our gazes locked over Denise's quivering head, and I raised my eyebrows.

"I'll take care of these bodies. You should get her home." He paused, seeming to debate whether to say something else.

"What is it?" I asked.

"Will she talk?" He jerked his chin at Denise who still shook in my arms.

"No!" Denise stiffened in my arms. "No. I would never."

Pierre narrowed his eyes and pressed his lips together.

"What would she say? Two guys tried to kill us and we acted in self defense?" I held Denise tightly. "As for the other stuff, these two were off the mark and making wild accusations based on some pretty bold assumptions." I needed to keep up the act. I wanted to trust Denise I really did. But I couldn't confirm I raised baby vampires for the local master vampire, even if she probably suspected it. I needed her to have plausible deniability.

Pierre grumbled but didn't press.

I'd already seen two too many deaths tonight and I hadn't begun to process what happened with my magic. I didn't want Denise in any more danger.

"Take her home, *ma belle*," Pierre finally said.

I nodded and walked Denise slowly to my car. I settled her in the passenger seat and reached over her to click in her seatbelt. With one last wordless goodbye to Pierre, I slid into the driver's seat and closed the door.

Denise and I didn't speak for three city blocks.

"You just ripped his soul out," Denise whispered. "I've never felt power like that before."

I jumped in the seat but luckily didn't crash into the car in front of us. I settled back and took a deep breath. "Yeah. I guess I did."

"That was so fucking badass," Denise said.

I agreed, but what scared me was not knowing what it meant. I shouldn't have been able to do that. I certainly hadn't practiced rending souls from the living. Yet, something dark and angry inside me wanted to grip Cooper's soul and rip it from his body and it didn't need a set of instructions.

What the hell was I becoming?

CHAPTER EIGHT

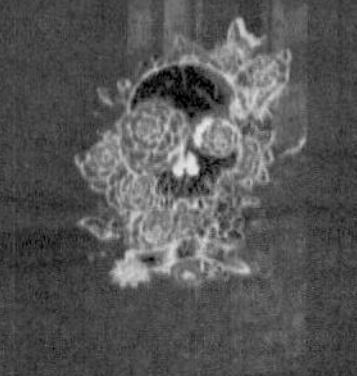

I stared at the laptop screen until my eyesight blurred. When I dropped Denise off at her apartment, I'd stayed for a couple of hours to make sure she was okay. She shook the entire time and spilled tea on herself, but after she came out of a hot shower and dressed in her pajamas, I'd wrapped her up in warm blankets and got her comfortable on her couch. She kept promising me she'd never say a thing and the magic around her vibrated with sincerity. I'd left Denise with a good book, a bottle of wine, and a promise to come back if she needed me.

I had returned home and went straight to researching. At first, I'd tried to find information on necromancers who could rip souls from living people, but that turned up nothing aside from conspiracy sites and some oddly specific fanfiction romance stories. I'd have to tell someone. Logan wouldn't judge me. Hell, he might even try to recruit me, but I wasn't fit for life as an assassin. It meant killing people unprovoked.

I should probably tell Kang, too.

He'd ripped a man to shreds for me, so I wasn't really worried he'd arrest me or turn me in. Part of me wanted him to have plausible deniability, but the other part of me recognized that this wasn't a secret that should exist between us.

After admitting defeat on researching super-duper necromancer skills, I'd turned to the other things currently plaguing my mind—the inability to call Lily's soul.

It wasn't a coincidence that her grave had been dug up and now her soul was missing in action. Cathy was my number one suspect, but what could she do to Lily's bones to prevent her from not just speaking to me but from answering my call altogether?

Had Lily's soul been destroyed as Levi suggested? Or had something else happened?

"What the hell are you doing here?" My brother walked into the living room and stopped long enough to growl at me.

His boyfriend, Brandon, followed close behind and flashed me a wide smile before winking.

"I thought I lived here?" I shot back. "Or did you two lovebirds evict me while I was out?"

They exchanged a glance. Brandon walked over and perched on the edge of the desk. "Shouldn't you be out getting railed by that hot cop?"

"Gross," Logan muttered.

Brandon smirked at him over his shoulder.

Logan sighed. "I mean…it's about time you got some action. Just would've preferred a different description." Logan flopped down on the sofa. "You are my sister, after all."

"I should have never told either of you about Kang."

Logan snorted. Brandon's smirk widened into a full-out grin.

"Look, if you're both going to be a pain, can you at least be helpful?" I asked.

Brandon's eyebrows rose, a sparkle in his gaze. He leaned forward. "Oh, how sweet. You're letting us in on a case."

Logan pulled himself off the sofa, casting the cushions a reluctant look before coming over to where I sat.

If I didn't also share their love for true crime documentaries, I'd be worried about their mental states.

"I'm trying to figure out how a spirit can be destroyed on Earth."

"As opposed to on Mars?" Logan asked, tone dry.

I narrowed my eyes.

Brandon elbowed my twin in the side. "Venus, obviously, you insidious fool."

Logan shook his head. "I love it when you get all medieval on me with your insults."

They leaned toward each other.

"Um, hello? Focus?" I snapped my fingers in the air

between them. "You two can make out later. A spirit wouldn't answer my call. According to Levi—"

"Levi?" Brandon asked.

"Leviathan."

Logan whistled.

"You're on a nickname basis with the Lord of the Veil, too?" Brandon's eyes widened. "Damn, sis."

Logan scowled. "I don't like this."

Logan didn't like anything that placed me in danger.

"Did you..." Brandon waggled his eyebrows. "Is that why you're not after the dick's dick?"

I reached out and shoved him away. My hand met his rock-hard abs and he graciously made a show of stepping back, but we both knew my push had little to do with it.

"No, I didn't sleep with Levi." Nor did I want to.

"So you still want the detective's peen?" Brandon asked.

"Yes," I growled.

They both grinned.

"No..." I winced and looked away.

Brandon and Logan started laughing.

"Ugh...you two are...you know what? Never mind. Let's stay focused." I pinched the bridge of my nose. "Levi told me the spirit most likely got destroyed. He figured that was the only explanation for why the victim didn't answer my summons and I have to agree with him."

"Did he destroy the spirit? Did you even ask, or did you get distracted?"

I glared at Logan. "Yes, I asked. No, he didn't. Which means someone else did. My number one suspect is a drab, though, so I'm missing a giant fucking piece to the puzzle."

"Which means someone else has the ability to kill spirits." Logan shivered.

"Yeah, that's not a pleasant thought. Nor is it likely to be a coincidence you just happen to work this case involving another powerful entity." Brandon shook his head. "I don't like this, Sparky."

"Are you positive the spirit's been destroyed? What if someone figured out a way to trap it? What about rebirth?" Logan leaned against the wall and folded his arms over his chest.

"She has only been dead for four years. Rebirth is so improbable we may as well assume impossible." A memory flashed through my mind of a time when I called a spirit that had been reborn. A shudder racked through my body. Not even rebirth could protect a soul from my call, but I'd never shared that story with anyone, and I didn't plan to now, not even with my boys.

"Natural rebirth, maybe," Logan said. "What if someone figured out a way to make it happen faster? I mean, vampires exist."

I paused and thought about his suggestion. "I guess...Her body has been recovered, so I think we can eliminate vampirism as a possibility, but yeah, maybe something else hocus pocus is going on right now."

Brandon already had his phone out, scanning the screen. "To summarize, we're looking for ways to destroy, trap or prematurely rebirth a soul?"

"Pretty much." I returned my attention to the computer and scowled at the screen. A trapped soul was unlikely. I knew what it felt like to call a trapped soul, but maybe the summoning slaughter victims weren't actually trapped so much as still living. Or maybe Lily's soul was just super-duper trapped to the point of being beyond my powerful reach. I really didn't know, and I couldn't rule out the possibility. "I'll focus on destruction."

We worked in silence for the next couple of hours, punctuated with heavy sighs and hissed curses.

"I've got nothing," Brandon said. "Investigating stuff sucks."

"Nothing like the shows," Logan muttered. "Way easier to kill people."

"I'm going to pretend I didn't hear that," Brandon said.

"Me too. Also, I think I'm done. I've found nothing." I pushed away from the desk. "I've spent entirely too much time on this and I'm going cross-eyed. I think it's time for a drink."

"Now, you're talking." Brandon perked up and tossed his phone on the couch.

"Wait." Logan held up his hand. "What about Giselle?"

"Who?" I sat back in my chair and swivelled around to face my brother. I'd never heard of Giselle, and I was all up in Logan's business since our birth.

"She's a witch. Mom sent me to her when we were sixteen to see if I had any necromancer powers. It was a little after Dad disappeared."

"You never told me that," I said.

He looked away. "Mom always scheduled it for when you had volleyball practice. Giselle didn't find out what was wrong with me. I'm not a necromancer and that's all she needed to know." Pain streaked across his face, but he packed it away quickly.

"You're not nothing, either. With or without magic." I reached out and grabbed his hand. Giving it a squeeze, I continued. "You are not defined by what you can and cannot do with magic. You've become what you are today because you are so much more than some number on a fucking magical scale."

Brandon nodded emphatically.

Logan waved his hand in the air. "I had a moment of sadness that I wouldn't follow in Dad's footsteps. It's gone. I realized I could make my own path and my powers, no matter where they rank on the glamy scale, serve me well for what I do. Now, I can gut all the magical snobs in their sleep if I want to and that helps me sleep at night."

Maybe we were a family of psychos.

Speaking of which... "Hey, I, uh, need to tell you guys something."

Both perked up, but as soon as Logan met my gaze, his expression closed off as if he mentally planned for war.

"Something happened earlier tonight. I want to tell you both, but I also don't want to make you accessories to a crime." Really, I was speaking about Brandon, and we all knew it. Logan was so steeped in committing his own crimes that trying to avoid adding accessory to murder to his list would be like eating an entire cake and then trying to refuse taking the last bite.

Brandon snorted. "Remember that time you gave me money to pick up curry and I never gave you back the change?"

"That happens all the time," I said. "Can you be more specific?"

"I don't need to be." He shrugged. "You'd given me money and that means I'm your lawyer on retainer. You can't make me an accessory to a crime."

"And we all know I don't give a shit about any of that," Logan said. "Though I appreciate you trying to protect Brandon, you need to start talking, Sparky."

I sighed and relayed the earlier events with Denise. When I got to the part where I stupidly met Denise in an alley, Logan shot up, shadowy death magic spiralling around him. He cursed and called me dense, and I didn't disagree. I'd grown way too complacent in my life and needed to act more cautiously.

Logan calmed down as soon as he found out I'd killed the guy.

Brandon listened to the whole story with rapt attention, probably cataloging all the details in case he had to defend me in a trial.

"You just ripped out his soul?" Logan asked. He'd taken a seat on the couch and leaned forward, gaze sparking with curiosity.

"Yeah. For the dead, I reach into the veil and pull them into the living realm. This was similar, except I didn't use a sacrifice or an incantation, and instead of reaching into the veil..."

"You reached into the man." Logan whistled.

"That's so badass," Brandon added.

I agreed, but part of me was still freaking out. "Is that...is that what you do?" I asked Logan.

My twin's expression closed off, his impartial mask sliding back over his face. "Not quite."

I nodded. Logan didn't like to speak about what he did or didn't do, but he had a monster of his own living inside him. "Guess I have another question for Mom."

"Right? Add it to the list, babe," Brandon said.

During my week off, I'd spent some of the time venting to Brandon about all the things I didn't know about my own family. He'd suggested making a list to keep track of all my questions, and I planned to bring it with me when I next saw Mom.

"Have you told hot cop, yet?" Brandon asked.

"No."

"But...you're going to, right?" Brandon pressed.

"Yes."

Logan grumbled.

"We can trust him, Logan," I said.

"Seems like you're putting a lot of trust in other people, Sparky," he said.

"Do you disagree? Don't tell me you haven't looked into the detective. You've probably followed him around and monitored his activity. He's always protected me." He'd killed for me, and I knew he wouldn't hesitate to do so again.

"It's not the cop I'm worried about," he growled.

"Denise?" I sat back in my chair. "She'd have to be a first-rate actress to pull off her reaction to the events."

"Did you ever pause to think she might be reacting to what you did, not the men?"

I stilled. The thought hadn't crossed my mind. Maybe I was entirely too trusting. I had gone to a remote location to meet Denise, not even questioning the text. But why would she be involved with those scumbags? I shook my head. "Cooper admitted to using her phone to text me and he was about to shoot her. His finger had moved to the trigger, and he'd started to pull back. So even if she was in on it, they planned to double cross her. But I really don't think that's the case."

"We need to monitor her," Logan said.

"Okay, fine. Monitor her. Just promise me that

doesn't involve locking her up in a cell or killing her," I said.

"I'll only promise to those terms under the condition she remains innocent. If it turns out she's involved, I will not work within those restrictions."

"Logan..."

"Sparky. You're my twin. My sister. It's always been us against the world and I'll fucking protect you, even if it's from yourself."

I threw my hands up. I was perfectly capable of protecting myself.

"Anyway," Logan continued. "Back to the other business. Giselle might help us."

My mind reeled to follow his subject change. Other business?

Lily's face flashed in my mind.

Right. We wanted to find out how a soul could be destroyed, and Logan had mentioned a witch. "It's worth a shot," I said. "Do you remember where she lives?"

"Not quite. Somewhere in Esquimalt, if I remember correctly. She's a witch named Giselle who offers her services for hire, though. I'm sure we can find her."

"And if not her, we'll find some other witch." Brandon already had his phone out again, tapping the screen and entering information into the search engine.

We might actually be getting somewhere with this case.

CHAPTER NINE

Brandon, Logan, and I stood outside the old Victorian-style house. The off-white paint had mostly peeled off the trim as had the dark blue paint on the siding. The result was probably due to the age and lack of maintenance, but it appeared as if the paint tried to escape whatever occurred inside the home.

One of the hinges holding up the lattice shutters had broken off, leaving the shutter to hang at an angle and detract from the beauty of the stained-glass window. The images depicted must've been striking in their prime, but the grime on the glass rendered the design difficult to make out.

"The business of magic doesn't look like it's been very lucrative," Brandon whispered.

"Are you sure this is the right place?" I asked.

Logan nodded. "She confirmed the address over

the phone, and this is where I came to see her all those years ago."

I shivered. "I wish she would have done the whole interview with us over the phone, this trip was completely unnecessary."

Moss covered the roof shingles and ivy crept up the sides of the house as if attempting to reclaim the wood for nature. The witch had used some sort of animal bones to line her property in a warding spell. Either it wasn't activated or we didn't trigger the spell because we crossed it without difficulty.

"Do you think it's safe to go in?" Brandon asked, biting his lip. "We have dinner with your mom tomorrow night, and I don't want to stand her up. Besides, you have all those questions to ask her, and I don't want to die before we find out the answers."

"Are you concerned about safety because of the structural integrity of the building or because we'll be in the domain of a powerful witch?" Logan asked before turning back to frown at the building. "I don't remember it looking like this when I visited all those years ago."

"How powerful can she be if this is what her house looks like?" Brandon asked.

"Powerful enough to listen to you disparage my home." An older woman stood on the front porch. How and when did she get there?

I straightened while Brandon made an impossibly

high-pitched sound and jumped back. Logan just scowled and shoved something back in his pocket.

Was he planning to throw a knife at her?

I couldn't take these two anywhere.

"I apologize for our comments," I said. "We didn't mean to offend."

"Yet, you did." The woman couldn't be more than five feet tall. She had white and gray hair that flowed down her back in soft waves and despite her age and wrinkles, her pale skin shone with the vitality of youth.

Surprisingly, she wore jogging pants and a matching sweater. Not sure what I expected, but a tie-dyed article of clothing wouldn't have stood out as much.

"My sincerest apologies," I said. "We should not have commented on the state of your property and your finances and will reflect on that to see how we can do better the next time." And I meant it.

Brandon shuffled his feet and looked at the ground. His face went red. Even the tips of his ears blushed.

"What do you want?" Giselle asked.

"We spoke on the phone," I said. "My name is Lark Morgan, and we have an appointment."

Logan stepped forward. "I'm—"

"I remember you." She waved her hand in the air. "The dud."

Logan winced.

Anger flared up inside me, hot and ready to burst from my fingertips. Not all witches could sense death magic, but regardless, Logan wasn't a dud. He wasn't a drab, either. And most importantly, he was my brother, and I would make her regret speaking to him that way.

Logan reached out and rested his hand on my arm. "I can take an insult, Sparky."

Though I knew he could very much take an insult, my opinion was that he shouldn't have to. I itched to grab my power and send spirits racing into the woman's home. If I had bones, I could draw blood and rip the witch from the safety of her doorstep and abandon her in the veil—I had my anchor with Gregor, after all, and she would have nothing.

The memory of ripping Cooper's soul from his body flooded my mind. I could do that again. It would be so easy.

My magic pulsed inside my chest.

Part of me loved this new murderous side of my personality that wanted to kick some ass, but another part of me was freaking out. Where was this all coming from? Was this voice emerging because I had spent more time in the veil? Did Leviathan healing me with death magic bring it out? Or was this voice and side of me always there but suppressed or ignored? Had I only learned to listen to my own intuition now, at the tender age of thirty-one, because of yet another near-death experience?

The old woman cocked her head and studied me. Maybe she could see the steam escaping my ears, or maybe she didn't miss how my hands had curled into fists. Or maybe she sensed her own death buzzing in the air.

I might hesitate to sacrifice chickens for estate disputes. I might even hesitate to defend myself. But I would rend the souls from everything and everyone who dared to harm my brother.

"Sparky," Logan said, his voice a low warning.

"Brandon insulted her home," I whispered. "She insulted you. Neither is okay, but we don't have to tolerate this. There are other witches."

Logan squeezed my arm again. "I'm a grown adult, Sparky. I've been called worse. Let's just go inside and get this over with."

A slow smile spread across Giselle's face as if she heard the entire conversation even though we whispered to one another.

Fuck sending spirits after her or ripping out her soul. If this witch tried anything, I'd leave her in the veil to make friends with Levi. I'd even wrap a bow around her scrawny neck.

I gathered my magic, pulling it from the ground and all the bones around us.

The animal bones may have offered the witch some protection, but not from me.

Never from me.

The bones gave me power and access to the veil.

The smile slipped from Giselle's face. She paled and staggered back. "Necromancer."

I frowned but kept the death magic close. Surely,

Giselle knew our family. Mom had sent Logan here for assessment, after all. Or had Giselle assumed we were all duds?

"I wish you no harm," I said. "We only came to ask a few questions with the hope you could share your expertise with us."

Giselle nodded, her gaze darting from side to side. She had thought she had the upper hand, and given her shaking hands, she must've realized she'd underestimated us. "You can drop your magic. I offer safe passage and promise to do no unprovoked harm."

I let my power slip away and we walked up the stairs. The wood creaked and groaned under our feet but held.

Giselle opened the door and waved us in. Warm air filled with herb and floral scents washed over my face as I stepped over the threshold.

The air shimmered. Unlike the outside, the inside of the house was opulent, clean, and stunning. Expensive rugs lined the hardwood floor, heavy, tasteful furniture sat in the living room and the kitchen, also viewable from the open floor plan, was gorgeous. Industrial-sized, the kitchen looked like something more aptly found in a Hollywood celebrity's home.

"A witch is only as good as her kitchen," Giselle spoke behind me.

"The animal bones," I said. "They're to disguise your home, aren't they?"

Giselle walked past me, an earthy sage scent

brushing by me in her wake. "The spell ensures the house is always the worst in the neighbourhood. I didn't used to have to resort to such carnival shenanigans, but crime rates have skyrocketed and I always protect what is mine. Break-ins have increased, but they always leave this house alone."

"It looks real," Logan said.

Giselle paused to peer over at him. "That's because it is. The spell is more than an illusion."

"Powerful spell," I noted. I wouldn't make the same mistake she had. I wouldn't underestimate the witch's magic.

Giselle nodded and waved at the living room. "Please have a seat. Would you like tea?"

"No, thank you. We don't expect our questions to take long."

Giselle narrowed her eyes. "My appointments have a one-hour minimum fee."

I bit my lip.

Logan stepped over to the couch. "That's fine. We may not use the full hour, that's all."

Brandon and Logan took a seat on one of the couches, leaving an armchair and a loveseat for me and the witch.

I took the loveseat. The wingback armchair with a tufted back looked like a throne and had been placed in front of the window by the fire. The small table beside it had a book splayed open, pages down, to mark a spot, and a half-finished cup of tea rested on a coaster. Without physically claiming a chair, Giselle claimed the armchair long before she offered us a seat.

As she should.

This was her home, after all.

Giselle sat down, crossed her legs, and folded her hands together to rest them on her knee. "How can I help you?"

"I tried to call a spirit from the veil, but she never answered my call."

"That happens all the time," she said.

"Not to me."

Giselle tapped her fingers on her knee and pressed her lips together. "To clarify, you're saying every time you've called a spirit, it's answered?"

"That's correct. I've never come across a spirit I couldn't call. And this wasn't a powerful spirit that resisted. This was a spirit that just wasn't there." I purposefully left out the summoning slaughter victims. The last one hadn't technically answered my call, either, but I'd felt the soul, I'd sensed its need and desire to answer. Lily was different.

"Were the bones old? Is rebirth a possibility?"

"The victim died four years ago. I saw and spoke to the spirit a couple of weeks ago. Rebirth is unlikely."

Giselle sat back in her chair, worry tugging at her mouth.

"We suspect the spirit has either been destroyed or trapped."

"Then why come to me?" Giselle frowned. "Why not seek answers in the veil?"

I exchanged a look with Logan. Though I didn't particularly want to expose the extent of my powers or my familiarity with Levi, I'd known going in, I might have to share some information.

"Leviathan confirmed he did not destroy the spirit. He didn't even know the name."

"You spoke with Leviathan?"

"Yes?"

"And you're still alive?"

"It would appear so."

Giselle snapped her mouth shut, her gaze shifting back and forth as she processed the information. "Is your surname truly Morgan?"

"Yes," I spoke through clenched teeth.

Giselle leaned forward. "What's your mother's maiden name?"

Irritation prickled my skin. What the hell did Mom's family have to do with this?

Okay, maybe I knew a little of why the witch asked —meeting and surviving Leviathan was unheard of— but we weren't here to discuss me. I still had a lot of questions about why I could do the things I could do, including grow talons and have my eye colour change in the veil. But I hadn't tackled Mom to ask her these questions yet and I certainly wasn't sharing what limited information I did have with a random witch.

"That's not relevant," I answered. "We need to

know how or if someone from the living realm could manage to destroy or trap a spirit."

Giselle pinched her lips together for a minute, looking quite ready to demand more answers from me, but eventually, she nodded and sank back in her seat. "There are ways of trapping a spirit, but if you're powerful enough to have never experienced a failed summoning, it's doubtful a trap could contain the spirit so well that you wouldn't feel it. You're most likely dealing with the destruction of a soul and other than the Lord of the Veil, there's only one way to do that. At least only one other way I know of."

The witch's mouth turned down and she looked away.

"And that would be?" I prompted.

"Disgusting magic. Dark defiled magic that shouldn't exist. A spell so despicable, it's been struck from most grimoires."

"I don't want to do the spell or even learn it. I just need to know how to find the person who worked it."

"The spell itself is easy. The weakest of witches could pull it off," Giselle said. "It's the active ingredient that's hard to find."

I leaned forward in my seat. If the ingredient was hard to find that might help us identify the spellcaster. "What's the ingredient?"

Giselle finally looked back at me, her gaze sad, her expression pinched. "The bones of a barghest."

CHAPTER TEN

After thanking Giselle and leaving her house in quiet shock, I dropped the boys off at the apartment and made my way to Kang's home. He opened the front door, a large smile on his usually serious face.

"You made good time," he said, his gaze raking my body.

I'd texted as soon as we left Giselle's and he told me to get my "leather-covered ass" over here, followed shortly after with another text giving his address. Showing up on his doorstep wasn't a surprise, yet nerves still knotted my stomach.

"Don't you mean, 'about fucking time'?" I asked.

"If that's what does it for you, I'll greet you like that next time."

"Kang, you always greet me like that."

Amusement flashed in his gaze, and he leaned forward. "And you like it."

I cleared my throat. He was right. "You mentioned food?"

Something smelled great. He was making food, instead of ordering out.

He snorted and stepped back so I could enter the home. Straight and to the point, the open floor plan and minimalist décor with its sleek, clean lines, suited Kang. A large leather sectional sat off to the side in the living room and looked as though it would swallow me whole. The walls were all painted in shades of gray that seemed to absorb the light and give the space an almost otherworldly atmosphere.

Or maybe that was just my feelings talking—I never thought I'd walk into Kang's home voluntarily. Stepping into his house now felt surreal.

Thick black curtains were drawn tight, shielding the inside from prying eyes and the glittering lights of the city outside. Stacks of books decorated the low coffee table by the couch, and though I had a lot of other things I'd like to do in this place, part of me wanted to grab the gray knitted throw blanket, one of Kang's books, and curl up on that monstrous couch to get lost in another world.

And maybe that was just my feelings talking, too—though I desperately wanted to find comfort in Connor's arms, I needed to come clean about a number of things first. Reading was preferable to facing the possibility Connor might not want me after he learned how truly horrifying my magical talents were.

No, wait. That wasn't quite right. Connor would still want me despite my soul ripping powers. It wasn't my magic I feared he'd take issue with. It was my secrets.

"Not that I don't find your motivation to break every speed limit on the way here flattering," Kang said. "But your face doesn't match." He shut the door behind me and crossed his arms over his chest. "What's wrong?"

Where did I start?

Giselle's words replayed in my head as I took off my shoes and padded farther into the house. "I've been looking into Lily Zheng's case and Brandon and my brother helped me with research. We suspect her spirit was destroyed and met with a witch today to figure out if there's some way for someone to do that in the mortal world."

His dark gaze scanning my face. "And you found an answer."

"Yeah."

"And you don't like it." Again, he spoke as a statement, not as a question.

I took a deep breath. "I don't like it and you won't either."

He nodded and waited, his brain probably already preparing to compartmentalize.

"Apparently, the spell, though dark and disgusting,

is relatively easy to do, but it requires the bones of a barghest."

Kang stilled.

We stood like that, staring at each other, about two feet apart and I hated the distance. I hated not knowing what he was thinking.

While his actual thoughts remained a mystery, his feelings were easy to read.

Rage vibrated from within, and his magic leaked out from behind his shields.

"With the risk of being completely insensitive," I continued. "May I ask about your family?"

He grimaced before he pulled his shoulders back and lifted his chin. "What would you like to know?"

"If someone were to procure barghest bones, how likely would it involve someone from your family?"

"If they got the bones locally, very likely."

I winced and looked away. "I was afraid of that."

"There are few barghest families left. There are families from Northwestern England like mine, but also families from Northern England, Wales and Scotland. Over the years, our kind were given different names in folklore, but in essence, we are all the same."

"I thought you had Korean and Scottish ancestry." He mentioned it once, I was sure of it.

He nodded. "I do, but that's not my only ancestry—it's just easier to list two. My dad's father is from Seoul, and two of my other grandparents are from Scotland. But my barghest power came from my maternal grandmother. Her family is from Lancashire." He paused. "How much do you know of our kind?"

"The important parts." Heat rushed up my face.

Kang paused to reach out and cup my face. He stepped forward and brushed his thumb along my cheek. His expression softened and he leaned in to press his lips to mine briefly before turning away. "Barghests can use death energy to travel to the veil and to change shape. That's where the death omen rumour came from, but we don't cause the deaths, we just use them."

"And there aren't a lot of you left?"

"Not that I know of. Barghest genetics are complicated. Inheritance, even more so. But the over-simplified explanation is we inherit barghest power through the maternal line. My parents would've contacted me if they were aware someone had our bones."

"Grave robbing?"

"Not a lot of people are aware of our true identities." He scowled. "Either they found out, which places me in jeopardy, or they got the bones without knowing the connection to my family, or they got the bones somewhere else."

"Does your family have a plot?"

"They do." He glanced out the window at the darkening sky. "I don't feel like traipsing through a cemetery at night. I know it's your thing, but it invites the interactions of night creatures, and I don't want to deal with it."

"We'll go tomorrow?"

He nodded, stepping in close to run his hands up my arms, his expression darkening. "Besides, I have other things to deal with."

I swallowed, trying to desperately ignore the heat rising in my body in response to the promise in Kang's gaze. "Before you deal with me...there's something else."

He stilled, his dark gaze laser-focusing on my face.

"I...I killed a man yesterday." Nausea rolled in my stomach. Even though I would do it again to save my friend, I'd never taken a human life before. And I felt no remorse or regret. Only sadness for the waste of a human life and anger for being placed in the position where I had to end things. What did that say about me?

Connor blinked at me. "Why am I only finding out now?"

"Well...the manner in which I killed him required some processing. I also had to help my friend and then I got sucked into researching and finding out about the barghest stuff. I needed to distract myself."

He remained eerily still. "You couldn't text?"

I sighed. I had thought about doing exactly that multiple times since the alley. "And you wouldn't have demanded answers? You wouldn't have stormed over to Denise's apartment in full interrogation mode while she was still in shock. Also, this wasn't something I wanted to explain over a text message or phone conversation."

"I would've protected you. I would've...shit...I don't know. But I would be there for you. I'd like to think I have more control over myself than to bulldoze my way into your life and mess things up." He squeezed his eyes shut and took a deep breath. He balled his hands into fists. "Why don't you tell me what happened? From the beginning."

So I did.

Kang grumbled at the part where I naively met Denise in a deserted alley with no questions asked. He should form a "Lark is an idiot" support group with my brother. I already knew, before Kang and Logan's reactions, that meeting Denise in an alley hadn't been a smart decision, but as I reminded Kang, there was a precedent set. I'd met Denise in all sorts of places as a necromancer, so I really hadn't thought much of it. Should I have exercised more caution? Absolutely. But hindsight was always twenty-twenty.

"So you ripped out his soul and one of Gregor's vampires killed the other guy," Connor summarized the events.

"Yup."

"And are you going to finally tell me what your connection with Gregor is?"

I hadn't expressly told Kang that information, not because I was ashamed of my choices, but more because I wasn't sure how he would react. I also didn't want there to be any secrets between us. Though we'd only technically been on one date, this thing developing between us felt so right and real and serious.

"I made a deal with him," I said. "My mother is suffering from sanguimort and he cleans her blood."

He waited, letting none of his thoughts show on his expression.

"In exchange, for each healing session," I continued. "I raise a baby vampire."

He waited for what felt like the longest moment of my life before he leaned in and whispered, "I know."

What?

He what?

He knew and waited for me to nervously share the information? I swatted his arm lightly. "What the fuck, Kang?"

"I smelled his bond and did some digging myself. You mentioned your grandfather once and that helped me figure out the connection along with seeing your mother's health considerably improve."

My mouth fell open.

"I understand why you didn't share this information with me right away," he said. "I'm glad you chose to finally trust me." He leaned forward. "I will never betray your trust, Lark. But now I'd like to deal with something else."

"What would you like to deal with?" I asked and held my breath.

A slow smile spread across his face. He'd compartmentalized the news about his family's possible involvement with his case, and my murderous activities and connection with the local vampires, seemingly shutting the mental door on all of it.

Now, his entire focus settled on me.

"Right now? I'd like to deal with the soul-rending vampire-bonded necromancer standing in my home."

"That sounds very ominous."

He nodded solemnly.

"What about the food? Your cooking smells great."

"Fuck the food." He released his magic, the power flowed over me in delicious waves. "I'd rather feast on you."

Pleasure bloomed where the energy caressed my skin. Intoxicating, overwhelming, addicting. I wanted more. "You're not put off by..." How should I phrase it? "You're not put off by me?"

He pulled the magic back, and I whimpered. "I've never wanted someone more than I want you, Lark. Before and after I learned the extent of your magical strength."

"How exactly do you plan to deal with me?" I asked. "This feels like torture."

His grin widened, his gaze flashing with promise. "I've been thinking about how to deal with you all day."

"Oh?"

"Yeah."

"And?"

"And I thought about how you'll feel in my arms,

how you'll sound when you gasp and how you'll taste." He ran his magic down my skin.

My body hummed with anticipation. Surely, he could hear it.

He pulled me close, slipping his arms around me.

"You must've been unbearable to work with," I said.

"Pretty sure Jacobs wants a reassignment."

I reached up, slipping my fingers through his thick, silky hair and pulled his head down. His lips quirked against mine before he kissed me back. I opened my mouth to him and his tongue swept in, tasting of steak sauce and sin. His magic caressed my body like a million invisible hands while his mouth quickly moved to kiss my jaw, neck, and shoulders. At some point, we moved because my back slammed into a wall as we continued to kiss, trying to inhale each other.

He scraped his teeth along my skin. "I've thought about what I'd like to do to you in my bed for a long time."

"What happened to taking me on another date?"

He pulled back, his expression serious. "I can do that if that's what you want."

"Dates are for getting to know strangers, Connor. I know you. What I want is for you to take me to your bedroom and start showing me the things you keep promising." I unclasped his belt and pulled it free from the loops. "Unless you want to have some dinner first? You might need to load up on carbs."

A wicked smile flashed across his face and in a blink, he had me pinned to the wall.

"You have no idea what you do to me," he murmured into my skin as he kissed his way down my body and removed my clothes as he went. He tugged my pants so they pooled at my ankles, and knelt to pull them off. Flinging the clothes to the side, they hit the ground with loud flops, but Connor didn't seem to notice. He was too focused on other things.

He pulled off my socks, one by one and kissed his way up the inside of my leg.

All I could do was breathe.

Or pant.

Semantics, really.

Connor hooked my knee over his shoulder and looked up, gaze wild, magic flowing over me. He looked at me like I was the most beautiful woman in the world and the sight of him kneeling in front of me stole my breath away.

With his face at my waist, he paused, his warm breath fanning my core. I wore a blue lace thong with pretty scalloped edges. They were my favourite pair, and I might've put them on when I got up hoping this would be where I ended up at the end of the day.

"Are you sure?" he asked.

"Mmmm." If he didn't do something right now, I might die.

"I would beg," he said. "For you, I would do anything."

"If you don't rip these off and start touching me, it's me who'll end up begging," I said.

"Can't have that." He reached up and with a sharp tug, ripped the underwear from my body. The fabric snapped and Connor flung the destroyed panties over his shoulder to join my pants. Without pausing, he clamped his mouth on me. The immediate warmth threatened to make my leg buckle. Connor moaned as he licked and sucked, the sound vibrating along every nerve ending in my body. He feasted on me as if he'd been starving his whole life and tasted dessert for the first time.

All thoughts of my underwear fled.

All thoughts, period, disappeared.

His tongue had a way of stealing my ability to form comprehensive thoughts, let alone words and I gave up caring. Instead, I threaded my hands through his hair again to hold on and leaned back. Connor's magic wound around me, playing with my senses and coating my skin. This exposed, I should feel cold, but a hot fire burned within me, threatening to combust and Connor kept stoking the flames, one swipe of his tongue at a time.

This man would be the death of me, and I didn't care.

I gripped his head and held him in place while I arched my back against the wall and closed my eyes as pure pleasure swept through my body. Connor released more of his power. He must have a deep well of it. Smooth as silk, death magic curled around my body and licked my skin. Wisps of power teased my hair and danced along my spine to curl my toes, and I reveled in the taste of his power. I consumed it. I brought it into my body and let it delight my own magic.

Release slammed through me, hard and fast, and I cried out, holding Connor's head in my hands as my thighs clamped him in place. He lapped it up. His tongue still stroking and tasting and drawing out every ounce of my pleasure until I sagged down the wall.

My thighs dropped to the sides and Connor unhooked my leg from his shoulder, but he kept his hands on my waist to steady me as he knelt in front of me. I looked down, still gasping for breath, to find him watching me intently.

"I'm not religious." He licked his lips. "But I could pray at this alter every day, all day."

"I think I'd let you."

He leaned forward and placed a chaste kiss on my hip as if he hadn't just done wicked things with his tongue moments ago. Without warning he stood, picked me up and threw me over his shoulder.

"Wha—"

He slapped my naked ass playfully. "If you think I'm done with you, you're sorely mistaken. That was merely an appetizer. My hunger for you is not sated."

My whole body clenched at the promise in his words, and I remained silent, enjoying the aftershocks of my orgasm while he carried me through the house to his bedroom. He kicked the door open and flung me onto the bed. I had a brief moment to take in the tasteful décor, the tufted headrest, king-sized bed and a large painting of an angry ocean scene before Connor was climbing over me.

"You're overdressed," I pointed out. All I'd managed to remove was his belt.

Connor paused, poised over me like a large cat stalking its prey. "You're right."

He hopped off the bed and flung off his clothes with quick efficiency. I'd seen him without clothes on before, but he'd been splattered with blood. Now, he stood in front of me, gloriously naked and unapologetically aroused. Strong defined abs tapered down to a narrow waist and drew my gaze even lower where his large erection jutted out.

"Are you sure about this?" he asked.

I sat up and trailed my hands over his strong chest. "I'm unsure of a lot of things, Connor. But not this. Not you."

He shuddered but still hesitated. "I...My magic is so erratic around you. I might lose control."

"Connor, you're the epitome of self-control."

"Not around you."

My chest tingled with warmth at the thought. I'd wanted to watch Connor lose control since the moment we'd met. "I can take whatever you give."

He squeezed his eyes shut and growled a warning. "Lark..."

"Connor." I waited until he opened his eyes and met my gaze before I repeated, "I trust you."

Connor's gaze darkened and he leaned over to open his bedside table and pulled out a condom. He kept his gaze locked with mine as he ripped the packet open and rolled it on, an intense promise sparking in his gaze the entire time. Anticipation trilled inside me, and I didn't breathe as I watched.

When he finished, I licked my lips and reached out to grab his hand, pulling him back to the bed and on top of me. My whole body ached with need, with the desire to feel him move within me.

His magic reached out, caressing my body and stirring the heat already building again. His power was mesmerizing, seductive and I wanted it inside me as much as I wanted Connor.

He stretched out beside me, trailing his fingers along my collarbone and then tracing the curve of my breast. He was stalling, trying to calm things down, trying to calm himself, but I didn't want to take it slow. I didn't want gentle, and I certainly didn't want to be teased mercilessly. It was time for Connor to shed that self-control and I would be the one to make him unravel.

I reached out to grab his head with both hands. Pulling him to me, I claimed his mouth with my own. I nipped at his lips, tangling my tongue with his. Connor groaned. He tried to pull back, he tried to resist so he could torture me some more, but I was having none of it. I hooked my leg around his and rolled onto my back, pulling Connor on top of me.

Connor growled and slid his mouth off mine to kiss along my jaw. "You're impatient."

"And greedy." I wrapped my arms around his neck and curved into him as he settled between my legs. "You've given me a taste and I want more."

He chuckled and moved his kisses down my neck. "It's me who's had a taste and now I'm addicted."

Nothing lay between us now except his raging hard on, and nothing would ever come between us again. The tip of his shaft pressed into me, and heat pooled low in my body. Anticipation raced through my veins. Connor raked his teeth along my shoulder and the last bit of control he held over his magic crumbled.

Death magic flowed over my skin, vibrating along each nerve and licking my power that simmered beneath, until Connor's power completely coated me like an invisible shield. Instead of being a barrier though, it acted like glue, bringing us together, molding my body into his as he worked his large shaft inside me slowly, inch by inch.

He palmed my breast, power cascaded over my chest while he kissed me, lapping up my panting breath as if he would steal the air from my lungs.

"Connor." I ground my teeth together. Was he

worried about hurting me? He was going to kill me if he kept this up.

He stilled on top of me and lifted his head to meet my gaze. He looked feral, driven wild with need. His whole body vibrated, and his magic pulsed along my skin. Slowly, he pulled back his magic, all of it, every delicious drop of power until there was only him. Connor.

He waited, laying himself bare to me, as if asking whether I still wanted this, wanted him, without the addictive taste of his magic. He'd never been more beautiful than now.

I pulled my magic in as well and held his intense gaze, a slow smile pulling at my lips. "Just us," I said.

He groaned and thrust all the way in.

Nothing had felt more right than this moment.

He paused, hovering over me as my body stretched to accommodate him and need thrummed between us. He watched me as if drinking in my reaction, noting my gasp for breath the erratic beating of my heart, my fingertips digging into his skin, my thighs clamping his body to mine. I felt full and content, and yet I wanted and needed more.

"You are stunning." Connor released his control on his power again, slamming it into me as he began to move. "And you are *mine*."

I cried out. My fingertips tingled and I held onto Connor as he pumped into me, stirring a heat that threatened to burn my entire world down.

This was it. This was how I'd die. How could I survive something so profoundly intense? He was my death and I'd drown in a pool of bliss with a smile on my face.

"Fuck, you feel so good," he growled into my neck, his voice teasing the sensitive skin.

I raked his back with my nails and arched into him as another release slammed through me. I cried out. My power lashed out, gripping Connor as pleasure rolled through me. As the orgasm ripped through my body, Connor kissed me again, swallowing my cries.

Our magic danced together, tangling in tune with our tongues. The bands of power stroked my skin and bound us together as we moved. His magic called out to me, and I pulled it inside, making it mine, making Connor mine.

"More," he growled. His brown gaze turned black, his skin tinged gray. He snarled and revealed his teeth, his canines elongated into fangs. He lengthened and thickened inside me as well as he continued to move. The beast had risen, but he did not scare me.

Connor would never hurt me.

I held his face in my hands and met his feral gaze before pulling his head down to capture his mouth again.

He answered by changing pace. Alternating between grinding in circles against me with one hip swivel after another and thrusting deep, he wrung more pleasure from my body. I moaned as my head swam, and pressure built and built. And just when I thought I couldn't take anymore, couldn't give any more, another wave of pleasure slammed through me, and I cried out again.

Connor's movements became erratic. He thrust one last time and roared his release. He stayed like that, fully seated inside me, throbbing while my muscles clamped around him and our magic tied us together.

Things between us would never be the same.

I would never be the same.

And it felt so right.

CHAPTER ELEVEN

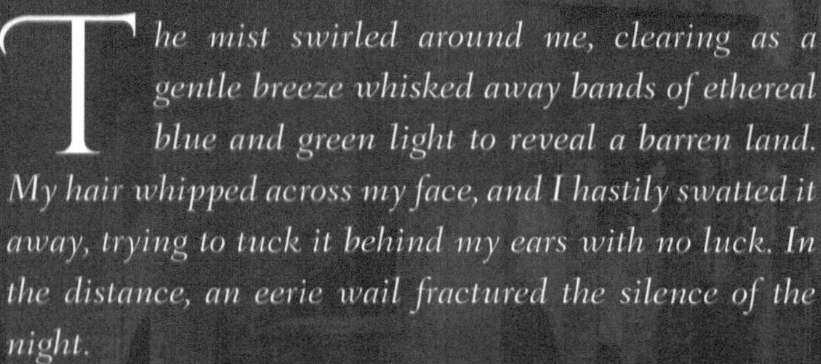

The mist swirled around me, clearing as a gentle breeze whisked away bands of ethereal blue and green light to reveal a barren land. My hair whipped across my face, and I hastily swatted it away, trying to tuck it behind my ears with no luck. In the distance, an eerie wail fractured the silence of the night.

Where was I? The last thing I remembered was cutting myself in the backyard to see if I could raise our family pet from her remains and now, I was here.

I should've listened to Logan. He told me I was too young to try. We'd only turned fifteen last week. But the power had called within me for release, and I needed to see if I would be a strong necromancer like Dad.

A flash of light illuminated the mountains in the distance and highlighted the peaks of a castle far away. The castle had a tall curtain wall and many towers, and after the light disappeared, the mysterious castle faded into the inky darkness.

"You shouldn't be here," a craggy old voice spoke behind me.

I turned around to find an old lady with a wrinkled face. I squinted and leaned forward, but I couldn't make out the details of her features, like a hazy film covered her entire body. "Who...who are you?"

She cocked her head, and her dead gaze studied me. "A friend, and one you desperately need."

"Am I dreaming?"

"No child," she said. "You've travelled to the veil."

Warmth fled from my body, replaced with ice and an overwhelming feeling of dread. My limbs began to shake, my lips trembled. I shouldn't be here. I couldn't be here. Mom had warned me so many times. And like an idiot, I'd carelessly ignored her rules.

I hadn't been completely careless. Raising Muffin shouldn't have brought me here. "I...I need to go back. How do I get back?"

I shouldn't have used my own blood.

Now, without an anchor in the living realm, I was stuck in the veil. Unless, somehow, I miraculously found a way back.

"Take my hand, child." The old woman held out her hand.

I looked down at her open palm, the paper-thin skin lined with wrinkles. "Can I trust you?"

"I have seen a glimpse of your future, sweet child, and not a single one of my kind will seek to harm you."

"Your kind?"

She smiled, a toothy grin that revealed a dimple on one cheek. "I may not pose a danger to you, but there are others who might, and some are headed this way. Take my hand, child, so I may help you travel home."

A deep howl rose in the distance, a rumbling growl that shook the ground I stood on. I slapped my hand in hers and squeezed my eyes shut. Nothing happened.

The old woman smiled again and for a brief moment, the haze blurring her features slipped and I caught a glimpse of her green eyes and a face that seemed vaguely familiar.

"Reach down inside you, daughter of Bedoe, blood of Morcant. For the key lies within you." Her power reached out and coated me like a warm blanket, and like a guiding light it reached inside me and showed me a well of power I'd barely tapped. Deeper, farther within, a secret awaited, and when I drew near the hidden door and touched the handle, power erupted from within me. Magic shot out and burrowed a doorway between this land and the living realm, a hazy portal forming in front of me.

I jerked back and turned to the woman. "How...how is this..."

"You must keep your powers secret. No one can know. Not even you." She waved a hand in front of my face and her magic swept my body again. When it left

me, I swayed on my feet, my mind fuzzy, my heart beating rapidly. The woman had taken something from me, I felt its loss.

"What...who..." I looked around, confused and scared. What was I missing? Who was this woman?

"It's time for you to go home, Lark." The woman pointed at the portal and let my hand go.

I stumbled toward the portal. As I stepped through, I tried to focus on the old woman, tried to memorize her features, any detail, but her face kept slipping away. This woman had helped me, but I couldn't quite remember how or why. "Thank you."

"We will meet again someday, I promise." Her craggy voice faded as I slipped from the veil and reformed in the backyard of my family home in the living realm.

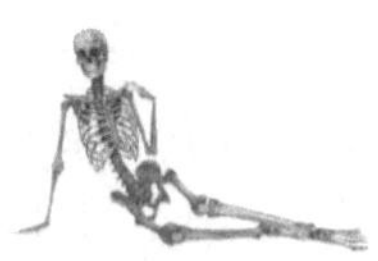

THE DREAM SLIPPED from my memory as I grasped to remember what vital information I'd recovered—something about the veil and an old woman. Like all the other times I dreamed of when I'd first travelled to the veil, the memories faded and the details fled, leaving me as clueless to the events as before.

With a groan, I fluttered my eyes open and found myself flung over Connor's body as if my sleeping state worried he'd somehow escape. He didn't look like he planned to go anywhere. He lay on his back, gently running his fingers along my spine. His eyes weren't fully open, and he blinked slowly. He looked like a content cat, laying in his favourite sunspot.

Just over a week ago, he'd ripped a man's body apart as revenge for kidnapping me and out of frustration, fear and grief because he'd believed at the time he'd been too late to save me. Nothing about his physical prowess scared me, though I guess it probably should. He'd never harm me, and his magic made my body sing.

My only regret about finding Connor in that clearing with Steve's blood splattered all over his body was that I hadn't been there to see that fucker's demise. Maybe that said something awful about me, but I couldn't bring myself to feel a minutia of sadness or remorse for having such dark thoughts.

I'd been in the veil, biding my time with Leviathan and dodging deals like a pro. I'd figured out that the soul Leviathan had held right before he sent me back to the living realm must've been Steve's. It hadn't been a soul spy after all, like I originally assumed. Leviathan had caught Steve's soul, realized what that meant, and fulfilled his promise to send me back.

And he'd told me to say hello to Connor.

I stiffened.

The Lord of the Veil knew who Connor Kang was, and in all the hubbub afterward, I'd forgotten this crucial detail. At the time, I assumed the spirit Levi had held in his grasp—most likely the newly-departed Steve—had told him, but I never had a chance to follow up. After melting into Connor's arms, shock had set in and with everything else involved with the healing and therapy over the last week, Leviathan's off-hand comment got pushed to the side.

Connor stopped strumming my back and rolled a little so he could look at me. "What's wrong?"

"Why would Leviathan, Lord of the Veil, know your name?"

Connor frowned. "I'm not sure."

I sank back into the bed and ran my hand down his chest. "He probably said it to mess with me, but I still don't like it."

"Did you want to go and ask him?"

"Fuck no."

"Is there anything you can do about it now?"

"Also, no."

"Then let's log the information and see if it's a piece to a bigger puzzle later." Connor sighed and slipped from the bed. "I guess that's as good a segue as any for getting up to visit the family plot." He peered down at me, his expression softening. "Unless you're too tired?"

He had worked my body like his personal play putty through the night. I was tired and sore but in the most wonderful way possible. My skin tingled, and my body hummed with energy. I felt like I could hike up Mount Finlayson in thirty minutes.

Which was ridiculous. I'd never climb that mountain that fast. Even if I lived closer and hiked it every day.

"I feel amazing," I said. "But I'm a little conflicted. While I personally feel great, I know this won't be an easy outing for you, which makes me feel awful. Maybe I should do this part alone?"

He leaned down and flung the covers off my naked body. His gaze raked my exposed skin, and he reached out to pull me close. Starting with the softness of my stomach, he kissed his way along my body until he made it to the sensitive skin of my neck, just below my ear.

"I'll be okay, Lark." He gently bit my earlobe. "Unless you don't want to get dressed. If you stay naked in my bed any longer, I'm going to have to assume you intend to kill me and neutralize the threat accordingly."

I snorted and pushed him away. When he straightened, he held out his hand and I placed mine in his and let him haul me from the warm cocoon of his bed.

CHAPTER TWELVE

The tombstones sat in tidy rows upon rows as the late afternoon sun shone down to illuminate the engravings. A gentle wind wove around the strategically planted trees and bushes that separated the various areas. We'd entered one of the oldest sections of this cemetery, the tombstones no longer uniform, some listing to the side, others with crumbled edges to show the passage of time and long exposure to the elements. I studied the ones with statues as we quietly moved through the rows, the eerie angels and cherubs silently watching us as we passed.

After we'd showered together, which ended up being a lot longer and steamier than either of us intended, we'd thrown on our clothes from last night.

Well, most of our clothes.

My underwear was ruined, and Connor didn't even try not to look smug about it.

"I'll get you a new pair," he'd promised before we hopped in my car and headed for the cemetery.

"Do you ever get used to it?" Connor asked as we walked along the rows of tombstones.

"Visiting graveyards?"

"Being surrounded by all the death energy."

"You have death magic yourself."

"Yes, but I avoid cemeteries for that exact reason. I can handle the death magic at a crime scene, but being surrounded by so many corpses in a graveyard sets my own power off. Like it has a mind of its own and it's uneasy. Do you not experience the same thing?"

I shrugged. The magic hummed along my skin and made my own power pulse in my veins. "I guess, but I must've acclimatized to it. Do you get used to visiting murder scenes?"

His expression closed off. "No. Those aren't quite the words I would use to describe it. Desensitized, maybe. No crime scene is the same and I always arrive with apprehension. I block out the feelings and focus on what needs to get done."

"I think that's a fairly accurate way to describe how I feel about graveyards, though I know the experiences are not the same." I paused as a thought crossed my mind. "What do you do as a barghest, anyway?"

"I'm a detective, Lark. That's what I do. I just happen to be a barghest. I can sense death magic, see and hear spirits, talk to them if they're present and I can use death magic to transform into a hideous beast that can rend flesh from bone."

"But..."

Connor sighed. "Do all Italians play soccer and cook pasta?"

"Well..."

He grimaced. "Do all tall people play basketball, all pretty people model, all necromancers turn evil? Just because I can do something, doesn't mean I do it. Being a barghest doesn't dictate my path in life."

"Okay. I get your point." Sort of. Connor completely defied all the detailed bedtime stories casting barghests as evil monsters. But most children's stories were cautionary tales meant to convey safety rules and life lessons. Mom adamantly and repetitively stated I was to avoid barghests at all costs. Why? What was I missing? I took a deep breath before asking, "So you're not planning to eat my soul or smite me in the veil?"

"No." His lips twitched into a small smile, and he reached out to grab my hand. "This way."

I was too shocked to pull my hand away. Connor didn't come across like the PDA type, but his large hand wrapped around mine sent warmth spreading through my body.

Not that the cemetery was very public. But still. We hadn't spoken about our relationship and frankly, I didn't want to. Things between us were going so well that a "what are we" or "what are we doing" conversation might mess things up. It might complicate things when everything felt so simple and easy.

We walked in silence through the cemetery, Connor leading the way.

Each row of gravestones was punctuated by fresh and decaying flowers. Though evidence clearly indicated frequent visitation, the grounds were currently empty.

"Do you come here often?" I asked.

Connor jerked and looked at me sideways.

"Sorry." I winced. "I didn't mean for that to come out like some sort of cheesy pick-up line. I genuinely wished to ask if you visited your family's plot often."

"I don't like to dwell on the dead." Connor glanced over at me. "Not when everything I want is here in the living realm."

I swallowed and met his fierce gaze.

"I've never visited," Connor continued as if my heart hadn't just exploded. "The death energy messes with my control. I can use it to travel to the veil, but I have no need or desire to go there."

"Then how did you know..."

"I always knew this cemetery had our family plot, and I've been here before for funerals. But I haven't stepped foot in this cemetery since I was a child." He squeezed my hand. "It was for my grandmother's funeral. She was the matriarch of our family, and her death shattered me."

"I'm sorry."

"She always had these hard candies in her purse, and came to all of my Christmas concerts." He looked away and shrugged. "Everyone learns the fragility of life at some point."

"It's still a hard lesson, no matter the age. Do you remember which way to go?"

"Of course. Their remains call to me." He peered down at me. "Can you sense the difference in the energy? The power?"

I hadn't thought to try.

Reaching out with my magic, I let it flit through the cemetery, flowing past each death signature. Like a bear drawn to honey, a power, still distant, pulsed. I directed my magic toward the source.

Yes. The magic felt different. Stronger. Darker.

I shivered.

"I'll take that as a yes."

We turned in unison down the path toward the power source. I no longer needed direction. When we reached the family plot, Connor released my hand and paused.

A large statue stood in the centre, a giant stone barghest looking over the plots. Shaped like a wolf, only much larger, with thick fur covering its body, the barghest statue had a row of horn-like tufts around the base of its skull, poking out of the long fur to look like a spiky mane. When I saw one in real life, I'd had a passing thought that the spiky tufts looked like some sort of demonic halo.

The barghest in real life had a glowing whitish-blue gaze and greenish death energy had swirled around its massive body. The stone statue didn't have either of those things, but it still sent chills down my body.

"A bit obvious." I glanced at Connor.

He shrugged. "It wasn't exactly my decision. Most people, if they even venture this far, would just assume it's another gargoyle. Hell, no one really goes to cemeteries except for funerals now anyways."

I raised an eyebrow.

"And you, of course," he said. "If another necromancer came this way, given your lore about our kind, if they managed to somehow recognize the magic, they'd most likely turn and go the other way."

I most definitely would've walked the other way if I came across this prior to learning Connor's true identity. I wouldn't have known what the power signature meant, but it vibrated with potency and menace—not something I'd take lightly at any given time, and definitely not something I'd raise. "Makes sense."

I walked around the statue to the other plots and froze.

The upturned dirt was the first sign all was not well in the graveyard.

Connor cursed.

I quickly scanned the tombstone: Frances Sharrock.

"My grandmother."

"Not to be insensitive, but why would they go for the most recent burial?" I knelt by the open grave and ran my hand through the dirt to send my magic into the ground, searching.

If I had to retrieve bones, I'd go for the older graves so there'd less likely to be tissue and other remains inside.

What a morbid thought.

My magic flowed through the surrounding earth, relaying information about the nearby remains and death magic.

Connor walked up to the open grave. "It's empty, isn't it?"

I swallowed and nodded. The person who dug up his maternal grandmother's grave had taken everything. I didn't need to open the casket to know not a single bone remained.

"I'm screwed," Connor whispered.

I straightened and turned back to the statue. "Maybe the person didn't know your family's identity as barghests. Maybe they just searched cemeteries until they found this. And it's your maternal side of the family, your identity may still be safe because you have a different last name."

"And it may not be," he said. "They might know exactly who and what I am." And his whole family was now vulnerable to exposure. He could lose his job. His friends. Everything.

No. That wasn't quite true. He wouldn't lose me, Jacobs or his family.

Connor curled his hands into fists. Anger and power radiated from him, and his whole body vibrated. He opened his mouth to say something, but only a snarl came out.

"Connor?" I stepped forward.

He didn't look at me. Instead, he squeezed his eyes shut as a low growl escaped his lips. "Run."

I didn't need to be told twice. Spinning on my heel, I took off, running as fast as I could toward the car. I knew enough about Connor to know I likely had nothing to fear from him harming me in his barghest form, but he didn't want me to see his transformation. He didn't want to risk me at all. And he didn't want to risk losing control.

So I ran.

I ran to give him space and now he had one less thing to worry about. As I reached the car, an ear-splitting howl shattered the calm night.

CHAPTER THIRTEEN

I pulled up outside the house of Lily Zheng's parents and shoved the gear into park. Originally, I'd planned to come here with Connor, but he never returned to the car and hadn't replied to any of my messages, yet, so I decided to cross some things off the list while I waited for him to return to his magnificent human self.

My phone vibrated with a text message from Jacobs. I'd asked for Connor's sister's number.

Is he okay? Jacobs asked after supplying the number.

He's fine, I replied before hitting the contact information. I might be overstepping, but Connor in barghest form running around the city and an unknown grave robber in possession of barghest bones, I felt compelled to tell someone in Connor's family, and a sister seemed more approachable than parents.

She picked up on the second ring. "Hello?"

"Hi. Is this Jane?"

A hesitation. "It is."

"Hi. My name is Lark Morgan and I work with—"

"I know who you are."

Oh.

I paused and stared at my phone screen for a couple of blinks. How did Jane already know my name? Obviously, Connor had spoken about me, but what exactly did he say? "Uh...okay. Cool."

Cool? Seriously?

I groaned and mentally face palmed. Denise was right. I was awkward. "Look, I'm probably overstepping, but I wanted to call someone in Connor's family to warn you."

Silence answered me. Then, "Is he okay?"

"Connor is fine, just...unavailable for phone conversion right now."

Jane snorted. "Tactful."

"Thank you." I took a deep breath. "Someone has raided your maternal grandmother's grave. They've taken all the remains and we believe they've used some of the bones to destroy at least one spirit. I'm sure Connor will call once he's able to, but I wasn't sure how long he'll need, how pressing this information is or how immediately you needed to be informed."

Jane spat out a string of impressive curses.

My eyebrows rose. "I'm sorry if I should've minded my own business."

"No," she said. "No, you did the right thing. I can see why he likes you."

My heart caught in my throat.

"I don't mean to be rude, but I have to hang up now and make a bunch of calls," Jane said.

"Of course. Understandable. Please let me know if there's anything I can do."

"Take care of my brother and don't break his heart," Jane said before hanging up.

I sat in my vehicle and stared at my phone again for a few moments before collecting myself. I'd left Connor alone to lose control and ran off to interview the parents of a murder victim. Did that count as taking care of him?

I winced and shoved my phone into my pocket. Guess I'd find out. Barghests didn't exactly come with a dating manual.

Walking up the steps, I approached the solid oak door, painted a tasteful dark blue to go with the gray siding. I used the gold knocker. A breeze blew past me, bringing with it scents of ocean salt and pine needles.

An older East Asian woman opened the door and blinked at me, her brows pinching in, her body posture tensing.

The full necromancer outfit had a way of intimidating people. In hindsight, I should've gone with jeans.

"Mrs. Zheng? I'm sorry to impose on your day. My name is Lark Morgan and I'm a contractor with the

Victoria Police Department. I was wondering if I could have a moment of your time?" I held up my identification.

Mrs. Zheng stepped back, her mouth dropping open to form a perfect O. "A necromancer?"

"Yes, ma'am."

Her arms fell to her sides, slack. "Is this about Lily? The police have already contacted us."

"I'm afraid so. I understand if this isn't a good time."

"No..." She looked off into the other room, her chin trembled. "No. Now is as good a time as any." Mrs. Zheng opened the door more and stepped back to allow me space to enter.

As I stepped into the tidy West Coast styled home, crisp and refreshing air washed over me.

I nodded to Mrs. Zheng and removed my boots before following the woman into the living room. The walls were painted a soothing shade of seafoam green that complimented the natural wood panelled ceiling and exposed beams. Sunlight streamed in through the large picture windows.

An older East Asian man sat in an armchair, a newspaper open and spread across his lap. The paper forgotten, the man stared out the window.

"Tony!" Mrs. Zheng snapped.

The man jerked upright in his seat, his gaze focusing first on his wife and then on me. "Who are you?"

"This is Ms. Morgan from the VicPD. She's a necromancer," Mrs. Zheng said, her accent so soft, I hadn't caught it right away.

"Oh." Mr. Zheng nodded to himself. "Oh. Have a seat." He waved at the plush, cream-coloured loveseat adorned with soft, teal and navy blue accent pillows to his right. Mrs. Zheng excused herself to make some tea.

I sat down and folded my hands over my lap. "I am very sorry for the intrusion. I know this can't be easy for you. We were hoping you might answer some questions to help us make sense of recent events."

Mr. Zheng shook his head, his mouth flattening into a thin line.

"It's been awful." Mrs. Zheng carried a tray with a teapot and cups into the living room. She must've already had the water prepared. "We struggled with saying goodbye the first time and just when we're finding a sense of peace, we have to relive it all over again."

She set the tray down on the intricately carved wooden coffee table before picking up the teapot. She first poured for me, then her husband and finally for herself before setting the teapot down and taking a seat.

I thanked her for the tea and lifted the cup to my face. Hot steam lifted from the surface bringing a light, fresh orchid aroma to my nose.

"Tell me about your daughter Lily."

Mrs. Zheng placed her cup down. "There is so

much to say. Where do we start?" She glanced over at her husband. He had left his tea untouched and was staring out the window again.

"Maybe we should start with what I know," I said. "I know she was fatally injured at a busy intersection four years ago while waiting for her boyfriend to pick her up. She was four months pregnant. Although the boyfriend was a suspect, no one was arrested for the hit and run, and her murder has remained unsolved. Days ago, her body reappeared at the same intersection as if the accident had just happened except she bore no wounds." I paused to collect my thoughts. "Her grave had also been dug up and her bones removed. This indicates that something supernatural is involved, at least in part. Was Lily into the occult? Did she have any magical abilities? Did she know someone who did? That is the kind of information we're looking for. Anything to help us find the person or persons responsible."

Mrs. Zheng nodded again, gaze darting back and forth. "If you're a necromancer, can't you...can't you just ask her? If you need our permission, you have it. I'll sign whatever you want."

I didn't need parental permission to raise a spirit for a police investigation, but that's not what sent ice flowing over my skin and pain squeezing my chest. Under no circumstances did I want to tell them the soul of their beloved daughter might've been destroyed. "Lily didn't answer my call."

Mrs. Zheng blinked at me. "Why...why would that happen?"

"There are many reasons, but none of them change the outcome, so we're trying to focus on the glamy angle that could explain her reappearance."

Mrs. Zheng bit her lip and looked away.

"Mrs. Zheng?"

"Please, call me Alice," she said. "Lily had so many talents, so many things to live for, but she didn't possess any magical or supernatural abilities. She was a drab like the rest of us. I think she may have known a witch or two through school or sports, but no one major in her life."

"Not even the boyfriend?"

The dad scoffed. "The only thing significant about that boy was how deep his parents' pockets went."

"Tony," Alice warned.

"Well, it's true. A rich kid was seen fleeing the scene and doesn't get arrested. If that's not money talking, I don't know what is."

"Do you think he did it?" I asked Tony.

He turned his gaze to me. "I know he did."

I sat back on the couch and tapped my teacup. "Why would he do it? Because she was pregnant?"

Tony grunted and looked out the window again.

Alice reached forward and tapped his knee. "Tony always thought the parents gave that boy an ultimatum—the money or the girl."

Still, that was a big leap to murdering your lover.

"The part that hurts the most is that she didn't come to us," Alice spoke softly. "Sure, we were strict. Our parents came to this country with nothing, and we had to work hard to get where we are today. We wanted to instill that work ethic and drive in Lily. But we would've helped her. We wouldn't have shunned her or turned her away because of an unplanned pregnancy. That's what cuts me the deepest." Alice's lips quivered. "She died thinking we didn't love her unconditionally and now it's too late...it's too late to tell her."

"I'm sure she knew in the end." I put the teacup down and pushed back the feelings threatening to overwhelm me. I'd just lied to Alice. And now, because Lily's spirit had most likely been irrevocably destroyed, their daughter would never get to hear the words from her parents.

I managed to ask a few more questions before thanking them for their hospitality and choking out a goodbye. One thing was perfectly clear to me—Lily's parents loved her very much.

When I reached the car, my phone started buzzing.

"Morgan," I answered.

"It's me," Connor's deep voice rumbled through my phone's speaker.

"Are you okay?"

"Yes." A pause. "I'm sorry for that."

"Don't be. I was worried, though."

"I don't think I'd ever hurt you in that form, but I didn't want to risk it, and frankly, I didn't want you to see the transformation. It's not...pretty." Another pause. "Do you happen to know why I have a number of missed calls from Jacobs, my sister and my parents?"

He'd called me first. Not that it was a competition because I'd never get in the way of Connor and his family, but knowing he was concerned about me enough to call right away sent warmth spreading across my chest. I didn't know what to do with the upwelling of emotions, so I went with verbal diarrhea. "I'm sorry. I was worried about you and your family and didn't know how long you'd be...away. I called your sister and gave her a heads-up in case this situation needed immediate attention. And I got her number from Jacobs. I hope I didn't overstep."

"That...that was really thoughtful. Thank you."

"You're welcome."

"Where are you?"

"Just finishing up with Lily Zheng's parents."

"How'd it go?"

"Well, I'm super sad now and we don't have any more answers than before, so not good. Father thinks the boyfriend did it."

"No answers still provide information. You're eliminating possibilities and narrowing down the suspect field. Thank you for doing that. My next stop was the boyfriend. Would you like to come?"

I thought of all the witty responses, especially since I did a lot of coming last night, but settled with, "Yes."

CHAPTER FOURTEEN

I pulled up to the blue and gray townhouse wedged in a row of complexes on the west shore. Jacobs and Connor waited for me on the sidewalk. Connor had changed, so he must've gone home first and had his partner pick him up.

I shut the door and joined them on the sidewalk. "Hey."

"Hey, Morgan." Jacobs smiled. "Kang filled me in on your visit with Lily's parents. Next time, take one of us. I know part of this investigation is a little off the books with all the soul stuff, but you should have backup."

"Okay." I glanced at Connor...Kang.

He'd filled in his partner? Exactly how much had he shared?

"I am glad to have your help on this one," Jacobs

continued. "I wish they'd hire necromancers as officers."

Connor didn't say anything. He settled his dark gaze on me and nodded.

I rocked back on my heels and shoved my hands in my pockets. I'd rather run them down Connor's chest to make sure he was okay, but apparently, we were being standoffish.

Jacobs looked at me expectantly.

"Yeah, sure. No problem," I said.

Jacobs frowned and glanced between the two of us. Awkward silence settled over the sidewalk.

"You two really need to just make out already." Jacobs turned and walked up the stairs.

Probably for the best because the heat burning my face meant I must've turned so red I'd blend in at the fire department.

Connor leaned over. "You're blushing."

I shoved his shoulder. "You obviously didn't fill him in on *everything*."

He clicked his tongue and shook his head. "A gentleman never kisses and tells."

I snorted and walked past him. "Sure you're not trying to keep your options open?"

"With Jacobs? Neither of us swing that way, but if we did, he'd have already broken my heart by now."

I stopped and gaped at him.

Connor winked and sauntered up the stairs to join me.

"Are you two coming?" Jacobs called down from the top of the stairs before turning to knock on the door.

I pushed my feelings for Connor to the side and joined Jacobs at the door. "Interesting choice of words."

Jacobs barked out a laugh.

Connor smirked at me, but I focused on the entrance as it opened to reveal a young, attractive man. He had brown hair, brown eyes, and an olive complexion. He stood over six feet tall with wide shoulders and looked like he should be on the header for some bougie sailing club's monthly subscriber's newsletter.

"Hello?" the man asked.

"Mason Miller?" Jacobs asked.

"Yeah?" His gaze flicked over us.

"My name is Detective Jacobs, and this is my partner Detective Kang and our DM Consultant, Lark Morgan."

"DM Consultant?" Mason asked.

I silently thanked him for the question because Jacobs had never used that term before, and I was completely out of the loop.

"Death Magic," Jacobs said, somehow keeping a straight face. Fuck police work, this guy should've gone into acting.

I managed not to groan or snort.

Connor remained silent and observant, a big ball of dark energy at my back.

These detectives probably didn't need me here for anything other than show and to protect Kang's true identity.

Shaking off the thought, I smiled when Mason's gaze snagged on my face.

He flinched and quickly looked away. Maybe I smiled a little too hard.

Connor stepped forward, positioning himself between us. "We'd like to ask you a few questions about Lily Zheng."

"Lily?" Mason paled. He looked away and swallowed. "I heard...I heard her..." He swallowed again. "I heard the news."

Jacobs nodded. "May we come in?"

"Yes," Mason said and stepped back. "Yes, please come in."

We walked into the entranceway and paused.

"Would you like us to remove our shoes?" Jacobs asked.

"No, that's okay," Mason said. "Please come in and have a seat."

With the compact layout, the townhouse had a kitchen immediately to the left after the linen closet and a staircase to the right led up to the bedrooms. I didn't need a tour or to see the floor plan to know the short hallway ahead would open up to a living space and dining room. Almost all the townhouses in this area had the exact same layout.

Mason stepped into the area that bordered the two

open spaces and waved back and forth. "Couch or dining table?"

Connor nodded at the wood dining table, and we all took a seat. Mason sat with his back to the wall, Jacobs took the chair at the end, and I sat with Connor on the side opposite of Mason.

A professionally taken photo of Mason with a pretty woman hung in a frame on the wall.

"My fiancée," Mason said when he noticed what held my attention. "She's at work."

"When did you meet?" Connor asked.

"Just over a year ago? It took time to...took time to grieve. It's hard to forget your first love, you know?"

We all dead-panned and it made me wonder if the three of us were all broken. I hadn't experienced that big love. I'd had relationships, of course, but they always had a temporary feel to them. My relationship with Connor was probably the most serious feeling thing I'd ever had, and it had only started. I didn't want to jinx it into oblivion.

"What would you like to know?" Mason asked after none of us responded to his last statement.

Jacobs and Connor spent the next ten minutes confirming the information they already knew from previous police reports. Mason had been in a relationship with Lily four years ago, knew she was pregnant and planned to meet her at the corner where she died.

"What happened?" Jacobs asked.

"What?"

"You planned to meet her at 1:45am in the early morning at the intersection. A car fatally struck her at 2:00am. You were not at the scene. Did you not intend to show at all?" Jacobs asked.

"No!" Mason straightened in his seat and leaned forward. "No. I loved Lily. The pregnancy was unexpected but not unwanted. I...fuck. I still love her. I miss her. And the baby..." His voice cracked, and he looked away. "I lost the two things I loved most in the world that night and I hadn't even met one of them yet."

Silence fell over the table while Mason swiped his shirt sleeve over his face.

"Why were you late?" Connor asked.

"My car was stolen. I had to wake up and beg my parents to use their van. They never really approved of Lily, and I suspect they stalled on purpose—some weird way of theirs to sabotage our relationship."

"They must've stalled for a long time."

Mason winced and bowed his head. "Look. My parents got an expensive lawyer that told me to keep my mouth shut, but I...I just can't anymore. Not if it will help find who did this to Lily."

Jacobs and Connor waited, their expressions remaining open and relaxed.

I sat on my hands and tried not to vibrate with anticipation.

"I arrived on the scene in my mom's van shortly after the accident happened. First responders had just arrived. I freaked out. I freaked out and drove away."

He kept his head bowed. "I didn't have anything to do with her death, but it's my greatest regret in life that I wasn't on time and that I didn't park and get out of that fucking van to be with her in her final moments."

Mason paused, grief pinching his features. He clamped his mouth shut, but the corners quivered. He blinked rapidly and looked away, swiping again at his face with his shirt sleeve.

Jacobs cleared his throat. "If it provides any relief, the autopsy indicated she died on impact. She was already gone when you arrived."

"She still died thinking I deserted her." He choked back a sob and rocked a little in his seat.

We sat in silence again for a minute or two, allowing Mason to collect himself.

"There were witness accounts of a black Honda Civic leaving the scene, the exact make and model of your stolen vehicle."

Mason shook his head. "I swear that wasn't me."

"Why were you meeting her so late?"

"She was spending time with a friend and planned to come home with me." Mason swiped at his face again and sat up.

Jacobs flipped through his notebook. "Lia Holland?"

The detective had been busy pulling the previous police report.

"That's her," he said. "They were best friends and grew up together. We lost touch after...after the accident. I couldn't stand to look at her and I think Lia felt the same way. We both reminded each other of her. Last I heard, she was planning to move to Vancouver. To start over, you know?"

Jacobs nodded. "One more question."

Mason looked up.

"Were both your parents present when you asked to borrow the van?" Jacobs asked.

Mason stilled, his gaze shifting from one detective to the other.

"Mason?"

"Y...yes," he stammered. "You can't think they had something to do with this."

Jacobs shrugged. "Just trying to get a complete picture of the night in question."

"Did you go to Lily directly from your parents' place, or did you make a stop?" Connor asked.

Apparently, they still had more questions.

Mason flustered, blinking at Connor. "I stopped at the drug store to pick up some antacids and folic acid before heading over. Lily had only told me about the pregnancy a few days before and I hadn't reacted..." He looked away. "My reaction wasn't the best. I started thinking about all the ways the baby was going to change my life without considering how Lily felt, how she must've been freaking out just as much, if not more than me. Not only was the baby going to change her life, but also her body. I'd already apologized profusely, but words are only words. I planned to show her how much I loved her and our unborn child." He sniffed and finally looked back at us. "I wanted her to know I was all in."

Shortly after that, we gently excused ourselves and left the townhouse. Jacobs and Connor shared a look when they reached the cars.

"Any magical stuff?" Jacobs asked, directing the question to both of us.

I shook my head.

"Nothing," Connor answered. "No smells, either."

Jacobs grunted in agreement. "He was telling the truth."

"Do you think the parents are involved?" I asked.

Jacobs shrugged again. "If they had his car stashed nearby, they still could've beaten him to the scene after he left, especially since he made a stop first."

"So, they could still be involved..." I said.

A slow, wide smile spread across Connor's face. "Would you like to come with us and find out?"

CHAPTER FIFTEEN

My phone buzzed as I slid into my car, and I quickly looked at the screen to see a text from Logan. *Bring something starchy to dinner tonight.*

I'd forgotten about dinner with Mom and the boys tonight. I was a terrible daughter and sister. Already addicted to Connor, I'd mentally planned another night of debauchery with him, and forgot all about my plans to confront Mom about her rules and why I grew talons in the veil.

Sighing, I quickly texted my twin back. *What's in it for me?*

Your continued existence, he replied. He followed it up with a knife emoji.

I laughed and slid my phone into the holder. Logan wasn't lying. Mom had taken simple carbs out of her diet, and Logan loved bread. He got cranky without it.

The passenger door opened, and Connor slipped into the seat beside me.

I jumped and spun toward him. "What are you doing?"

"Getting a ride."

I stared pointedly at Jacobs' car as it pulled away from the curb.

"I'd much rather ride with you," he said. "You smell nicer."

"Aren't you worried your partner will figure it out?"

He raised his eyebrows. "It?"

I waved my hand back and forth between us. "You know what I mean."

"Well, you weren't exactly hiding it with your joke earlier." Connor chuckled and shut the door. After snapping on his seatbelt, he leaned back in the seat and closed his eyes. "But Jacobs already knows."

I shoved the gear into drive and navigated the vehicle into traffic. "I thought you didn't kiss and tell."

"With Jacobs, I don't need to. He figured it out right away." Connor didn't open his eyes to respond.

"You were both just teasing me?"

A slow smile spread across his face.

"You're both assholes."

He popped open his eyes briefly to look over at me. "You're just realizing that now?"

"Well, no. I already knew about you. Jacobs comes as a surprise." I turned down the next street. Jacobs had already sped ahead, but I didn't need him. The address was in my phone and the map app gave nice directions.

Connor closed his eyes again, a soft smile still spread across his face.

"Does shifting take a lot of energy? Is that why you're so tired?" I asked.

"Shifting? No. I'm tired because I had a hellion in my bed who kept me up all night."

My cheeks warmed. "You were hardly an innocent bystander."

"No. I wasn't." His smile somehow widened. "What are you doing tonight? After this?"

"I'm meeting with my brother, his boyfriend, and my mother for dinner."

He grumbled.

"Why?"

"I was hoping you'd say me."

I rolled my eyes and took the next left. "You need to work on your propositioning skills."

"Funny. I don't recall you complaining about my skills last night."

Hah. I shook my head and pressed the brake pedal to stop for the light. I had zero complaints about last night and he knew it.

"Come home with me tonight, Lark," he said, his voice a deep purr.

I hesitated, my chest growing warm at the softness in his voice. "I really do have dinner with my family."

"Then come over after."

The light turned green, and I released the brake to apply the gas. "It'll be late."

"I don't care."

I glanced over to find him alert and sitting up. He studied my face and waited for my answer.

"I *guess* I can make an appearance."

He reached over and squeezed my hand. "Promise?"

I navigated the car into a parking spot outside a large property in the South Oak Bay area of Victoria.

I stepped from the car, shut the door, and whistled. Wow. This was one hell of a house. On the other side of a well-manicured hedge, golden sunlight bathed the smooth, cream-coloured exterior adorned with delicate carvings and intricate details.

Jacobs had already parked and walked over to a break in the hedge where there was a wrought-iron gate. "Ready? Or do you two need a little more time?"

I narrowed my eyes. Exactly how had Jacobs figured out my involvement with Connor? Had it been his stellar detective skills or something else?

Jacobs winked before swinging the gate open. "I tried coming by yesterday to ask some questions and got turned around at the door," Jacobs told me, speaking over his shoulder. "They required me to schedule a meeting."

"You know what that means?" Connor asked as he held the gate open for me.

"He's a busy person?" I answered.

Connor shook his head and leaned down to whisper in my ear as he closed the gate behind us. "He wants a lawyer present."

"Why do you sound happy about that? Aren't lawyers a pain?" I silently whispered an apology to Brandon. Obviously, he was an exception to the rule.

"Absolutely," Connor said. "It also means Mr. Miller likely has something to hide."

"Let's discuss later," Jacobs hissed from up ahead. "I don't want to have to reschedule."

I followed the detectives down a cobblestone path lined with fragrant lavender and blooming roses and a grass lawn so lush I was tempted to lie down on it to see if it was as soft and cushy as it appeared.

"What exactly do Mr. and Mrs. Miller do for a living?" I asked no one in particular.

"He's an investment broker and as far as our records indicate, her job is to spend his money. They had multiple nannies, house cleaners and cooks over the years," Jacobs said.

Sounded like a sweet job to me. "I'm sure there's a downside even to that job."

Connor shook his head. "Always the pessimist."

"And you aren't?"

Before he could retort, a bonafide butler opened the door and led us to a quiet study where Mr. Miller and another man, both in expensive suits waited.

Mr. Miller looked like an older replica of his son—same brown hair, brown eyes, and olive skin tone. Gray streaked his hair at the temples and wrinkles lined his forehead and mouth. He looked like someone who frowned more than smiled.

"Thank you for coming, detectives," James Miller stood and shook our hands. "This is my attorney, Felix Colburn. He will be joining us for this meeting."

The cost of Felix's designer suit alone marked him as a successful lawyer, even if the keen glint of intelligence in his dark brown gaze didn't give him away. He wasn't as tall as his client—probably standing around five-foot-ten compared to Mr. Miller's six-foot-something, but he had presence and carried himself with confidence.

Jacobs flashed his wide, people-pleasing smile. "Of course. Will Mrs. Miller be joining us?"

"Sadly, no. Rebecca had a prior engagement." Mr. Miller sat down and waved at the seats across from him and the lawyer.

Felix, the attorney, stepped forward and rested his hand on Mr. Miller's shoulder. "My client is meeting with you and answering your questions on a voluntary basis. He reserves the right to withdraw his cooperation at any time, and I'd like to remind you to keep your questions focused."

"Of course," Jacobs continued to wear his fake smile. "We're just following up with a cold case that had some recent developments and would like to ask a few questions to clarify events on the night of Lily Zheng's unfortunate accident."

Mr. Miller made a circular motion in the air with his hand—as if to say, "Get on with it."

I suddenly developed an instant, intense dislike for the man sitting across from me.

The interview started in a similar manner as the one with Mr. Miller's son—the detectives established his whereabouts and the sequence of events leading up to the time of Lily's death. So far everything aligned with Mason's story.

"Your son indicated that on the night of Lily's death, his vehicle went missing," Jacobs said after pretending to consult his notes.

"That's correct," Mr. Miller said.

"They filed a police report," Felix added.

"That you did. You also indicated that Mason came to you prior to the incident and asked to borrow your vehicle. You eventually relented, but why did you delay granting permission?"

Mr. Miller exchanged a look with his attorney before turning back to us. "I didn't approve of the relationship. We hoped our delay would make him late enough that she would leave."

"You didn't like her?" Jacobs asked.

"I didn't approve of her. They were too young to be so serious. But I didn't dislike her, and I certainly didn't disapprove enough to do anything more than create conflict between them. I hoped a real argument would make them see that life wasn't a bed of roses. I certainly would never hurt the girl. Geez. Lily didn't deserve what happened to her." He looked down at his hands where he folded them on the table in front of him. "If I hadn't delayed our son from going to her, she never would've been harmed, and I have to live with that. We didn't know she was pregnant. Our son lost his girlfriend, and we lost a grandchild."

A moment of silence washed over us.

"Just one more question. After Mason borrowed your vehicle, what did you and your wife do?" Jacobs asked.

"We stayed home," Mr. Miller said.

"Together?" Connor finally broke his silence.

"Yes, of course, together," Mr. Miller said. "It was the middle of the night. We went back to sleep."

"Did you at any point during that night know the whereabouts of your son's vehicle?" Jacobs asked.

"No."

Jacobs and Connor exchanged a look and stood up together.

I scrambled to my feet to follow suit.

Mr. Miller focused on me for the first time in the conversation. "What did you say your role was?"

"I didn't."

"Nor did you share your name," Felix added.

"My name is Lark Morgan," I said.

Felix and Mr. Miller waited expectantly.

"She's our consultant." Connor reached forward and pushed my chair in for me.

"A consultant for what?" Felix asked.

"Magic, mostly." Jacobs shrugged.

Both men stiffened.

A cold mask slid over the lawyer's face. "Obtaining information by magical means requires consent or a warrant. You had neither and any information she gathered is inadmissible in court."

"Relax," Jacobs said. Obviously, he hadn't learned that telling someone to do that had the opposite effect.

Or maybe he did know that and hated James Miller's attitude as well.

"She didn't gather anything," Connor said.

"I'm a necromancer," I said. "Not a witch."

Both men paled but didn't say anything more, and we followed the nameless butler out of the house.

After we cleared the property and stood outside the hedge, Connor turned to Jacobs. "So?"

"He told the truth the entire time," Jacobs said.

Connor rocked back on his heels. "Son of a bitch. His lawyer thought he was guilty."

"Oh, he's hiding something, but it has nothing to do with our case. My guess is money laundering or something else financial. I'll tip off the boys."

I cleared my throat.

Both men turned to me. Jacobs raised his eyebrows. Connor's expression didn't change except a small tug on his lips.

"Would one of you care to explain why or how Jacobs is suddenly a walking lie detector?"

Jacobs opened his mouth to start speaking but

stopped when I held up my hand. “Don’t try to tell me you’re really good at reading body language. I’m about done with my bullshit quota after being in the same room as that guy.”

Jacobs sighed and shared another look with Connor. “I was really hoping she’d figure it out by now.”

“You can scent a lie, you have annoyingly good hearing and you’ve been off when there’s a full moon—at least the more recent ones when I started to pay attention.”

Connor smirked. “Our supervisors aren’t aware of that last tidbit, but only because I cover for his furry ass.”

Jacobs grumbled.

“Come on, man. We haven’t exactly been discrete or subtle around Lark.”

I gaped at Jacobs.

He had the audacity to stop grumbling long enough to wink at me.

“But...but...” I shook my head and jabbed my finger in the air at each man. “You’re a werewolf and you’re a barghest?”

They nodded.

“We figured each other out within seconds of meeting, and—” Jacobs started.

“Exactly why the fuck am I your magical consultant?” The answer smacked my brain. “I’m just a cover, aren't I? You don't need me at all. These six years, you've been using me as a shield."

I wanted to throw up. I needed to throw up. I thought I had made a difference. Six years I'd participated in this sham without realizing.

I really was an idiot.

Jacobs snarled.

Connor stepped in close, blocking out everything else and stole the air from my lungs. He grabbed both my arms. "Don't you for one second doubt your significance to us. You have helped us catch countless perpetrators. For all our extra senses, neither of us can do what you do. We need you, Lark." His gaze smouldered and threatened to melt me on the spot. "I need you."

Jacobs clapped Connor on the shoulder. "Plus, it's been enjoyable watching the two of you dance around each other over the years."

Connor stepped back and narrowed his eyes at his partner. "About that. You could've helped speed things along, you know."

Jacobs' grin was positively scandalous. "Why would I do that? You two have been the best form of entertainment."

I squeezed my eyes shut. "What exactly did you know? And how did you know it?"

"Elevated heart rates and the smell of arousal can be very telling, Lark." Jacobs used a matter-of-fact voice, but it did little to prevent the heat from flooding my face. "Connor might have a sensitive sense of smell—he can detect arousal when it's in full bloom, but my nose is far superior. Even the slightest hint of attraction causes a change in body chemistry, and I can pick it all up."

Just great.

I could never work with these two ever again.

"And of course, today, I could smell you on him and—"

A loud smack was met with momentary silence.

I opened my eyes to find Jacobs rubbing his shoulder and watching his partner warily.

"She gets it," Connor snarled.

Jacobs shrugged and flashed his teeth. "Well, we're done here. Are you coming back with me, Connor?"

Connor glanced at me, a question in his gaze. I'd already told him I planned to have dinner with my family. Why would he...

Did he want to join me?

Meet my family?

I shifted on my feet. I'd love for him to come along but hadn't asked because everything was so new. "Would you like to come with me? I wasn't sure if it was your...thing."

Jacobs snorted and walked away. He would probably hear the rest of our conversation anyway, but I appreciated his attempt to give us privacy.

"My thing?" His gaze danced, and he stepped closer, crowding my space again in a way that made it almost impossible not to touch him. "Let me make this very clear. My thing is you, Lark."

"But..."

"Will you be there?" he asked, his tone dropping dangerously low.

My body heated at his close proximity, the vibration in his voice caressing my skin. He'd whispered all sorts of dirty things to me in that tone last night and now my mind had spiralled all the way back into the gutter. "Of course."

"Then I want to be there," he said. "The real question is if you want me to join you."

I sighed. If we didn't have a witness sitting in a parked car a few feet away, I would've done a lot more than breathe heavily.

"I want you there," I said.

A slow smile spread across his face. He straightened and nodded in Jacobs' direction. His partner started the car and pulled away from the curb while I unlocked my own vehicle and slid into the driver's seat. Connor joined me.

After closing the door, he turned to me. "Why did you hesitate to invite me?"

"Well..." I started the car and pressed on the gas to follow Jacobs. "We haven't even gone out on a date yet." That wasn't entirely true. We'd been on a date. Connor had taken me dog walking and I'd realized exactly how much I didn't hate him.

But then I'd been abducted and shot. So that date felt like eons ago.

"I made you dinner," he said. "That counts as a date."

"You fed me after three orgasms," I clarified.

"Are you complaining?"

Heat spread through my body at the memories. "Absolutely not."

"I don't really care about a proper sequence of events, Lark. Not unless you do. We don't lead typical lives, so I don't expect typical."

"What do you expect?"

He didn't answer right away. I continued to focus on the road and made my way to the nearest grocery store to procure Logan's much-needed carbs. When I pulled into the parking stall and turned off the engine, I waited expectantly. Connor wasn't the type to leave a question like that unanswered.

What did he expect from me? From this relationship?

"Everything," he said.

CHAPTER SIXTEEN

Silence greeted Connor and me when we stepped into Mom's apartment. She had an open concept two bedroom, one and a half bath condo in Saanich. She'd sold the family home a long time ago, accepting Dad's unlikely return, the pragmatism of downsizing and the need to have more cash flow for the experimental treatments not covered by the provincial health care system.

Stepping into her place was like stepping into a second home, the familiar scents and furnishings bringing forth a flood of warm memories. The main entrance opened to a kitchen and dining room combo with the living room to the left and the hallway to the bedrooms straight ahead.

Since we'd stopped to pick up wine and a baguette on the way over, the boys had beat us to the apartment.

In the kitchen, Logan moved with efficient grace to collect plates and cutlery while Mom and Brandon stood on the other side of the kitchen counter, wine glasses in hand. The smell of spaghetti sauce, garlic and cooked meat hung heavy in the air and made my mouth water, but the look from Mom made me freeze where I stood.

"Everyone, this is Connor." I waved at each person as I introduced them. "This is my mom Harper, my brother Logan, and his boyfriend Brandon."

Logan recovered first, placing the plates on the counter before walking over. "It's nice to meet you."

Connor placed the wine and baguette on the small table by the entrance to grasp my twin's offered hand.

Brandon arrived second, pushing his boyfriend to the side so he could gush something incoherent before pulling Connor in for a man hug.

Connor patted Brandon's back awkwardly before they both stepped back.

Logan stood beside me, watching Brandon's gushing, and leaned down to hiss at me. "You should have texted."

"I did," I snapped back.

"Oh." Logan straightened.

Brandon snorted, rolled his eyes at my brother, and went to the kitchen to grab more cutlery, presumably to set another place.

Mom stayed a few feet away while this all transpired. Unlike Logan and Brandon's openly appreciative glances at my date, Mom studied Connor critically, her lips pressed together in a firm line. "You brought a barghest into my home."

A fork clattered to the floor. Brandon, who wasn't even a necromancer or raised by one, understood the significance, and he stood there stiff and slack-jawed, his open hand now forkless.

Logan pulled a gun.

"What the fuck?" I waved my hand. How did Mom know Connor was a barghest when I couldn't tell until he told me? I jabbed my finger in the air at my twin. "Put that away."

Logan hesitated and glanced at Mom.

"Guys. Please." I lifted my hands and did that slow up-and-down waving motion that everyone did in the movies to calm people down. So far, it didn't seem to work. "He promised he'd be on his best barghest behaviour and wouldn't eat any souls."

Brandon paled.

Logan scowled, still pointing the gun at Connor's face, but his finger stayed off the trigger.

Connor tried to smile reassuringly, but flashing his teeth had the opposite effect. He looked more menacing than ever.

"Logan put the gun away. We can't have a conversation with you pointing that at our guest," Mom said.

Logan grumbled and holstered the gun under his sweater.

Connor tracked the movement, and I knew I would

be answering some awkward questions later. Concealed carry permits didn't exist in Canada, yet here was my brother packing like he was prepared to strut down some dusty road in the Wild West.

He'd mentioned before he knew who and what my brother was, but not wanting to reveal there was so much more to Logan than met the eye, I hadn't asked for clarification, yet, on what he meant. Connor's lack of surprise at getting drawn on suggested he already knew quite a lot.

"How did you know?" I asked Mom. I hadn't told her about Connor. Well, actually that was a lie. I used to complain about Connor all the time, but I used his last name, and I only discovered his true supernatural nature after my near-death experience on Murder Island. I hadn't planned on telling her anytime soon, either. Not until she answered some of my own questions.

"His power is leaking out." She kept her focus on Connor. "What line are you?"

"Sharrock."

I frowned. I'd never noticed his magic unless he let it out. Now that I knew he was a barghest, I had noticed a slight vibration around him, even when he shielded, but the energy could be explained by so many other things and was almost undetectable unless I knew to search for it.

If Mom recognized the energy, it meant she either

already knew Connor was a barghest before he stepped into her apartment, or she'd knowingly met another of his kind before.

"Plus," Mom added. "His energy signature is all over you, dear."

Logan and Brandon raised their eyebrows in unison.

Ugh. I'd hear about this later.

"I guess we know why she didn't come home last night," Brandon said.

My face heated and I pointed an accusatory finger at my brother's boyfriend. "I used to like you."

He laughed, somehow breaking the tension in the room, and he finished setting the extra place at the table. With a fork, he pointed at me. "Please. We all know I'm still your favourite."

Mom narrowed her eyes at Connor before sighing and letting the tension drain from her face. "I'm sorry, dear," she said to Connor. "That wasn't a nice welcome. My daughter was placed on this Earth to test me, and you're just an agent of her chaos."

"Hey." I folded my arms over my chest.

Mom waved at the table. "Welcome to my home. I'd be honoured if you'd join us for dinner. I feel like we have a lot to discuss."

Connor nodded and bent to take off his shoes. I'd already shucked mine. Apparently, shoe removal was a very Canadian thing to do. I had an American roommate once and she thought we were all bonkers for the habit. She just stomped around our place with her shoes on like an animal.

"I should have told her," I whispered to Connor. "I didn't think she could tell since I had no clue until you told me."

"It's okay, Lark."

"No, it's not. That wasn't the greeting or introduction I wanted you to have." I straightened and bit my lip while I watched my family take their places around the table.

Connor neatly placed our shoes side by side on the mat near the door before reaching out to hold my hand. "You asked me in the car what I expected. Do you remember my answer?"

"Yes." I swallowed.

"What did I say?"

"Everything."

He nodded. "I meant it, Lark. I want everything. That includes the good and the bad. That includes trying to win over your mother."

"And convince her you're not a soul destroyer?"

He smirked. "I suspect your mom knows a lot more about barghests than she's letting on. She's met at least one before."

"I have and it's not an experience I wish to discuss before our meal," Mom called out from the dining room.

Mom's apartment wasn't large, but Connor and I had been whispering.

"Stop eavesdropping," I yelled, but mentally, I cursed. I'd forgotten my list of questions for Mom at home, and now I'd have to go off memory.

Crap.

"Stop whispering by the door and get your asses to the table," Brandon yelled back. "I'm starving and Logan's about to go into carb withdrawal. No one wants a cranky ass...ass at the dinner table."

I snorted. The more I thought about it, the more I was convinced Connor knew my brother was an assassin. Knew and didn't care. Knew and didn't report him to the very authorities he worked for.

Connor picked up the wine bottle and baguette we'd picked up on the way over and walked with me to the dining table.

"I'm not sure either of these will pair with spaghetti." He placed the wine bottle on the table next to two additional bottles that the boys must've brought over.

Logan grabbed the nearest one, making quick work of uncorking it. "That implies we're classy enough to care about that kind of shit—"

"Logan," Mom warned.

"To care about that kind of thing," Logan corrected himself. "Wine is wine. And I told Lark to bring carbs so this works perfectly."

Brandon held up his glass for Logan to pour wine into it. "And wine is delicious."

Mom nodded and held out her own glass.

Once everyone had wine and a plate of food in front of them, conversation faded into sounds of appreciation while we ate. But I couldn't relax. I knew it was only a matter of time before Mom reopened the conversation of a barghest in her home and if the increasing frequency of Mom's less-than-subtle side glances were any indication, that moment was fast approaching.

Sure enough, after Logan and I cleared the dishes and the wine glasses had been refilled, Mom turned to me and asked, "What do you know about the history between barghests and necromancers, Lark?"

"Er..." I glanced at Connor.

His lips twitched, and his gaze danced. He appeared genuinely amused and at no apparent rush to jump in and help me out.

"Not much," I admitted. "Most of what I know is from those bedtime stories that scared the crap out of me."

Mom nodded. "Fairy tales are often used as cautionary stories to warn children of real dangers. What did you learn from those stories?"

"Barghests are dangerous, especially to necromancers," I recited.

"Why?"

"They can wield death magic and destroy souls. If they die before their mates, they linger in the veil and will hunt necromancers because we're their sworn enemies."

Mom nodded to herself and took a sip of wine. "Barghests pass on their genes through the maternal line. Or at least, that's the guaranteed pathway. Unless a male barghest finds a female from another clan, they will not sire barghest children."

I glanced at Connor. He remained silent but dipped his chin. He wouldn't have barghest babies if he stayed with me. That made me a little sad, even though babies weren't even on my radar.

"Okay..." I said. "I don't see what that has to do with anything."

"To help barghest males find appropriate mates, they have a built-in ability to detect death magic. This makes them particularly dangerous to necromancers because they can find us easily in the veil and identify us in the living realm."

"But why would they want to? I'm still not understanding why they're a danger to us."

"Male barghests can only produce children with the aid of death magic. Either they find a female barghest and have barghest children, or they find a female necromancer and have necromancers. If they can't find either, they don't have children. Because of this, male barghests kill male necromancers on sight to eliminate competition."

My brain stuttered.

Mom continued as if she hadn't dropped a huge

knowledge bomb on me. "And even though female barghests don't need a barghest or even a necromancer to procreate, they often see female necromancers as competition as well."

Mom took a casual sip of wine.

Well, that just sounded awful.

Also, not exactly something I needed to worry about. If anything, it explained why Connor was attracted to me.

"But that's not all." Mom set her wine glass down.

I risked another glance at Connor. His expression had shut down, his shields had wrapped around his magic, holding it tightly in place.

"When a male barghest meets a compatible mate—either a barghest or necromancer—they can imprint on them. This allows them to sense and find their potential partners and they're often ruthless and single-minded in their pursuit. If the pair ends up bonded, their magic entwines, and they can have children."

Connor sucked in a breath but looked away when I raised an eyebrow.

"This is where the true danger lies," Mom continued, apparently unfazed by the emotional beatdown she had already given me. "If the barghest dies, or their partner dies, one half of that bond is destroyed, and the survivor becomes a shell of their former self. A husk. Nothing is left, almost as if their whole soul is destroyed."

"Is it?" I asked Mom. "Destroyed?"

"No. But half of it moves to the veil and that's where it waits until the other half can join it."

Silence descended on the room, each of us focused on our own thoughts.

"How do you know so much about barghests?" Connor asked.

"Oh, that's simple." Mom shrugged and took another long sip of wine. "My father was one."

CHAPTER SEVENTEEN

The silence that settled over the dinner table didn't last long. Chaos erupted, mostly a battering of questions from Logan and me.

"We're part barghest?" Logan's eyes widened. A shadow passed over his expression and he sat back in his seat, his lips pressed together.

"You told us Grandpa was a necromancer," I pointed at Mom accusingly as if she wouldn't know I spoke to her.

"I said he had death magic." Mom lifted her chin. "You just assumed."

Well, that was a bullshit excuse, and she knew it.

"Wait," Brandon interjected. "Just so we're clear. Of Lark and Logan's grandparents, two were necromancers, one was a barghest and the other?"

"Was a drab," Mom said. "My mother was a necromancer, my father a barghest. My husband's mother, bless her heart, was a drab and his father was a very well known, powerful necromancer."

"My brain hurts," I complained. "You know I barely passed my biology classes in high school."

"Who was your father's family?" Connor asked. He spoke quietly, but somehow his words cut through the barrage of questions forming in my mind.

Connor had told me there weren't many barghests left. That his kind had dwindled in numbers and only a few major families remained. "Oh, god. We're not related, are we?"

Mom shook her head. "My father was adopted, but he comes from the Bedoe line, not Sharrock."

"Well, that's good news," I muttered and reached for my wine. The Bedoe name sounded familiar, but I couldn't place it.

Connor grunted.

"Wait...how did Grandpa know what line he was from if he was adopted?" I asked.

Mom pursed her lips. "He always knew what line he was from. After both his parents died, family friends took him in and ensured he understood the danger of sharing his biological family's information."

"Why did you always tell us to stay quiet about his name and abilities, then?" I asked. "He wasn't a necromancer anyway, and he wasn't using his birth name. We would just be spreading the same lie."

"Because it would take two seconds for someone looking to figure it out," Mom snapped. "Maybe it was overkill to swear you all to silence, but I wasn't willing to risk your lives to find out."

Okay, I could understand where she was coming from, maybe. Maybe more than a little bit. If my grandpa's parents were killed and then their friends magically had a son appear with necromancer skills, anyone looking for barghests might make the connection. "Are there many barghest slayers running around?"

"Not anymore," Mom said. "Now it's more societal suicide to out yourself as a barghest. You'd lose your job, sweetheart. And if there were any barghest slayers, you'd find out the hard way. Safer to hide in anonymity."

I squinted at Connor. "I'm surprised you didn't run a background check. Surely you already knew this?"

He leaned back and took another sip of his drink. "I did run a background check, but obviously wasn't thorough enough."

I'd bet my entire stash of sour gummies he'd rectify that the next time he was in the office, and I wasn't upset about it. I wanted him to share the results.

Unsure of how to actually say that without saying it, I pointed at Mom. "Why wouldn't you tell us all this?"

Mom sighed. "My father died when I was a child. I didn't know the truth until much later. I was thankful for the information. I finally understood why my own mother became a husk of her former self and why she told those horrific bedtime stories. She didn't want her daughter to hurt the way she did."

"And that's why you continued with the stories?"

"No, dear. I continued because barghests still pose a danger to necromancers in the veil and in the living realm and learning caution might save your life."

"Culling the competition is a barbaric custom," Connor said. "I don't know any of my kind who participate in that."

"Not anymore." Mom nodded. "But that wasn't always the way."

"Why is the Lord of the Veil scared of barghests then?" I asked. "It's not like he has to worry about being culled as competition."

"Culled, maybe not," Connor said. "But barghests are one of the few supernatural beings capable of destroying him. He hides behind his magical shields because he risks being destroyed if he's caught outside them."

"Barghests are that powerful?" Brandon asked.

Connor nodded.

"Wait..." My mind still raced to catch up. "Is that why I'm so powerful? Is that why I grow talons and my eyes turn black in the veil?"

Mom's mouth dropped open.

Connor shifted in the seat beside me, his hand slid over my thigh and squeezed.

Logan remained quiet on the other side of the

table, his gaze flashing and flicking side to side as he remained lost in his thoughts.

Brandon, bless him, kept drinking wine.

"Do you remember much about your first trip to the veil?" Mom asked quietly.

"You know I don't." I'd blocked the memories.

"When you returned, you had black eyes and long, pointy talons instead of nails. Your skin had a blackish gray tinge to it. You kept saying *she* helped you come back."

I swallowed. Having seen Connor after a shift, I knew where this was going.

"We knew then that you had inherited more than necromancer skills from my side of the family," Mom said. "And you likely came across a barghest who helped you home instead of killing you. They had to be one of our ancestors."

"Barghests only pass along the maternal line." Connor frowned.

"Well, maybe it's different if the individual also has necromancer lineage on both sides. Maybe this resulted in the death magic powers being expressed differently." Mom's gaze cut to Logan. "Barghests and necromancers already defy drab understanding of genetics. With magic, anything is possible."

"Anything is possible," Logan murmured the words under his breath, speaking for the first time since Mom's absolute bombshell. "Anything is possible? How is it you're barely a hedge witch when both your parents were so powerful?" Logan asked, his gaze flashed, his tone clipped. "If a male barghest mates with a necromancer to have babies, why aren't you either a necromancer or a barghest?"

Brandon shushed him.

"No." Logan turned to Mom. "How?"

I scrambled to catch up with my twin's thoughts. Where was he going with this?

Mom looked down at her hands, her face going pale, her lips trembling.

"You're not just a hedge witch, are you? You're not weak at all," Logan whispered. "You're like me."

Mom flinched.

My stomach sunk as if someone punched me in the gut.

Logan's face twisted in pain. "You're like me and you hid it. You sent me to that witch to be evaluated and you let me feel so...so helpless and alone."

"I was hoping the witch could awaken latent necromancer magic." Mom bit back a sob and shook her head. "I was trying to protect you."

Logan slammed his hand down on the table. "You left me to feel like a freak."

The table grew quiet.

"What am I?" Logan asked. "What are *we*?"

Connor cleared his throat and opened his mouth.

"No." Logan held up his hand. "I want to hear her say it."

Mom nodded and finally looked up to meet

Logan's angry gaze. "You have to understand. If you had told anyone growing up, we would've been hunted. Killed."

"By whom?" I asked.

Mom flicked her gaze to me. "The better question to ask is who wouldn't hunt us? That's why I never wanted you to talk about our family or lineage. Why we needed to keep it secret. That's why I kept everything to myself."

Logan growled like a feral animal from the other side of the table. His body vibrated. "What am I?"

"Sometimes..." Mom took a deep breath. "Sometimes when a female necromancer and a male barghest mate, they produce something known as a reaper." Mom reached out to hold Logan's hand.

"What the fuck is a reaper?" I asked.

"Someone capable of merging with the veil to take a spirit-like death form," Mom whispered. "Someone who rips the souls from the living and forces them to join the dead."

My brother never went into detail about what he did or how he did it, but now everything made sense. Including my ability to rip souls from drabs. Logan might be a full reaper, but I'd apparently nabbed some reaper skills, too.

Logan snatched his hand away from Mom.

"I tried to protect you from this," she said to my twin. "I tried to keep you from a life of death."

Logan laughed bitterly and shook his head. "Well, that fucking backfired, didn't it?

"Yes." Mom pulled her hand back and stared down at it in her lap. "With or without magic, children don't come with an instruction manual. Parents aren't perfect. We do the best we can with the information we have in the situation we're placed in. You both showed signs of death magic around fifteen when I found out I was sick. Less than a year later, shortly after your sixteenth birthdays, your father disappeared. There was a lot going on."

"Whoa, whoa, wait." I held up my hand. "What do you mean you found out you were sick? You've only been sick for about seven years. I know because that's when I started looking into contract work with the police and I've been with them for six years."

Mom grimaced. "I guess tonight is the night for a lot of truths to be revealed. I was first diagnosed with sanguimort about sixteen years ago. Before your dad went missing and shortly after your magic started expressing itself. I did my best to hide the illness. You two already had so much to deal with. It's only when it progressed so drastically that I had to come clean about my diagnosis."

I clenched my hands together. Sixteen years.

"You had no right to keep these things from us," Logan said.

"I was a single parent with a terminal illness and two children going through puberty and dealing with abandonment issues. You were already so angry, Logan. You were acting out, doing drugs, getting in fights. If I had told you I was dying and revealed you had the ability to steal life from a living being, what would you have done with that information?"

Logan snarled. "I probably would've killed the entire hockey team. Especially Chad."

I choked on my own spit. Remembering some of the assholes on that team, I couldn't say they wouldn't have deserved it. "Fuck Chad."

Brandon murmured an agreement and drank more wine.

"And if you had told anyone?" Mom asked Logan as she shook her head. "If our true identity got out, we would've been on the run for the rest of our lives."

"But why not later?" Logan asked. "I get why you kept the truth from us when we were young and impulsive, but why not tell us a week, or a month or a year ago? Or when we were twenty-five? Or...I don't know... sometime after puberty?"

Mom nodded. "That's the problem with lies, isn't it? They keep getting bigger and bigger. What starts as a snowball, turns into a snowman."

"Please don't use festive cheer to lighten this moment." Logan swiped at his face with his sleeve. "You know I love Christmas."

"You'd already found your calling by the time I realized you'd matured enough to handle the truth, and by then, what was the point? Knowing what you were called wouldn't change anything. All it would do was upend your life. You'd found a great partner, you and your sister were and are doing well. If I dropped this bomb on you, would you spiral again? Would you self-sabotage? I didn't know, and I wasn't going to risk it. I was willing to take the secret to my grave. I've only ever wanted you to be happy."

"If you'd shared the information sooner, I would've dealt with it like I'm dealing with it now, like an adult, because that's what I am," Logan snapped. "You should have told me. Us."

"I know," Mom said. "I'm sorry."

Silence fell over the table and my heart ached for Logan. If he sat beside me, I would've reached out to hold his hand. Brandon had that covered, placing his hand over Logan's clenched fist on the table.

My mind still reeled from the information. My brother was a reaper.

Logan snatched his drink from the table with his free hand and took a long sip. "Now, I understand why we had those awful and traumatic stories growing up."

Yup. Just scare us into compliance and the truth would never get out. I was pissed. Part of me understood why Mom had done it. She'd just lost her husband and feared losing us, too. And then when we got older, she feared she'd lose us because of the lie. She definitely should've told us sooner, and it shouldn't have taken a barghest walking into her home for the truth to come out.

"Did you know?" I asked Connor.

He shook his head. "I knew your brother was an assassin and I knew you were both descendants of two powerful necromancer lines. I didn't know you were part barghest, but after your mom's reaction to me, I suspected, and started putting the pieces together."

"I still don't understand why you greeted Connor the way you did," I said to Mom. She had better manners than that, even with her treasure trove of secrets. If she wanted to keep those secrets, she should've kept quiet.

Mom dabbed her eyes with a napkin and sniffed. "Don't you?"

I frowned.

Connor looked ready to breathe fire, which made no sense. He was a barghest, not a dragon.

"He's imprinted on you," Mom said, tone deceptively light. "If you let him into your heart, you'll end up like my mom."

I froze. My thoughts stuttered. Logan stilled on the other side of the table, his own pain momentarily pushed to the side as his gaze slid to Connor.

Brandon perked up as if our daytime soap opera just got to the juicy part.

I continued to slow blink at Mom as I processed what she'd said. *If* I let him into my heart? A bit too late for that warning...

In slow motion, I turned to face Connor. "Is that true?"

He took a deep breath and settled his dark gaze on me. Magic snapped between us, fierce and exhilarating. I didn't need to ask him the question again. Frankly, I didn't need to ask him at all. The truth was in the magic humming between us and the flash in his gaze.

"When?" I asked instead.

"Our first case together," he said.

"Our first?" But... that made no sense. "That was six years ago."

He nodded and slowly placed his wine glass on the table. "Imprinting isn't like a fated mate kind of deal. It's a completely one-sided barghest thing unless we bonded. I wanted you to have a choice to get to know me and decide without the added pressure."

"Are we..." I waved my hands in the air. "Bonded?"

"No." A slow smile spread across his face. He didn't say a word, but I'd swear he mentally added, "not yet" to the end of that single-word answer.

"Is that..." I swallowed, not liking the question bubbling up from my gut, but needing to ask it anyway. "Is that why you like me?"

Connor stilled. Silence descended on the room while my heart raced. Slowly, Connor turned to me in his seat. "I could've released the imprint six years ago. I originally held on because I wanted to get to know you. I continued to hold on because I do like you. I like how you're fierce and funny, and that you care so deeply for your family and animals you'll make sacrifices to see them happy. Imprinting doesn't dictate my feelings, Lark. It doesn't control my heart."

"Oh."

"But you do."

Brandon chose that moment to elbow my brother. "Maybe we should give them some privacy?"

"Don't be preposterous." Logan balked, the darkness plaguing his expression clearing a little. "It's just getting good."

Brandon shook his head.

"Besides, I want to be here for Lark if she needs me to stab him," Logan added.

Connor narrowed his eyes.

"Logan," I warned. "No one will be stabbing anyone at the dinner table."

"I'm a fucking reaper." He puffed out his chest. "Just watch me."

Connor tore his calculating gaze away from my brother and reached out to hold my hand. "Consent and choice are very important to me. I would've told you all of this in time. Everything is so new between us right now and I wanted to find the right moment."

And place.

He probably wouldn't have chosen Mom's dining room with my family surrounding us.

"Wait a minute." A thought snapped its way to the forefront of my mind. "Is that how you found me on the island?"

I ignored Mom's deep frown from across the table.

Logan's eyes widened momentarily before understanding cleared his expression.

Connor's smile spread and he winked.

In front of my family.

The audacity.

I loved it.

"What island?" Mom asked. "When did you go on vacation?"

Right. I hadn't told her about that incident. I hadn't planned on doing so either. All it would do was stress her out and make her worry and the danger had already passed. Obviously, I couldn't hide it from the boys. Days after I'd gone missing, I'd returned to the apartment with Connor, covered in blood, dirt and bruises. The gun shot wound, though mostly healed by Levi, left a red mark of angry skin that had ripped open and bled a little on the trip home.

I already had to deal with the over-protective side of Logan, and he still threatened to stab anyone who entered my personal space.

"I think we might head out. I hope you guys don't mind cleaning up. I'll make up for it next time." I pushed away from the table.

Connor raised his eyebrows.

"Connor and I have a few things to discuss in private."

Mom nodded, her expression closed off, her posture stooped as if we'd exhausted her. She'd spent her entire life living a lie to prevent Logan from turning into a killer and me from bonding with a barghest.

Part of me felt sorry for her.

Brandon got up and walked around the table. He held up his phone so I could read the screen. He'd made a list of all the questions I'd meant to ask Mom and had checked them off for me. "You got them all."

I wrapped my arms around him and squeezed.

"We won't wait up," Brandon whispered in my ear.

Logan scowled, probably already mentally planning a security detail.

Shockingly, we walked out of the apartment within ten minutes of making my intention to leave known. Mom hugged me before we left as well but said nothing else.

I didn't know what to make of this night, but I did know I had to clarify some things with Connor.

"So...." I broke the silence as we approached my car. "You imprinted on me."

"I did."

"Like a cute little hatchling."

One minute I fumbled for my keys in my purse and the next I was pressed into the side of my car, Connor's hand fisted in my hair. He leaned into me, his body warming my back, his groin pressed into my ass, his breath teasing the sensitive skin of my neck. "Like a man who wants to do very bad things to you."

"Don't you dare distract me with your body," I said.

"I've tasted the honey of your lips, and now I'm

addicted." He shifted, leaning his weight on me even more, squishing me between my car and his rock-hard body. "We were meant for each other, Lark."

I stilled.

Not from fear, from overwhelming desire racking my body. Somehow this man knew every right button to push.

"You are my weakness. My sin and my redemption." He pulled my head back, just a little more, just enough that I arched my back and lifted my ass into his erection even more. "You are the light that anchors me to this mortal plane."

"Son of a bitch," I whispered.

"I've made no secret about wanting you. Fuck, I'd take you against this car right now, public indecency be damned. But you will always have a choice. Do you want me, or do you want to walk away?"

He wasn't talking about fucking now. He was talking about us, our relationship. "What about the imprinting?"

"That's not your problem to deal with." He kissed my neck and dragged his teeth along my skin. "What do you want, Lark?"

I bit my lip and tried really hard not to squirm. I might be enjoying this position a little too much, but I refused to dry hump in front of Mom's apartment building.

"I think a couple orgasms sound pretty fucking good right now."

He snorted and released me. Cold air washed over my back.

"Is that all?" He stepped away from the car to give me room to turn around. I did and found him studying me, the moonlight glinting in his dark gaze and playing with the chiselled angles of his face.

"No," I admitted. "I want a whole lot more than just orgasms."

"But?"

"There is no but. I'm just not sure I'm ready to talk about more right now. My mind feels like mush."

A slow smile spread across his face. "Then let's start with the orgasms and work from there."

I'd never heard a better deal before in my life.

CHAPTER EIGHTEEN

The next day, in the early evening, I stepped onto the blood-spattered floor and met Connor's dark gaze from across the empty room. "Seriously?"

He winced.

I knew not to expect a romantic rendezvous when I received Connor's text with an address and a dagger emoji, but a little heads up that I'd walk into another summoning slaughter scene would've been nice.

Connor joined me where I stood near the entrance. He didn't touch me, but the heated look he gave me warmed my entire body as if he had. Last night, he'd ruthlessly exploited all my sensitive areas and made me scream for release, delivering the promised orgasms and more—the man took his promises seriously—and then he'd made me breakfast and coffee before we both headed out for work.

Connor leaned down and whispered, "I'll make it up to you later."

More heat flooded my body, a completely inappropriate reaction for the horror scene around me. "You better start talking about this scene."

Wicked promises flashed in his gaze and his lips quirked up at the corners, but he straightened and turned to give me a view of the room. Like the two crime scenes before it, white powder and five dark patches of pooled blood arranged in a circle marked where bodies should have been.

"Any remains?"

"Not this time," Connor said.

"Then why call me in?"

"I wanted to see you."

"I thought we already established you don't need a murder scene to call me, Connor," I said.

His dark gaze swept my body and lingered on my throat. Could he see my pulse? Could he see the effect he had on me just by standing close?

"I'm aware," he said, shifting his focus back to my face. "I was going to message you to see if you wanted to get something to eat but then this call came in. I thought I'd bring you in anyway. We might not have recovered any bones, but the occult specialist was just here and confirmed this was a summoning and someone went to great lengths to magically clean the scene—again."

"To get rid of what?"

"Everything. Hair, fibres, fingerprints, scents, aura...there had to have been other people in this room but there will be no way to forensically connect them to this case by scientific or magical means."

"And they'd somehow even prevented the dead from speaking to me." Something I still wasn't pleased about.

Connor snapped his mouth shut and nodded.

"And me? How do I fit in?" I asked.

"You fit in by scanning the room to see if you can detect any death...just in case. And then you let me take you out for sushi because I'm fucking starving and I'd appreciate something else to focus on than this."

I released my magic, enjoying Connor's shiver as my power caressed his skin before spreading out to search the area. The magic hummed in my veins, eager to find death and release and connect with the veil. I needed bones, blood and power, and after another sweep of the room, I had to concede I had only two of those things.

"No bones," I confirmed.

Connor nodded. "Thank you for checking. I'm going to take a few more pictures and seal the scene back up. Do you want to watch, or wait outside?"

"I'll wait outside." Part of me wanted to watch, but I also knew the faster he got this done, the faster we could leave. "Where's Jacobs?"

"Following up with the crime scene investigators and lab results."

I nodded and hesitated. Connor studied me, amusement dancing in his gaze. I planted my hands on his chest, rose on my toes, and placed a gentle kiss on his lips. "See you outside."

Before I could step back, Connor gripped my hips and pulled me into his body. His mouth claimed mine. Before he could deepen the kiss, I pushed away, relishing the taste of him on my tongue.

"We've already come close to messing up one of your previous scenes," I said.

His gaze darkened and he reached for me.

"Connor..." I warned.

He growled. "Fine, but you're coming home with me tonight."

I would've leaned up and kissed him again, but I didn't trust either of us to keep it tame. So instead, I smiled and spun around, making a quick exit. Connor's chuckle followed me into the hallway. I ducked under the crime scene tape and made my way outside. The moon bathed the neighbourhood in a soft glow and dried pine needles lined the pavement. The weather would turn soon, the skies murky with dark clouds and torrential rain.

I closed my eyes and breathed deeply, taking in the fresh air. Death energy coiled around me, and I popped my eyes open.

Reaching out with my magic, I searched for the source. Death was nearby and it was moving. I reached inside and let my magic pool out.

There.

Around the side of the house.

Conscious of my last dark alley experience and my stupidity for walking right into a trap, I walked over to the side street cautiously, my magic ready to strike out at the first sign of danger.

A familiar vampire waited in the inky darkness.

"Pierre?" I rocked back on my heels. "We need to stop meeting like this." I walked farther into the narrow side street. The tall buildings towered high on each side, surrounding us in dark shadows. "What are you doing here?"

"I'm worried about you."

"Why? Am I in trouble?"

"When are you not in trouble? You were injured. You live in an unsecure apartment. If anyone else found out your connection with Gregor, they'd try to use you like those two men."

"Did you..." I swallowed.

"I disposed of the bodies, and no one will ever find them or connect them to you. Will your friend remain silent?"

I nodded. "I believe so."

"Was she involved?"

"No, definitely not." If she was, she should quit her job as a necromancer and take up acting. I'd called her earlier to check in and she seemed fine. Or at least as fine as someone could be after getting abducted and held at gunpoint.

I would know.

She planned to take a week off work and had a therapy session booked for tomorrow. I hoped that would help her heal but still planned to visit.

He nodded, concern etched in his brow. He took my safety seriously and had told me he'd always protect me.

A thought crossed my mind, and I mentally swore. "Pierre...Did you leave me roses?"

Pierre ducked his head, his long brown hair falling in front of his face.

"Pierre?" My skin prickled.

"*Je suis très désolé, ma belle.*"

"My high school French is a little rusty, but I'm pretty sure you were just apologizing." I took a deep breath. "That second rose scared the crap out of me, you know. My brother went manic trying to secure our home from a rose-wielding stalker."

"I know and as soon as I realized my error, I stopped."

Okay, he had been in the dirt for who knew how many years. I could look past some social etiquette blunders. "But...why?"

"You were the light that led me out of the dark," he said, as if it made all the sense in the world.

I stammered. Connor had said something similar to me before, but Pierre's words had a different effect. I didn't like him like that. Bringing him out of the veil didn't mean the same thing to me as it did to Pierre.

He held up his hand. "I know your heart is not available. I stopped leaving the roses because you found them unsettling, and my intent was never to unnerve you."

"What was your intent?"

"Isn't it obvious? I planned to court you. Or date you. Or whatever it is they call it these days. I stopped pursuing you altogether when I realized your heart already belonged to someone else."

"Oh..." That was reasonable.

"But I hoped and still hope we can be friends. I will look out for you regardless. I don't need to have you in my life romantically. I just..." He shook his head. "I want you in my life. It's like everything makes sense when you're near."

"Pierre..."

"I know how that sounded. You're not some drug I'm addicted to, you're someone I like being around. Someone I want to protect and someone I want to see happy, even if that's not with me."

My brain stuttered as I processed his words. He was the first vampire soul I'd retrieved from the veil, and I'd probably overcompensated with the magic I used to call him. Had I somehow tied him to me with my magic? Though stomping around the veil to find a vampire soul had been a new and scary experience for me, it really had no other impact on my life, whereas it appeared to have dramatically and irrevocably affected

Pierre to the point he followed me around like a super-powered guard dog.

At least, I assumed he followed me around. How else would he have found me in the alleyway with Denise, or here at this crime scene?

I frowned. I'd left for this crime scene before the sun set. "How are you tracking me?"

Pierre shook his head. "I'm not. I do follow you from your apartment sometimes."

"Then how did you find me here? Or was this just some happy coincidence?" Another thought crystallized in my mind. "Did you have something to do with this?"

"Me? No."

An awful thought chilled my bones. "Did Gregor?"

He looked away, the muscles along his jaw bunching as he clenched his teeth. "I was sent to watch over the scene to report when it was discovered by authorities. I wasn't supposed to be seen."

My stomach twisted in a knot and nausea bubbled up. Gregor was responsible for the summoning slaughters. I swallowed and took some shallow breaths. My heart thudded loudly. I always knew Gregor was capable of great violence, but it was one thing to know it and another thing to see the aftermath of it. "Do you know what he's doing with the circles?"

"No, but it has something to do with the veil. I can feel the pull. I'm...I'm still connected with it."

The veil? Gregor had sent a vampire to the veil to

try to steal the Book of the Dead from Leviathan. The vampire had threatened to kill me, I controlled him with my magic, and then Leviathan killed him. At the time, I'd wondered how Gregor managed to get a vampire into the veil. With everything else that had happened since then, I'd kind of let that question fall to the backburner with all my other unanswered questions and hadn't bothered to follow up.

The summoning circles must allow Gregor to send vampires to the veil. That had to be it. Was he still trying to steal the Book of the Dead? He'd completed at least three rituals and I only knew of one vampire in the veil. What was he up to?

"Thank you for telling me," I said.

Pierre nodded. "He's dangerous."

"Gregor? I'm aware."

"No, not Gregor. Well, actually, yes. Gregor is capable of truly heinous things. But it wasn't Gregor I referred to." He jerked his chin at the street behind me.

Connor waited outside the alley. He leaned on the side of the building with his arms crossed over his chest. He looked calm and relaxed, but the tension in his shoulders gave him away.

"Be careful of that one, *ma belle*. He has the power to destroy your world."

Too late for that.

Pierre nodded and without another word, slipped into the shadows, disappearing in the night, and leaving me alone to face a grumpy detective.

"I'm surprised you didn't come running in, guns blazing," I said as I walked out of the side street to join him.

"I know you can handle yourself," he said.

"And if I couldn't?"

"I wouldn't run in guns blazing."

"Oh?" I stopped short of running into him, a mere foot separating us. I reached out and placed my hands on his chest. "What would you do?"

"I'd shred all my humanity and tear that bloodsucker to shreds with my teeth."

"Lovely." An image rose in my mind of Connor standing in the middle of Steve's bloody remains.

I shivered.

Connor would protect me with whatever means were necessary.

"Are you okay?" He studied my face, concern etched in his brows.

"I just found out a bunch of things." I ran my hands down his chest. "I think you should take me out for a drink instead of going for food."

"Done."

CHAPTER NINETEEN

Connor stirred in the bed to answer his phone and woke me up. With my head on his chest and my limbs draped over him, I'd trapped him in my sleep again. My whole body hummed with satisfaction.

Last night, Connor had taken me to a local pub and while I consumed a few drinks I told him about the vampires' connection to the summoning slaughters. He'd quietly eaten a burger and I had picked at his fries while I explained how Pierre was behind the roses. Connor hadn't liked that part. He'd grown still and his gaze had darkened.

"You're mine," he'd said.

"I know."

"Does he?"

"Yes," I'd said, reassuring him. Connor had grumbled after that, but after paying for our meal and drinks, he'd taken me home and spent hours proving how well we went together. He'd been very thorough, leaving no part of me unexplored.

A memory of my leg thrown over his shoulder so he could pump into me at a different angle surged up and flushed my body with warmth. His expression had turned so serious like he needed me to get off or he'd die. And after I'd fractured into a million pieces after yet another orgasm, he finally shed what little self-control he had left.

He truly was beautiful.

I peeled my cheek from Connor's chest in time to watch him place his phone back on the side table.

"Everything okay?" I asked, though I knew no one called a detective in the middle of the night to just catch up.

He caressed my back with his hand and turned to plant a kiss on the top of my head. "I've been called in."

"Boo." I glanced at the clock. Four in the morning? Fuck that.

I pulled away to let him slip from the bed.

Maybe I should get up, too, and make my way home. The boys didn't need any more time to plan their interrogation, anyway. If they were even planning one—my brother might be too busy processing and facing his own truths after Mom's big reveal. When I'd texted Logan earlier he'd said he was *fine*, but he was full of shit.

Brandon had reached out moments later to reassure me my twin was coping and to enjoy my night, but I still wanted to see them both and debrief after our visit with Mom.

Flinging back the sheets, I shifted to the edge of the bed.

"No." Connor turned to smooth my hair from my face. "Stay."

I fell back into the bed, sleep still clinging to my limbs. I had no desire to fight his command, and as for my brother, I wasn't worried. Brandon would text if sisterly intervention was needed.

"I like seeing you in my bed." He said something else as well, but I'd already started to drift off to sleep, reliving our time together all over again. I nuzzled my face into Connor's pillow, his scent curling around me in the most delicious way. My body sank into the pillowtop mattress...

Only to be rudely awakened by my phone ringing.

I slapped my hand on the side table and fumbled along the surface to find the offensive device.

Prying my eyes open, I read the screen: 8:00am.

I'd just closed my eyes a second ago, but somehow four hours had passed, and Connor was now calling me.

"Hey," I answered.

"Sorry for the early call," he said.

"You interrupted the best dream."

"Oh?"

"You were doing that thing with your tongue." I rubbed the sleep from my eyes and sat up.

Connor cleared his throat and dropped his voice. "I could do that again."

"Don't be a tease. I know that's not why you called."

"Sadly, no," he said, his voice back to normal. "We need you at a crime scene."

I'd figured as much and had already pulled free of the sheets. I slipped from the bed, the floor cool on my bare feet. "Where should I meet you?"

He rambled off an address before stating, "There's a new toothbrush in the middle drawer in the ensuite bathroom and fresh towels in the linen closet. I left a spare key on the kitchen counter beside the coffee maker so you can lock up. I'll see you in an hour."

We said goodbye and I padded to the washroom to get ready.

Other people would use this as an opportunity to snoop, but I didn't want to, nor did I need to. Connor wasn't the type to try to hide something he thought I'd dislike. He was upfront and honest. Brutally blunt, even.

His interior decorating reflected his no-nonsense attitude in life. Smooth, clean lines, no clutter. His linen closet contained precision-folded towels stacked in orderly piles.

Connor would have an aneurysm if he saw what

the linen closet looked like in the apartment I shared with the boys.

I got ready in record time and headed straight for the crime scene after hitting the nearest drive-thru for coffee. Connor had set up the coffee maker for me, but chugging one coffee wasn't enough.

Traffic, like always, was atrocious. I hit the morning commuter traffic and Victoria drivers didn't get the memo about maintaining the nice Canadian image.

By the time I pulled up to the crime scene and parked near the yellow tape, I was half an hour late.

I hopped out of the car, shut the door, and hit the lock button on the key fob.

"About fucking time." Connor leaned against a telephone pole, his arms crossed over his chest, a smile tugging at the corner of his lips.

Stepping around the vehicle to join him on the sidewalk, I scowled. "And here I worried how we'd navigate this."

He straightened and unfolded his arms. "Navigate what?"

I waved my hand back and forth between us. "Navigate working together at a crime scene in front of all your peers, not just Jacobs." I sighed and dropped my hand. "I see we're going with the status quo."

Connor's gaze darkened. He stepped forward, grabbed a fistful of my shirt and pushed me into my car. Without pause, he ducked his head and kissed me.

Not a sweet friendly kiss. A claiming one. One that marked me as his to anyone who dared to look our way.

I squeaked in surprise, pushing against his solid chest.

Instead of easing off, he caught my lower lip with his teeth and parted my lips. His tongue touched mine and if he'd claimed me with his lips before, he devoured me now.

Everything around us faded away. All that existed right now was Connor and his kiss and how he stirred a fire deep inside me with each flick of his tongue.

He still tasted faintly of me, even though he'd obviously brushed his teeth and used mouthwash before leaving, and it made me feverish, sending memories of last night to help fuel the flames.

Someone whistled.

Probably Jacobs.

Connor hesitated before pulling back, face flushed, gaze wild.

"That's how I plan to navigate this," he said.

Huh?

He ignored the riot of catcalls and cheering from the crime scene staff, his gaze locked on mine. "I've heard you moaning my name and felt you coming on my cock, Lark. The status quo will no longer fucking cut it."

I blinked at him.

"Any questions?"

Tons, but that would involve speaking and the ability to form words was currently beyond me.

"Now that you two are done...whatever the fuck that was, can we move along to solving heinous crimes now?" Jacobs called out as he approached closer.

"You know exactly what that was," Connor grumbled.

Jacobs shook his head. "Not really, but I think I might be pregnant."

Connor snorted.

I laughed.

For a moment, we stood there, smiles on our faces and then the flashing lights, the wind tussling the yellow tape and the sounds of swishing fabric from the crime scene technicians' coveralls brought reality crashing back.

Jacobs sighed and spun on his heel. "This way."

A woman lay sprawled and broken behind a bush, one shoe resting on the weeds nearby and the other still on her foot with the heel snapped off. Blood spattered the cement. A thin white sheet covered half the body. They must've pulled it back in anticipation of my visit.

The woman's head faced our direction, her mouth open, makeup smeared. Her eyes had been closed, most likely by a technician after they took the crime scene photos.

She'd been beautiful.

And also familiar.

"I've seen her before," I said. "Her face. I've seen it."

Connor nodded and leaned in. "Want me to tell you?"

"Yes, please."

"Maria Espinoza. Twenty-five years old, educational assistant."

I frowned. So far nothing rang a bell.

"And Mason Miller's fiancée."

I snapped my fingers. Memories of the photographs I'd seen in Mason's home resurfaced.

"Wait a minute." My brain kept turning. "Lily dies when she was in a relationship with Mason, and now Maria." I frowned. "Maybe Lily's murder had nothing to do with Lily. Maybe this has been about Mason all along."

Connor and Jacobs nodded along as I verbally worked out what they'd obviously already figured out before I arrived.

"Where's Mason?" I asked.

"Sent a patrol car over just before you got here," Connor said.

"I'll go get the chicken," Jacobs said.

It took ten minutes, one chicken and three attempts for me to declare another failure "It's like Lily. No soul. Not even a recognition of my call. No tingling. No fight. Just...absence."

Connor cursed and stalked away.

That meant the same killer must be involved and

likely used Connor's ancestor's bones again to do their bidding.

What could I say to make him feel better?

Nothing.

Words weren't needed right now.

Jacobs had already taken the chicken from me. I cleaned and sheathed my dagger and walked over to where Connor seethed. Everyone else had given him a wide berth.

He stiffened when I stepped up beside him. We both faced the street. Slowly, I reached out and held his hand.

He tightened his grip on me but didn't say anything for a long while. Neither did I. Instead, I stood beside him, quietly being there for him until he was ready to speak.

"They're fucking using my grandmother's bones," he hissed.

I nodded. "We'll find the person responsible."

He pressed his lips together in a grim line and nodded.

"Patrol car called," Jacobs announced. "Mason wasn't home. Door was ajar, but no sign of a struggle."

Connor cursed again but kept a hold of my hand.

"What do you want to do?" Jacobs asked.

"I want to see it for myself," Connor said. He hesitated and glanced down at me. "Would you like to come?"

"You don't have to invite me to make me feel included," I said. "I can meet up with you later."

He pulled down on my hand while turning toward me until we fully faced each other. He lifted his free hand to cup my face. "I want you with me."

I smiled. I hadn't been fishing for compliments. I just needed him to know I understood the demands of his job and wouldn't throw a tantrum if he had to leave me behind to do his job.

"Besides," he said. "If there's death magic present, I might sense it, but I sure as shit won't be able to call the spirits or get them to cooperate."

"I'm shocked the mighty Connor Kang is admitting a weakness."

He barked out a laugh before dipping his head to rest his forehead on mine. "I only have one weakness, Lark."

"Oh?"

"You," he said simply. "It's always been you."

Warmth spread through my body. If he wasn't holding onto me, I would've floated away.

"Kang being sweet just feels...wrong," Jacobs grumbled. "I think I might throw up."

We broke away from each other and a light blush tinged Connor's cheeks.

"Are you coming in our vehicle, Lark?" Jacobs asked.

"No. I'll meet you there."

It didn't take long for us to make it to Mason's home, and even less time to figure out something was incredibly wrong.

CHAPTER TWENTY

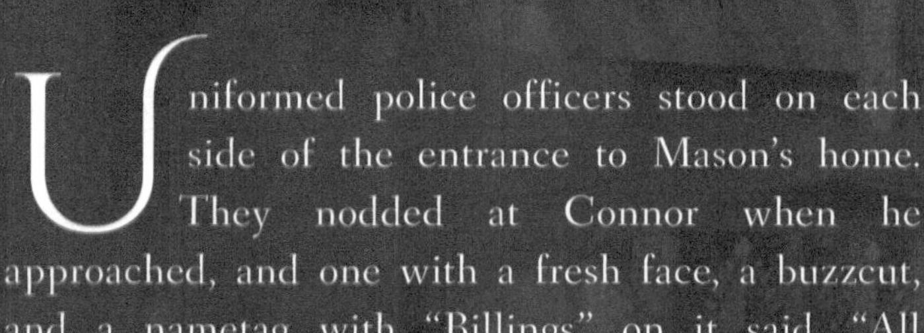

Uniformed police officers stood on each side of the entrance to Mason's home. They nodded at Connor when he approached, and one with a fresh face, a buzzcut, and a nametag with "Billings" on it said, "All clear."

Connor and Jacobs nodded and walked into the home.

I followed suit.

We'd been here the other day and now it felt like a moratorium.

The air might've been fresh, but the silence and atmosphere were stifling. Despite the gloom and doom ambience, the air sat still and devoid of death energy. My whole purpose for being here evaporated. "No recent death."

Connor nodded.

"I'll take the bedroom." Jacobs pulled out a pair of latex gloves.

Connor nodded and mirrored his actions. "I'll start in the living room."

They both turned to me.

"Stay put and don't touch anything?" I guessed.

Connor's gaze sparked and his mouth twitched.

I pulled out my phone and went through my messages from work and then my private ones. It didn't take long. I'd already touched base with the office to discuss my upcoming clients and made plans with Denise to meet for sushi.

Gregor had been suspiciously quiet. He had a graveyard full of vampire babies who needed raising and he had yet to proposition me. Maybe he was turning a new leaf or trying reverse psychology.

I checked my text messages to Estelle, the master vampire's human servant. She'd read my last three messages but hadn't replied.

Ouch.

Last time I checked, I hadn't done anything to justify being ghosted by my human servant friend, but I couldn't exactly find out how I fucked up if Estelle refused to talk to me.

Connor finished searching the living room and moved to the side table in the dining room.

The framed pictures of Mason and Maria still hung in the same place.

Pictures.

I swiped my phone screen and navigated to a social media app. People put their entire lives on the internet. Connor, Jacobs, or someone from their team would complete a comprehensive internet search later, but maybe I could find something helpful while I waited.

Mason didn't have any privacy settings.

Idiot.

I clicked on his albums and started scrolling. Picture after picture painted an image of a man happily in love with his fiancée.

I kept scrolling.

Whatever this was, it started before Mason met his current fiancée.

The pictures morphed into ones with Mason alone or with friends. His smile never reached his eyes and his sunken cheeks and the way his shirts hung on his torso spoke of significant weight loss. That must be the time between Lily and Maria. I checked the date stamps. Yup.

I kept scrolling.

He'd kept his pictures of Lily up.

I raised my eyebrows. Maria must've been an understanding fiancée.

I grimaced.

Or she knew she didn't need to worry about a past girlfriend when she was dead.

I shook my head. I needed to keep my thoughts focused. Obviously, Maria supported Mason's need to grieve and remember Lily. But at the end of the day, it didn't matter. Lily and Maria were both dead.

Could Mason have done it? Did he kill them both?

I kept scrolling. Lily and Mason had an adventurous relationship. Pictures of kayaking outings, volleyball gatherings, picnics and hikes filled his feed.

They played beach and grass volleyball.

I paused on one picture, another familiar face snagging my attention.

No.

It couldn't be.

I tapped the screen and zoomed in.

"Son of a bitch," I said.

Connor straightened from where he stooped over the garbage, his eyebrows lifted.

"She knew them." I swore again. "She fucking knew them."

Stalking over to Connor, I held up my phone so he could see the picture of Mason and Lily, standing arm-in-arm with none other than Cathy.

Lily and Cathy wore sporty bikini tops and shorts while Mason wore only board shorts and burned shoulders and chest—the perfect attire for playing beach volleyball at Willows Beach. The cerulean blue summer waters of Oak Bay sparkled behind them, and the glaring sunlight highlighted their sun-kissed skin.

"Mason tagged her." I pointed at the name, my stomach sinking. Lily's best fucking friend. "Lia Holland."

Jacobs peered over my shoulder to look at my phone screen. "She must've changed her name."

"Or it's her middle name." Connor stripped off his gloves, pulled out his phone, punched in a number and started rumbling off directions—half in English, half in cop code.

I didn't speak cop code, but I caught enough to understand Connor had put out a BOLO on Cathy. Now every cop in the Victoria area would be on the lookout for my shady client.

When he hung up, he shoved the phone into his pocket. "I could kiss you."

"Please don't." Jacobs walked out of the living room. "You two already knocked me up earlier."

CHAPTER TWENTY-ONE

I followed Connor into his place and kicked off my shoes. Today had been a long day. I'd left the detectives to raise a grandmother to settle an estate dispute between her two children while Connor and Jacobs continued working on the case. They'd sent uniforms to pick up Cathy, but she'd already taken off.

Then I'd met up with Connor for a late, very-late dinner. He fed me tacos.

This had to be true love.

We made it three steps and one hot kiss into his bedroom when his phone started ringing.

Connor cursed and ran his hand through his hair.

"It's okay," I said.

"It's not."

"Connor." I waited until he met my gaze. "This isn't going to make me run away. I know what your job is."

"I've had people tell me that in the past," he muttered.

And then they realized they couldn't handle it and left. I didn't need him to elaborate. The worry tugging his brow down said enough.

"Well, I'm not them." I placed my hands on my hips. "How many of these women actually worked with cops? I'm sure they were wonderful people. This isn't a dig at them, but unlike them, I already know what I'm getting into and what a grumpy ass you are."

He looked away.

"Exactly. Remember my hours are just as ridiculous as yours."

He grumbled. His phone started ringing again.

"Now answer that or Jacobs is going to have a fit."

Connor shook his head, a smile tugging on his lips. "Can't have that."

"Not in his condition."

Connor laughed and answered the phone.

I followed him out and made my way to the front entrance to get my shoes.

Connor joined me shortly after, shoving his phone into his pocket. "What are you doing?"

I paused having bent over with my shoe in my hand and frowned. "Going home."

"The fuck you are." He crossed his arms over his chest.

I straightened and dropped my shoe. I didn't

bother voicing my question because it was likely already plastered all over my face.

"You're staying here," he said, matter of fact.

"Is that so?" I raised an eyebrow. "Are you going to cuff me to the bed?"

"Don't tempt me."

I folded my arms over my chest to mirror him even though my heart raced at the idea of Connor tying me up. Tempting him was exactly what I wanted to do.

"You're exhausted. It's been a long day," he said.

I narrowed my eyes. "I wasn't too tired for you about five minutes ago."

A self-satisfied smile spread across his face. "That's different."

I snorted.

"Stay," he repeated, his tone losing the playful edge. "I like the idea of coming home to you."

The tension in my shoulders slipped away, along with any lingering irritation. Hard to get upset with an admission like that.

"Okay," I said.

My phone vibrated in my pocket, and I frowned. I rarely got actual calls unless it was an emergency, Connor calling to request a consult, or Denise trying to get me to do a last-minute raising. Logan, Brandon and I all preferred to text.

I pulled out my phone and glanced at the screen. "It's Cathy."

Connor froze, his gaze flicking back and forth. "Try

to keep her on the line as long as possible." He started tapping away on his phone.

I accepted the call and held the phone up to my ear. "Hi, Cathy."

"I'm in need of your services," she said without greeting, her usual timid tone gone.

"You're in need of a necromancer?"

"I'm in need of protection."

I winced. Necromancers didn't have the best reputation, and although I was powerful and capable of doing a lot of damage, most necromancers needed three chickens to speak to a single spirit. When would society stop painting us as ruthless killers? "I'm not sure I'm the best person to hire for that. I'm a death raiser, not a bodyguard."

"Oh, forget it..."

"Wait!"

A pause.

"I don't want to discuss this over the phone. Why don't we meet, and you can tell me more about the job?"

Another pause. "You're helping them, aren't you?"

"Helping who?"

"The police. The drabs."

I flinched. There went any hope of getting her to meet with me and give away her location the easy way. Now I needed to get her to stay on the phone.

"You should turn yourself in," I said. "If you cooperate, they'll take it easy on you. Isn't that what you want?"

"What I want?" Cathy snapped. "What I wanted is gone now. Thanks to them. All I ever wanted was him. I wanted a family. Those bitches kept taking him from me."

"Let me help you," I said. "I'm sure we can find a way out of this."

"What would you know about wanting something you can't have? What would you know about rejection or family?"

"A lot. Or at least enough to know you can't force someone to stay with you and love isn't an obligation."

Cathy cursed.

I glanced up at Connor.

He kept waving his hand in a circle for me to keep talking to her while he continued to text madly with the other hand. Did he already get someone to trace the call? Could they get a trace on the call without a warrant? Did they have enough on Cathy to get a warrant? Though we now had proof Cathy knew Lily and lied about it, that might not be enough for a warrant to search her home or tap her line.

"This is all your fault," Cathy hissed. "You're just like them."

Before I could say anything else, she hung up.

I looked over at Connor.

He sighed, his lips pressed together.

"No luck?"

He shook his head.

"Sorry."

"You did great." He stepped in close and gathered me in his arms. "I have to go, but you better sleep naked."

"No promises," I said. "I was planning to fully suit up so you don't get any ideas of waking me at three in the morning. I'm not into that."

He leaned down and kissed me.

Kissed wasn't the right word.

He stole my breath and heart away and replaced them with something else.

Something more.

I was in so much trouble.

As Connor's death magic fell away, he leaned in and whispered in my ear, "Liar."

CHAPTER

TWENTY-TWO

Persistent ringing dragged me out of my dream. I lay on my side, wrapped under a puffy white duvet, Connor spooning me from behind, his body pressing along my back with delicious warmth, his arm draped over my waist. Yesterday had been a regular workday while Connor and Jacobs continued to work their case and search for Cathy. My feet had felt like they were filled with lead, but Connor insisted I come over. He'd given me the best foot massage of my life, before making the rest of my body sing yet again. If he wasn't careful, I'd become addicted to him, if I wasn't already.

Connor nuzzled my neck. "Are you going to answer that?"

Shit. My phone was ringing, not his.

I stretched out my arm and fumbled my hand over the side table's surface until my fingers brushed along my phone's familiar shape. I blinked and plucked the phone from the table, tapped accept and brought the phone to my ear.

"Hello?" my voice cracked.

"Ms. Morgan," Gregor said in greeting.

I stifle a yawn and rolled onto my back. "It's three-thirty in the morning, Gregor. A little past my bedtime."

Connor withdrew his arm and propped up his head with his hand to watch me, concern etched on his face.

"I know what you did," Gregor said.

My brain still foggy, I rubbed the sleep from my eyes and sat up to rest my back against Connor's headboard. "What are you talking about? I haven't done anything." Besides sleep.

"Exactly."

I frowned harder and a yawn escaped. "This would go a lot faster if you just told me what you were talking about."

"You did nothing and now I will do the same thing," he said. "And soon you will know what it feels like."

"Gregor, I just woke up. I'm uncaffeinated, hangry and confused. You need to explain explicitly what I did wrong for me to be properly chastised."

"You stood by and let the Lord of the Veil kill my son. You said nothing. You did nothing."

Oh.

That.

"What exactly did you expect me to do in the veil against Leviathan?"

Silence stretched over the call while Gregor didn't answer. He said he would do nothing as if that would somehow upset me. Nothing about what? What did Gregor know that I didn't?

"When you said you'd do nothing, what did you mean?" I asked.

"I can feel her, you know."

"Who?"

"Your mother."

Dread tingled along my spine and clamped onto the back of my neck at the base of my skull. Why was he mentioning Mom?

Connor was out of the bed, throwing clothes on and finding mine.

"My mother?" I stammered.

"Her life force is weakening. I didn't have a hand in whatever is causing her current condition, but her blood is calling out to me. The soul is trying to save the vessel and pulls on me to complete the change and turn her."

My mouth fell open. My mind scrambled to process. He couldn't possibly mean... He didn't say...

Mom was dying?

I flung the sheets back and slipped from the bed to pace. My scalp prickled and my stomach churned. No. He had to be wrong. Mistaken.

Connor had his phone out, talking to someone on the other end in his cop code gibberish.

"My mom is dying?"

"And I will do nothing," he said.

"Bastard." The despair clamping my skull sent cold shivers over my skin, every hair on my body stood up. Our agreement pertained to healing her blood disease, not saving her life from other sources, which meant something awful had happened.

"Maybe I am a bastard, but you deserve this," he said. "I'm not without mercy though. I could be persuaded to do something."

Ah. There it was. Even through my shock, alarm bells rang. He was using this situation to manipulate me.

And I didn't care. "What's your price?"

"A life bond."

A memory from a few weeks ago flashed in my mind. One from Mom's apartment living room after I'd landed unceremoniously at her feet. She'd discovered I'd made a deal with Gregor, a deal that saved her life because at the time, she didn't have much time left.

Mom turned back to me with narrowed eyes. "You must promise me, Lark, my beautiful Sparky. Promise me, that when my time comes, truly comes, you'll let me go."

I pressed my lips together.

"No more deals with vampires without my consent."

"Fine," I bit out.

Mom told me to let her go when her time came. She wouldn't want me to do this. Regardless of whether I paid nothing or permanently bound my soul to Gregor, Mom wouldn't want to be turned.

Connor leaned in and whispered, "Emergency responders are on their way."

"You don't have much time," Gregor said. "You need to make a decision right now."

"I respectfully decline your offer," I said.

Silence met my answer.

Time ticked by. I started to pull the phone from my ear when Gregor spoke again.

"Then you'd better get that hot cop of yours to drive fast if you want to say goodbye."

The dial tone filled my eardrum and I stood in the middle of Connor's bedroom, stark naked, as numbness spread over my body.

Connor's death magic snapped out and coated me.

I shook my head and looked up.

He held out my clothes. "Let's go."

CHAPTER TWENTY-THREE

I clutched the handle as Connor took another sharp corner and accelerated after the turn. My heart beat frantically and I tried to call Mom again.

No answer.

Again.

I'd already called Logan. He was heading over with Brandon, but we'd beat them there.

Connor had his portable siren on and raced through the streets.

"Can you talk?" I asked.

He kept his eyes on the road and swerved into the oncoming lane to cut around the few random motorists out at this time of night.

"I can do anything for you."

"Distract me," I said. "Tell me about why you got called out."

He closed his mouth, his lips pressed into a firm line. He navigated the vehicle back to the correct lane and punched the gas.

"It was Mason."

My stomach rolled. Had Cathy killed him before or after his fiancée? Or had she gone over there to confront him with her feelings, and he rejected her?

"Why didn't you call me in?"

"Jacobs picked up Cathy's scent on the body. If we need official evidence to connect her, we'll get it from you later. But I think we have enough probable cause to go after her without your testimony."

I nodded and swallowed. My mind instantly shot back to Mom. Had Gregor lied? Why was she dying?

Pain shot through my chest, and I squeezed my eyes shut.

We were still too far out.

I needed to stay distracted or I'd lose my mind.

"How did Jacobs know her scent?"

"He went over to her place when we went to look for possible evidence to pinpoint her whereabouts."

"How did you not catch her scent?" I asked.

Connor scowled.

"I'm not attacking you; I'm still trying to wrap my head around what you're capable of."

"I'm empowered with death magic. Although my sense of smell is heightened to some things, like when you're aroused or scared and standing a few feet away from me, my abilities are more geared toward catching the scents of the dead. It's a barghest thing. No one has a better nose than Jacobs."

"You still should've called me in."

He glanced at me quickly before focusing again on the road. "I wanted you to sleep."

"You need sleep, too."

"I have slept better with you in my arms these last few nights than I have in years."

The vehicle grew quiet again, and Connor made the final turn onto Mom's street. Emergency vehicles lined the road, the flashing lights turned off.

What did that mean?

"Lark—" Connor slammed the gear into park.

I was already out of the car and sprinting toward the entrance of the apartment building.

Some uniformed cop I didn't recognize stepped into my path. "Miss, you can't—"

"She's with me, Terrant," Connor yelled from somewhere behind me.

I'd already stepped around the officer, racing through the apartment foyer and heading straight to the stairs. I took two at a time.

The air burned my lungs. My heart threatened to bash its way free of my chest.

Flinging the emergency door open, I stumbled onto Mom's floor, startling a number of uniformed officers.

"Uh...you can't be here."

"Yes, she can." Connor pushed past me. He grabbed my elbow and pulled me along.

With a weary grimace to say thanks, I slipped through the apartment door and stopped dead in my tracks.

Mom lay on her back in the centre of the apartment in a pool of blood, the hilt of a knife protruding from her chest. Death magic spiralled up from her body.

Almost dead.

Not quite dead.

If Gregor had been here, he could turn her. The soul still remained in her body.

I squeezed my eyes shut and clenched my hands into fists.

No.

Mom wouldn't want that.

The surrounding emergency responders backed away as I approached.

Dropping to my knees, I brushed Mom's hair from her face.

"Smells like Cathy," Jacobs said somewhere behind me.

When did he get here?

Did it matter?

Mom was gone.

Fucking gone.

And it was that bitch's fault.

I dropped my hand in the pool of blood and pulled the death magic to me.

The dark energy rose, fast and furious, flinging my

hair from my face. My nails stung as my fingernails grew into talons and my skin tingled as rage swept through my body.

Mom jerked.

A paramedic cursed.

More power.

More magic.

I'd force Mom's soul to stay until her body could heal.

I pulled all my magic and poured it into Mom.

She fluttered open her eyes. "Lark..."

I bit back a sob and gathered her in my arms, trying to hold her up and hug her at the same time. "Mom."

"Lark, sweetie..."

"Who did this? Was it Gregor?"

"No dear, it was some weak witch armed with... barghest... She tried to...she tried to destroy me, but she didn't realize what I am...what I was..." Her body sagged in my arms.

I reached down with my magic and poured more power into her, anchoring her soul in her body. Her eyes fluttered open again. "Sparky...my beautiful Sparky. You need to let me go."

"I'm not ready," I said. "I'm not ready to let go."

"You are," Mom said, the light in her eyes already fading again. "I love you. You and your brother are the world to me."

"I love you too." I bit back a sob. "I love you so

much. I haven't had the time to tell you how thankful I am. How grateful. How much you mean to me."

Mom's mouth twitched into a sad smile. "I know, honey. I've always known. I'm so proud..."

Mom slipped away. Her soul left her body, leaving an empty husk on the floor beside me.

With too much of my magic mixed with the blood, Mom's soul pulled me into the veil with her.

My world tilted and I collapsed forward, my braced arms preventing me from totally face-planting.

"Ah, Ms. Morgan," an all-too-familiar voice crooned. "I knew you'd be back."

CHAPTER TWENTY-FOUR

Wind and spirits whipped my hair, flinging it up to create a halo of black strands. My nails elongated even more, and my skin tingled as death magic surrounded me.

Standing a few feet away, Leviathan vibrated with quiet menace. Obscenely tall and powerfully built, he wore armoured leather like a second skin. Despite knowing he intended to use my blood for his missing ingredient to break free of the veil, he remained beautiful—at least on the exterior. The dim light from the veil played with the angles of his chiseled features and made his fair skin glow, adding to the aura of malice that perpetually surrounded him. His inky black hair matched his black gaze.

But it's what he held in his hand that caught my attention.

Mom.

I didn't need to see her soul morph into an outline of her once-living body. I didn't need Levi to tell me who he held in his grasp. I'd recognize the vibration of Mom's soul anywhere.

With one arm held out, Mom's soul hovered above his open palm. Her soul pulsed, healthy and full of essence that made Mom who she was to her core.

All the things I loved about Mom now lay in Leviathan's clutches.

"What are you doing?" I asked.

Levi cocked his head and looked at me before his gaze drifted down to consider the soul he held. "Remember when I warned you not to be too hasty?"

"W...what?"

"You said there was nothing I could offer, do or say to convince you to help me."

Dread shimmied down my body as if someone dumped an entire bucket of ice water over me.

"Barghests aren't the only beings who can destroy souls."

Well, I knew that, but... "You wouldn't."

A slow smile tugged at his lips. "I won't if you work with me."

The souls continued to whip by me, creating a whirlwind, poking, prodding, slapping me as they flew by.

No.

I would not allow this to happen.

I called the death magic to me, drawing from my

surroundings while pulling it from my core. Power pulsed in my veins, thundering in my heart. I unleashed all my fury on Leviathan. Everything I had, I blasted at his hulking body.

And met an invisible shield.

"You think you can best me? In my domain?" He wrapped his hand around Mom's soul and squeezed.

"No!" I held my hand out and slumped forward. "No. Please."

I let the magic slip away. It broke into sparkling ice and fell to the ground.

"Wise choice." Levi stopped squeezing Mom's soul. His shield pushed out and wrapped around me. The power sank into my skin, suffocating my lungs. My vision narrowed, a wall of black closing in on each side as Levi loomed over me with Mom's glowing spirit cradled in his palm. "You will see things my way soon enough."

CHAPTER
TWENTY-FIVE

I woke up with my face pressed against a cold, hard surface and my body in a giant cramp. I groaned and rolled to my side. I lay on a rough and uneven stone floor in a tangle of limbs and thin, stale-smelling blankets.

A single cot had been set up a foot away. I must've rolled off it somehow.

Peeling my aching body from the ground, I stretched my sore muscles. The dungeon prison cell was a dank, dimly lit chamber, the air thick with the musty scent of mould and mildew. Moisture dribbled down the stone walls lined with rusted chains and manacles.

"Ah, you're awake." Levi's deep voice penetrated the quiet space.

I spun around to find the Lord of the Veil on the

other side of metal bars. The bars separated my cell from a narrow stone corridor with a heavy-looking wood door at the end.

He'd locked me in a cell like a criminal.

"What the hell, Levi?" I reached for my bond with Gregor to find it gone. "What did you do?"

A slow insidious smile spread across his face.

I was beginning to really hate his face. To think I'd kissed him. To think I'd rubbed my body against his and considered what it would be like to end up naked with him.

My stomach rolled.

"What do you mean?" Levi asked.

"The blood bond. I can't feel it."

"Ah, well..." He flicked his hand in the air and looked away. "If Gregor decided to release his claim on your blood, that's something you'll have to take up with him."

Release his claim...

Gregor had dissolved the blood bond?

How?

Why?

I grimaced.

Okay, I knew why, but I hadn't realized Gregor could do something like that.

"Of course, releasing some of his progeny early and providing him with an intriguing offer may have helped motivate his decision to drop you as a minion."

Bastard.

"You've trapped me here."

"I have."

"And you're holding my mom for ransom."

He lifted a necklace I hadn't noticed before and studied it. A familiar blue light glowed in the centre, encased in an intricate web of gold.

Mom.

He wore her like a fucking locket.

"Not for ransom. For compliance. Here's the problem. You can't help me in exchange for your mom's soul. It's too close to coercion, and I'm not willing to risk it. I'm keeping you here and providing you with an abundance of reasons why you should help me, and then you need to volunteer, without the promise of escape or payment."

"We definitely have a problem, but that's not it."

Levi frowned.

"We have a stalemate."

Levi released the necklace so it dropped back to his chest. "What do you mean?"

"A stalemate is when—"

"I know what a stalemate is. Why do you say we're in one?"

"I won't fight because you have my mom, but I also won't help you. You may threaten my mom's soul, but you won't destroy her. If you do, my assistance is most assuredly gone."

Levi rolled his hands into fists and leaned forward. "Then you will never leave this place. You will rot here as the world continues on without you, including that cop of yours."

I swallowed. That sounded awful. But releasing Leviathan on the entire living realm sounded worse. "Why, Levi? Why do you want this?"

"Why wouldn't I?" he snapped. "Don't I deserve some freedom? Don't I deserve to escape this prison?"

Prison.

So he had been trapped here.

"How? No, why? Why did you get chained to the veil?" I asked.

Levi narrowed his eyes, but he didn't respond right away. Instead, he nodded at the corner of the room. "I took the liberty of picking out a dress for you."

A dress?

I rarely wore dresses.

For a reason.

When I was eight, Logan had used the dress I wore to pin me to the floor and fart on me. I learned at an early age how cumbersome dresses could be and how detrimental the lack of free movement was on survival.

I still liked dressing up and feeling pretty, though, so a few dresses graced my closet.

I glanced over at a neatly folded bundle of fabric I hadn't noticed earlier. I didn't bother asking Levi what was wrong with my current blood-stained outfit. Not wanting him to derail my train of thought, I turned back to Levi. "What did you do to get trapped here?"

Something flashed in his gaze and then he shut it down. All emotion slipped from his expression, replaced with a cold mask of indifference. "It doesn't matter."

"Then I definitely won't be helping you." Not going to lie, I didn't plan to help him even if he dished his entire life story. Not only had he committed a crime so heinous he got sent to the veil to rot, he threatened Mom's eternal soul. He deserved his fate.

"In a few years, you will start to see things my way." He turned away.

"Or you could realize this is futile and let me and my mother's soul go."

He responded with laughter and walked away. He left through an open door on the far side of the room and pulled it shut after him, leaving me in dark silence.

His footsteps faded and another door shut in the distance, metal hinges creaking.

The eerie silence of the dungeon surrounded me, leaving me alone with my thoughts. It didn't take long for them to turn to my last moments with Mom—her expression etched with pain, blood soaking her white shirt with the pink hearts on it. She loved pink. When I was younger and got hurt or sad, she used to wrap me in a fluffy pink blanket, like a baby burrito, and just hold me. She'd stroke my hair and tell me everything was going to be okay.

Well, nothing was okay right now.

A sob escaped my lips.

Then another.

I curled up in a ball in the corner of the cold room and cried as memory after memory flooded my mind.

When she got sick, I watched her get frail. They called it the "long goodbye" because Logan and I watched her slowly fade in front of our eyes. We had resigned ourselves to her impending death despite our best efforts to get her more treatments. She'd already surpassed the doctor provided expiry date.

I'd made the deal with Gregor when she was quite literally on her death bed. It gave us more time with her. It gave her a better quality of life.

It gave us hope.

And that hope had been torn away from us. From me.

Now she was gone and if I wasn't careful, Levi would destroy her, and she'd never be reborn again.

Another sob wracked my body. I wiped the tears from my face and sat up. Mom would want me to be strong. I still had a chance to save her eternal soul.

A blue spectre formed in front of me, the death energy vibrating around the jail cell. I scrambled until my back hit the wall.

The spectre solidified into the familiar shape of Bernice, the lovely old lady from the very first VicPD case I had consulted on. I'd taken her cat in and

Bernie's spirit followed me to the apartment and occasionally visited until she ran out of energy.

"Bernie?"

She nodded, her expression sad and forlorn. "I'm so sorry, my dear."

"Did you see what happened?"

She nodded again, her gaze dropped to her empty hands. "I was powerless to stop it. I couldn't even warn you."

"You used up all your energy trying to warn me about Steve." I sniffed and swiped at the remaining tears on my face. "You made a big sacrifice to help me, and I'll never forget it. Thank you, Bernie."

"I'm sorry I didn't know his name."

"That's okay. I appreciate that you tried."

"I really miss Maggie."

"Me, too." I missed my cat—Bernie's cat—but I also missed my brother, Brandon, and Connor.

And Mom.

I missed her so much it hurt. My chest ached as if someone had reached in and ripped out my heart and my stomach dropped, leaving me with a hollow, empty pain.

"Oh, sweetheart." Bernie drifted closer and wrapped her arms around me. They didn't feel like solid, human arms, but the death energy provided a presence that emulated the same feeling. Comfort. "I know it hurts. It will always hurt, but it will get better."

I wrapped my arms and magic around Bernie, hugging her back.

She ran her hands down my hair and shushed me. "It's going to be okay."

I don't know how long I stayed like that, crying in Bernie's arms, but eventually I found sleep. It wasn't restful. It was filled with memories of Mom as if my mind wanted to cling to thoughts of her in a valiant attempt to keep her alive.

CHAPTER TWENTY-SIX

I fastened the last button along the back of the dress when footsteps echoed down whatever hallway existed on the other side of the door. I had never toured the dungeons during my previous visits to the veil's creepy castle, so I didn't know the layout. I couldn't see much beyond my own cell and Bernie had left long before I'd thought to ask anything about my surroundings.

Not that it would do me much good now, anyway.

Spinning around to face the door, the full skirt of the dress swept around, the satin fabric whispering along the rough floor. Without a mirror, I had no clue how the gothic-style dress looked on me, but it was gorgeous.

Black satin gathered in a sweetheart neckline, emphasized with a large gemstone that sat nestled between my breasts. A tight, corset-style bodice made the dress hug my form before flaring out at the hips in a voluminous skirt. A long slit up the front showed off my legs and the web-styled lace sleeves, caped with hard-armour shoulder cuffs, matched the tights. The door opened, the hinges creaking in protest.

I wiped my puffy eyes. Pain stabbed at my chest with each thought of Mom. I had cried until I ran out of tears and then I'd cried some more.

My body felt empty, hollow, like everything wasn't quite real anymore and I was just a leftover husk waiting to deteriorate.

"Hudson." I scrambled back into my cell as the man rushed forward.

"Shhh." He held his finger to his lips. He had short brown hair, blue eyes, fair skin and great teeth. He was tall, attractive and had a deep, sexy voice. Too bad he had a shit personality.

"What do you want?" The last time I'd seen him, he'd used me to find the Book of the Dead, travel to the veil, and become Levi's right-hand man.

I frowned.

No, wait. That wasn't the last time. The last time I'd seen Hudson, I'd come to the veil to escape a serial killer named Steve. I discovered Hudson wasn't dead, he was working with Leviathan, and that serial killer trying to murder me? Yeah, Steve turned out to be Hudson's brother. And to make everything more infuriating, the reason Steve set his sights on me was all thanks to Hudson. Apparently, Steve had a thing for offing Hudson's romantic interests.

Lucky me.

And what really burned was I was never a romantic interest to Hudson. He was just using me to get the book and inadvertently put me in the crosshairs of his brother.

To say I hated Hudson was putting things nicely.

And I loathed Steve, entirely.

"I want to help you," Hudson said. His gaze swept down, eyes widening as he took in the extravagant dress.

I snorted. "You want to help me?"

"Seriously."

"You already did the whole pretending to like me thing, Hudson. I'm onto you."

He scowled and straightened from the bars. "That might've been a dick move, but Levi did to me what he's currently doing to you. I didn't have a lot of choices."

"Why should I believe you? It's a little convenient that this is all coming up now, isn't it?"

"Ask Levi. The guy can't help but brag about it."

"Did he keep his word?"

"What?"

"Did he keep his word? Did he release your loved one's soul once you did his evil bidding?"

"Yes. Oaths sworn in the veil must be kept. If you do make a deal with him, make sure he swears an oath.

And do better than me. Make sure you negotiate your return to the living realm as a part of the deal."

I narrowed my eyes.

He held up his hands and shrugged. "I didn't exactly cut in line in front of the hordes of people here offering to help you."

He had a point.

"What's in it for you?"

He frowned.

"I don't know you well, but there has to be something in this for you."

"Your freedom might provide me with my own. I might not be in a cell, and my shackles might be invisible, but I'm trapped here as well. Just like you."

I considered what he said. Last time we spoke, I got the impression he planned to stay to gain more power. That's certainly what Levi believed.

"Okay." I rubbed my hands together and waved at the bars between us. "Let me out."

He winced. "That's the problem. I don't know how to get you out. I wanted to see the bars first and talk to you."

My hope dissipated and fell away.

Hudson leaned forward and examined the bars. His magic spread out, slow and tentative, feeling the energy around the cell without touching the bars.

I watched in fascination. What information did his magic provide? He was a necromancer like me but had less power. Could I use my magic in the same way he just did?

I pulled on my power.

Hudson snapped his head up, his magic falling away. "Don't."

I released my power and frowned.

"You'll set off the alarms."

I flicked my hand in his direction. "You're doing it."

"My magic isn't as strong as yours. It flies under the radar."

"You were strong enough to infuse a spirit to take over drabs and cause murder and mayhem."

He nodded. "I didn't say I was weak. I'm a pretty strong necromancer in the living realm, but not strong enough to raise that witch or touch the Book of the Dead with my bare hands, and certainly not strong enough to travel to the veil. You're next level and I have no idea why. But I've been with you when you've summoned spirits. You pack quite a punch. Levi will notice."

Part of me wanted to preen under the compliment, but the other part just wanted to argue and punch him in the face again.

Hudson's words sank in. I knew why I packed more of a punch, now. I wasn't just a necromancer. In addition to necromancer magic from both sides of my family, I had barghest ancestry. Death magic thrummed in my veins.

"So?" I prompted, nodding at the bars.

"So...what?"

"Did you learn anything about my jail cell?"

He nodded. "I think so." He backed away from the cell. His gaze dropped to the dress again. "Nice outfit."

"It's from Levi." Obviously.

I smoothed my hands down the skirt. I might hate the Lord of the Veil, but this gown was the nicest thing I'd ever worn.

Though my twin was thankfully very far away from this dungeon, I could hear what he'd say as if he stood right beside me. He'd tell me how impractical dresses were and how I'd be at a disadvantage in a physical altercation.

Then, I'd mention how many places I could hide weapons in this outfit.

And then, he'd grow thoughtful.

"Levi had me commission a number of dresses for you," Hudson said. "He had me travel to the living realm to get them."

My head snapped up.

"He wanted something fit for a queen."

"That's not going to happen."

Hudson clamped his mouth shut and nodded. "I didn't think he'd get you in that dress at all, yet here you are."

I narrowed my eyes. This asshole better not be judging me. I'd rather wear a paper bag than my mother's dried blood.

Hudson glanced at the door. "I have to go."

I lurched forward, instinctively wanting to keep him here, wanting him to stay. I might not like him, but being left alone in a dark dungeon was somehow worse.

I shook myself. I hated this guy, but he might get me out of here. He might find a way.

Hudson's expression softened. "I'll be back."

I took a deep breath and tried to settle the unease twisting my stomach into a knot.

"I'll be back and then we'll defeat Levi together."

"Right." I nodded. What did we have to lose?

Only our immortal souls...

CHAPTER TWENTY-SEVEN

Leviathan stared down at me from his side of the bars, his full lips curled down in a frown. "Surely, you'd prefer more comfortable accommodations?"

"Fuck off." I rolled into a sitting position, my side aching from the hard mattress. "Luxury isn't worth selling my soul."

He cocked his head to the side. "You wouldn't be selling your soul. You'd be taking your place by my side as my queen, and we'd become indestructible."

"Pass."

"Is it because of that cop? Connor Kang?" His gaze narrowed. "Steve told me his name before I crushed his soul in my fist. I can give you more than *Connor* ever could."

"Are you honestly still trying the seduction angle?"

"I have never lied about wanting you, Lark." His

gaze dropped down, taking in the dress again. "The dress is beautiful on you."

I crossed my arms over my chest. "This isn't about me or how good I look in a dress. This is about my blood."

"Sure, I want your blood to form a gateway to travel to the living realm, but I also want you."

"A relationship can't be built on lies, Leviathan," I said. "You've lied to me since the day we met. Sure, you might've lied by omission, but in my book, it's the same thing."

He rocked back on his heels. "You want the truth?"

"Of course."

"I haven't lied to you."

"But you haven't told me everything."

"What would you like to know?"

I touched the chain of the pendant hanging around my neck. I'd found it's twin here in the veil when Levi had provided me with a room to stay in.

"When I was last here, I found a family pendant like this one." I lifted mine so its golden surface would catch the glowing light from above. "It has the symbol for the descendants of Morcant. I'm assuming it belonged to someone from my family and that they didn't meet a happy end in your castle. Who did it belong to?"

Levi clamped his mouth shut, his dark gaze flashing.

"You promised the truth."

"You won't like it."

"Well, I don't really like you much anyway." I folded my arms over my chest. "You're threatening to destroy my mother's soul. Who did the pendant belong to, *Levi*."

"Your father."

I squeezed my eyes shut and took a deep, shaky breath. I had already suspected my father was gone, already knew that it was a real possibility he met his end here in the veil. The confirmation still knocked the wind out of me like a sucker punch to the gut.

"Explain," I said.

"Your father came to the veil looking for the Book of the Dead. He'd hoped to find a cure for your mother's illness somewhere in its pages. Sanguimort carries a death sentence, and he was desperate. I'm surprised your mother survived sixteen years battling the disease."

I sucked in a deep breath. "We paid for experimental treatments."

Levi's smile was slow and lacked warmth. "But it wasn't just those treatments that gave her a longer lease on life, was it?"

"No. We had help from a vampire."

"The one you bonded with." Levi nodded. "But that was only recent..."

Coldness clamped my spine. What was he getting at?

"Your mother's own blood helped prolong her life

and stave off the degenerative effects of the disease." Levi glanced down at the locket. "I see things so clearly now. She's the daughter of Bedoe. The leader of the barghest pack. That's why those mangy mutts were chasing us and threatening me. They were trying to protect you. I should've seen it. Your mother's soul sings with power as does yours."

"What?"

"I suspected, of course. The talons and eyes gave it away, but I couldn't figure out which line you came from. But now I know, and now you shall rule beside me. The barghests will have no choice but to yield under your power."

"I will never be your queen."

"Never is a long time."

My stomach sunk even lower. "Can we get back to my father? I'm assuming because he never returned, he had no luck finding a cure or evading you."

"As you know, I only recently acquired the book, but I have leafed through its pages. There is no cure. He never stood a chance," Levi said.

Pain stabbed my chest. He'd risked his life for nothing. "And my father? Did you kill him and eat his soul?"

"When he realized the book wasn't here, he tried to kill me to take my power. He thought he could prevent your mom's death if he commanded all the spirits in the veil."

I squeezed my eyes shut.

"So yes, I killed him, but I didn't consume his soul. I consumed his blood and tried to form a portal I could leave through. I failed but discovered a lovely side effect. I found a connection with his children."

"Connection with his children?"

He nodded.

"With me, you mean." As far as I knew, Dad only had two children and Logan had never been to the veil.

"Yes, though I assume it would work with your brother, too," Levi said. "Whenever he accesses his power, I feel whispers of his soul in the veil."

That's how Levi always found me here. I touched the chain of my pendant hanging around my neck. He had a connection with our blood. Because of Dad.

Tears stung my eyes. My father hadn't abandoned us. He'd been searching for a cure years before Logan and I found out Mom was sick.

"Where is his soul now?" We didn't have any of his bones, so we'd never been able to raise him, but knowing where he rested would help ease my mind.

"I staked the remains of your father outside my castle and waited for the day when one of the descendants of Morcant would stumble into my domain."

Nausea bubbled up my throat. Dad was one of the skeletons in front of the castle. The very same skeletons I'd viewed from my room the last time I'd stayed here. So close and yet so far away. Did his soul remain anchored there? Did he have to watch me skipping into the castle like the ignorant fool I was?

Tears stung my eyes. I didn't think I had any left to shed, but apparently a few remained. They slipped from my eyes and trailed down my face.

Levi's gaze snagged on them, and his frown deepened. "You're leaking."

"You're perceptive."

"Will you reconsider my offer?"

"Absolutely not."

"You will," he said, before turning around and walking away.

CHAPTER TWENTY-EIGHT

Magic vibrated in the air, something familiar in the essence tugged on my memory. A large animal formed in the space between my jail bars and the door to freedom.

A barghest.

The outline of this barghest's body was fuzzy and illuminated with ethereal blue light. Barghests could access the veil while in the living realm, but my understanding was they faced the same challenges I did—a safe way back. Unlike necromancers, though, they could remain in the veil and feed off souls.

This barghest wasn't a mortal-realm barghest—at least as far as I could tell. There was a lack of physical essence, or sustenance. This barghest had already shed its mortal shell and now lived in the veil. Did this one remain in the veil waiting for its mate to join it?

The barghest snarled, the snout pulling back to reveal freakishly long fangs.

The door behind the barghest opened and shut, and Hudson stepped around the foaming beast.

I perked up. Had Hudson brought the barghest to free me?

I hesitated.

Or would I be the latest barghest victim? Its midday snack?

Hudson winked at me before turning to the barghest. "Thank you for coming."

The beast shuddered and transformed. In mortal life, changing shape took longer and made a lot more mess. At least that's what Connor implied. Whatever the case, the shift occurred seamlessly in the veil. The barghest shed its monstrous appearance to reveal an older Caucasian woman wearing a pleated polyester pantsuit. With fine bone structure, fair skin and wispy gray hair, the woman's spirit shone like a brilliant, fragile gemstone, completely in contrast to the intimidating beast she'd been moments ago.

"It is nice to meet you, Lark Morgan," the woman said. "Although this isn't the first time we've met, is it?"

Her words shattered something in my brain and memories of my dreams came flooding back. The familiarity of her face clicked in place. It was the same face I never managed to focus on in my dreams.

"That was you?" I asked. "The barghest in my dreams?"

"Not your dreams, honey. Your memories. You stumbled into the veil, and I helped you find a way home." She smiled, revealing a dimple in one cheek.

"You saved my life," I said. "Thank you."

She inclined her head. "And it appears I will save your life again."

"Who..."

"My name is Frances Sharrock. I'm Connor's grandmother."

I blanched. The same ancestor whose bones had been removed.

"I don't have a lot of time. Hudson has already taken a great risk by bringing me through the wards. As you know, a nutcase has stolen my bones and might call me back with her vile magic at any moment."

"That was you? You destroyed Lily and Maria's souls."

Frances bowed her head. "To my greatest shame, yes. I didn't have a choice. The magic compelled me."

"We know," I said. "We found your empty grave and made some assumptions. Connor knows you had no choice."

"That woman tried to make me destroy your mother's soul as well, but your mother's Bedoe magic saved her. We can destroy the souls of drabs and glamies, with one exception."

"Other barghests."

Frances nodded. "I'm sorry for your loss. I truly am. I wish I could've stopped it from happening. Your mother was strong, but we caught her off guard and my own magic countered hers. I wish that hadn't been the case."

Invisible hands squeezed my heart and pain stabbed my chest. I couldn't falter right now. I couldn't let the grief win. "I don't blame you," I said. "I know exactly where I should direct my anger." I balled my hands into fists, letting anger wipe away the sadness.

Frances nodded again. "Please tell my grandson I'm sorry. And that I love him and miss him and am so very proud of the man he's become."

I swallowed. I had to make it out of this place first, but I would make sure Connor got the message. "I will."

Frances smiled a slow sad smile that I couldn't quite figure out. There was more going on here, but the pieces I held in my mind weren't forming a finished puzzle.

"You have a beautiful soul," Frances said. "I can see why he imprinted."

I froze. Did I have some sort of neon sign on me? I glanced over at Hudson.

The man looked confused as hell.

Good.

I didn't want the entire supernatural community to know my personal business.

"It's time." Frances turned to Hudson. "I'm ready."

I frowned again. "Wait. What's going on? If you're going to do something dangerous, we'll find another way. I refuse to let something bad happen to you. You're Connor's grandmother. He loves you very much."

Frances turned that sad smile on me once again. "I am atoning for my wrongs and do so willingly. This is something I want and need to do, and I will finally have peace. You are my grandson's light. You need to get home to him. Preferably before he does something stupid like try to come here on his own rescue mission."

"He wouldn't." He better fucking not.

"He would go to hell and back for you, my dear, and rip apart anyone who tried to stand in his way." She paused, hesitating before speaking again. "It won't matter to me anymore, but the family will want my remains returned. I'm not sure exactly where they are, but when I'm called, I still feel the power of my family and I get glimpses of angel wings."

I digested the information and committed it to memory. It made little sense right now, but it might be the missing piece we needed later.

And any information was more than what we had.

"I'll tell him," I said.

She nodded.

Hudson stepped close and Frances sighed. Without another word, she grabbed the bars and sank her magic into them.

Light flashed.

More and more magic flooded into the bars. They glowed brighter and brighter and still Frances gave them more. With each push of power, the brightness of her soul dimmed.

"You have to stop," I said, "You're giving too much."

Frances shook her dainty head, her gray hair floating in the air.

"She knows the price, Lark," Hudson said.

I snapped my head up and glared. "What?"

"She knows the price and volunteered."

"No." I stalked toward the bars. Energy zapped me, sending me flying back. The impact with the ground knocked the air out of my lungs. I lay stunned on the hard surface of the floor for a second, the silly dress pooled around me, before I scrambled to my feet.

"No." My heartbeat raced. "She can't do this," I told Hudson. "Make her stop."

He shook his head.

"She'll destroy her own soul."

"She knows."

"I'm not worth that price," I growled. "Nobody is."

Hudson studied the barghest, a soft smile spreading over his face. "She's not doing this for you."

I rocked back on my heels.

"Okay, she might be doing this for you a little. She's definitely doing this for her grandson. But most of all, she's doing this for herself."

My eyes prickled and I blinked back tears.

Frances kept holding the bars, shattering Levi's

magic with her own, piece by piece, her soul dimming with each pulse.

"I will make sure your sacrifice is known," I whispered. "I love him, you know. I love him so much, it scares me. But I will spend the rest of my time with him ensuring he knows how much he is loved and make him happy."

A smile spread across Frances's face—a true smile, wide and generous and full of light.

"I know," Frances said. "Your love is in your light."

And then her light snuffed out.

I gasped and staggered back. "No."

The bars disintegrated. Levi's power was dismantled and destroyed by Connor's grandmother. Nothing remained of her or the bars.

A magical shockwave blew outward, sending me flying back again. My ass hit the hard ground and once again my breath was ripped from my lungs.

Outside, a howl rent the air, followed by another and another.

"Come on." Hudson rushed forward and pulled me to my feet. "She didn't just free you. By breaking Levi's wards on this jail cell, she brought down the entire protective barrier around the castle. We have to strike now while he's weak."

"What?"

"It's time to kill the Lord of the Veil."

CHAPTER
TWENTY-NINE

We found Levi surrounded by a snarling pack of barghests outside the castle. On his knees, he struggled to stand while the beasts lunged and snapped.

He was bent over, his dark hair hanging in front of his face. The death magic rolling off him was a fraction of what it once was. Frances destroying his wards must've weakened him considerably.

"How did you know?" I asked Hudson.

"While I was helping him research ways out of the veil, I was conducting my own research."

Levi looked up at our approach. "Ms. Morgan," he snarled. "Have you come to watch them destroy my soul?"

I skidded to a halt, just outside the circle etched into the ground by his magic.

A thin shield surrounded him. With each barghest

attack, it flared and then dimmed. His power weakened even more.

If the barghests punched through the shield, they'd destroy him.

Along with Mom's soul and the only one capable of returning me to the living realm.

Hudson grabbed my hand and pulled me forward.

"Come on," he said. "We need to act fast."

"What are we going to do? If he's destroyed, we're trapped here."

"Do you trust me?" Hudson asked.

"Not even a little," I snapped.

He narrowed his eyes. "Do you trust Kang's grandmother? She gave her soul for this to work."

I hesitated a second longer before nodding.

Hudson raised his arm to point at Levi, jabbing the air with his finger like it would somehow inflict damage. "Just aim your magic at his shield and I'll do the rest."

I didn't bother asking why. The shield continued to dim as we spoke.

Pulling my magic from within and from my surroundings, I pushed a wave of power at Levi's crumbling shield. Magic surged around me. Souls whipped through the air. A weightlessness consumed my body as the sticky, inky power of death lifted me from the ground Energy thrummed in my veins as necromancer and barghest magic coiled within me. My hair rose from my shoulders, coiling toward the ethereal night sky to form a tornado of hair. I held my hands out and embraced the power surging around me to answer my call.

As I drifted forward, the barghests parted to let me through, I poured everything into the blast. All my anger. All my fear. All my grief.

There was still a chance Levi would destroy Mom's soul before we reached him.

Levi stood slowly. His muscles tense, his gaze flashing.

The shield shattered under the force of my will.

Instead of yelling at me, instead of begging, Levi tilted his head, his gaze shifting to something over my shoulder. He smirked.

A blast of death magic struck Levi's chest.

Not my magic.

"No." I crashed back to the ground. Releasing my power, I rushed forward and caught Levi before he toppled over.

I stumbled to the side, my knees buckling under the weight. I let go and Levi's body hit the ground seconds before my knees slammed into the dirt. Pain lanced up my legs.

"What the fuck?" I screeched over my shoulder. "We're fucking stuck here."

Levi was gone. The great, terrible Lord of the Veil lay dead on the ground along with my chance of escape.

I pulled the chain with Mom's soul in a locket and

slipped it around my neck. The locket hit my sternum, its warm weight pressing into my skin. Safe. Whole.

I placed my hand over Mom's soul, a tear slipping down my cheek.

Mom's soul pulsed.

Yeah. It was worth it.

I might be trapped here for all eternity but knowing my mom would be reborn made the pain and fear lessen.

The skeletons on the nearby spikes crumbled, falling to the ground in a pile of dust. Souls streaked out of the cloudy air, zipping away with their freedom.

All but one.

A blue spectre drifted closer to me, where I crouched by Levi's body and held Mom's soul in my hand.

"Dad?" I said.

The soul flared but didn't form into Dad's image. He must be weakened from being anchored to a spike for so many years.

I sniffed and blinked back tears. This was not the time to get sad. This was a time to let my anger rage. I pulled myself to my feet and spun to confront Hudson.

"What the fuck, Hudson?" I threw up my hands.

And froze.

Hudson levitated in the middle of the barghest pack, arms spread wide, head flung back, souls and death magic swirling around him, through him.

Slowly, I lowered my arms and walked closer. The

death magic trailed off and Hudson floated down, his feet pressing into the solid ground, his gaze settling on me.

"What the fuck?" I said for the third or fourth time. I'd lost count.

A slow smile spread across his face as the barghests settled quietly around him. "I'm Lord of the Veil now."

I sputtered. "What?"

"Who do you think all those people were in the portraits? I shall have one made for Leviathan."

"Make this make sense," I demanded. "I thought you wanted to escape the veil."

"I may have misled you a little," Hudson said.

"A little?" I said. "*A little*?"

"I wanted to escape the living realm and Levi offered a sanctuary of sorts."

"You wanted to escape your brother, but he's dead now."

Hudson nodded. "Yes, he is, and his soul is destroyed. But it's too late for me to return to the living realm. Levi locked my soul to this realm. Either I could continue to be Levi's errand boy, or I could take control. I chose me."

"But...but how? I don't understand how this even worked."

He dropped his hands to his side, magic swirling around him. "The person to take the life of the lord, assumes the mantle and responsibility of the position. Leviathan had been tricked into killing the last lord, not realizing it would transform the veil into his own prison. He deserved it of course. He'd been a powerful necromancer in the living realm and was known to callously rip the souls from anyone who defied him. Or just looked at him wrong. Be glad you didn't take Leviathan's life, or you'd truly be stuck here, locked in the veil just like me."

I glanced at Levi's body behind me. I'd never discover his full story, never learn his origins. That curious part inside of me craved to untangle the mystery. And the other part was just glad he was dead, and I was free.

"Don't feel too bad for Leviathan."

I didn't, not really. He threatened Mom's eternal soul. He'd killed my father.

"He got what he wanted. In a way," Hudson continued. "The Lord of the Veil is a position, not a person. In the end, Levi knew his fate. He could've let the barghests take him and destroy his soul for all eternity, or he could let me win. He chose wisely. Levi will be reborn, one day, finally escaping the veil. And I will rule in his place."

Hudson would finally get the power he craved.

All tied up in a neat bow. At least for Hudson. And I'd helped tie the fucking knot.

I clutched the locket hanging against my breast. "What are your plans for me?"

He smiled and turned partially away from me.

Raising his arms, magic poured from his body and formed a portal.

"It's time for you to release your mother's soul and return home."

I stared at the portal. "I...I don't understand."

"What's there to understand?"

We never had an agreement. He never swore an oath to me. Why would he let me go when he could try to use me as Leviathan did? He owed me nothing.

Hudson waited for me to ask more questions, but I snapped my mouth shut. I wasn't going to point out any of that shit to him.

"I made Frances a promise," he said. "I swore to protect you, to never harm you or your mother's soul and to always provide you with a safe way home should you become trapped in the veil."

Wow.

"You might not have known her, but she knew you. They all do, and though you might not be a barghest, you are a descendent of one, but more importantly, you belong to one."

One of the beasts stepped forward and butted its head against my leg. I looked around. The whole pack waited, some panting, some watching me with in eerie stillness. The fear I might've had in the past no longer existed.

"Thank you," I said to all of them. They had been in on the plan as well.

Hudson nodded, though my gratitude hadn't really been directed at him. He got plenty out of this deal. He'd needed me to get what he wanted as much as I needed him. "Frances also got to find peace, in her own way. Her mate's soul had been destroyed by Levi years ago. She was stuck here for eternity and wanted to join her mate in oblivion."

I sucked in a breath. That somehow made it better and worse at the same time.

"It's time to go home, Lark."

I took another deep breath and opened the locket that held Mom's soul. As soon as the gold case opened, Mom's soul popped out. It pulsed a few inches from my face, sharing its warmth.

She spun around the shimmering blue spectre of Dad's soul before they sped away. Together.

My feelings twisted in a complicated knot.

"Goodbye, Mom and Dad." My voice caught in my throat, and I swallowed a sob. With everything happening, I hadn't had time to grieve properly other than cry in my jail cell. I wouldn't ever have enough time to truly allow their loss to swallow me.

Grief was a complicated emotion. I now had two distinct personalities—one that shoved away all the sad feelings and acted as though nothing bad had happened, and the second who had the weight of loss threatening to drown them in sadness.

I couldn't allow the latter to take control. Not right now.

The grief would have to wait. So, I embraced the

first personality and persevered. Someone needed to pay for what had transpired and I wouldn't rest until Cathy paid.

"One more thing." Hudson's voice stopped me before I stepped through the portal. "The vampires know."

Fear finally clamped my spine. Hudson didn't have to elaborate. The only thing I'd needed to worry about was the vampires finding out I was powerful enough to control them. I'd guarded that secret, but Levi had caught me controlling a vampire assassin sent to his castle. "Levi?"

"Gregor has been using some heavy dark magic to rip seams into the veil. At first, he sent a vampire to try to steal the book. Once Levi realized how Gregor got his man into the veil, he was waiting for the next one and when Gregor used those drab sacrifices to tear open another seam, Levi was there to suggest a deal."

The sacrifice slaughters. Gregor was using them to access the veil just as we'd suspected after speaking to Pierre. But I never thought he'd use access to the veil to make a deal with Levi. I should've seen it, anticipated it.

"They met for a third time just recently to finalize everything. Gregor was to release his blood bond on you and in return, Levi would tell him the secret to releasing the vampires from their blood dependency."

"What is it?"

"The secret? I don't know. I've scoured that book

and though there was a section, I couldn't figure out the translation. Levi didn't trust me with the information," Hudson said. "But what I do know is Levi took great pleasure revealing your additional talents as a parting gift to Gregor. He didn't plan to let you escape back to the living realm and thought to rub it in Gregor's face. The master vampire never would've agreed to release his hold on you had he known the full extent of your powers."

Motherfucker.

Gregor would now seek to kill or control me indefinitely.

"It's time, Lark," Hudson waved at the shimmering air.

I nodded at Hudson and then at the barghests before walking through the portal on shaky legs.

CHAPTER THIRTY

I stumbled through the portal, legs weak, head light, heart heavy, into the destroyed living room of Mom's apartment. The heavy skirt of my dress swished around my legs. The lights had been turned off, along with the heat, and a cold bite lingered in the air. Blood spatter still stained the carpet, but there were no paramedics milling around or crime scene analysts collecting forensic evidence.

"Lark."

The sound of Connor's familiar deep voice growling at me broke the last semblance of self-control I had. Stepping into the room, I crumpled forward, a sob ripping from me.

Strong arms caught me. Connor gripped me, hard, and whispered into my hair, "Lark, Lark, Lark, Lark..." His voice caught and he clutched me harder.

I cried into his chest. He surrounded me with his

warmth as he wrapped his arms around me and buried his face into my neck. He breathed in deeply, inhaling my scent, over and over again. "I've got you. You're safe now."

With each deep breath of his, I cried harder and harder until I had nothing left to give.

Then I just clung to him as he rocked me back and forth, holding me so tightly, his fingers dug in and threatened to bruise me as if he feared I wasn't real or would disappear again.

I didn't know how long we stood like that, how long we held each other as if we were the only two people who existed in the world.

Finally, and so slowly, I pulled back. Though it had only been a few days since I'd seen him, he looked as though he'd lost a little weight. His cheekbones were more pronounced, and he had dark bags under his eyes. "Have you been waiting here the whole time?"

"Yes."

"Did you eat?"

"Jacobs brought me food," he answered, his voice gruff.

"Did you eat?" I repeated.

He pressed his lips together and squinted at me. So, basically no, he didn't eat. While I'd been away, locked in a dungeon in the veil for a few days, he'd stayed in Mom's apartment, waiting and starving.

"What exactly was your plan? Go on a hunger strike?" I asked.

Connor scowled. "I planned to take my barghest form and enter the veil."

I sucked in a breath. As far as I knew, Connor had never gone into the veil. Wouldn't he also have to worry about a way to return? "Well, no need for that now."

Connor smoothed my hair and tucked it behind my ears before his gaze shifted to study my face. He paused on the bruise near my neck, his gaze flashing.

"Who hurt you?" he asked, tone dangerously low.

"He's dead."

A long pause. His magic flared around us, violent and potent.

"Good," he said, finally. His gaze dropped down. "What the fuck are you wearing?"

"I have so much to tell you."

"You don't have to do it right now. Let's get you cleaned up and something to eat."

My stomach growled in agreement. But instead of caving and letting Connor take care of me, I placed a hand on his chest.

"First, your grandmother says hi. She wanted you to know she loves you, misses you and is very proud of you."

He blinked and snapped his head back. He sucked in a breath.

"Second, she gave me some information that might help us locate her remains."

"And possibly Cathy," he added, following my

thoughts like a champ. "She's probably hiding out with the bones."

"I want a lot of things, Connor. But bringing that bitch down is near the top of that list."

His gaze darkened. "Do you want her to pay the glamy way or the legal way?"

He'd just offered to murder someone for me. I should be appalled. Taken aback. Instead, warmth spread through my chest. "The legal way. I want her to rot in prison for a very long time. The veil is too kind a punishment."

He nodded, brushing his thumb over my cheek. "I'll get it done."

And I knew he would.

"You said making Cathy pay was near the top of your list," Connor said. "What's at the top?"

"You," I said. "You're at the top of my list."

Connor waited, choosing to rub my back while I searched for the words.

"I know I told you I wasn't quite ready to discuss things, but getting thrown into a dungeon in the veil for the unforeseeable future put a lot of things into perspective for me and not telling you how I feel was one of my biggest regrets while I sat in the dark and faced so many unknowns. I love you. The fear of losing you or messing this up...I don't think I could recover from that. I don't want to wait for someday. We've already wasted six years dancing around each other. I want to start that life with you now."

Connor crushed me to him, his arms wrapping around me like a vise. He said nothing, just burying his face in my hair again as he shook. He shook as if his feelings overwhelmed him just as much as mine threatened to drown me. Or maybe he shook because I did.

Finally, he pulled back, his gaze melting me on the spot. "About fucking time, Morgan."

CHAPTER THIRTY-ONE

The moon shone down and illuminated the gravestones as I made my way through the cemetery with Connor and Jacobs. After I told him more about what his grandmother had said in her final moments, we figured out Cathy must've hidden Frances' bones somewhere in the cemetery. It couldn't be too close to the family plots, or else we would've sensed the death energy from the bones, so we started on the far end of the cemetery, carefully walking through each section while Connor and I scanned the area with our magic.

I didn't want to wait to get Cathy in case she moved her hiding place. After showering at Mom's and grabbing some spare clothes—sweatpants and a T-shirt, I left the cold apartment with Connor to meet Jacobs at the cemetery.

The feeling of his power gliding alongside mine empowered me and searching for his grandmother's bones allowed all my rage to come to the forefront. Hopefully, we'd find Cathy with the barghest's remains. She needed to pay for what she did. Sadness still tugged at my heart, still left me feeling hollow inside, but the grief came in waves and right now, anger won.

Connor held my hand and walked by my side as Jacobs trailed behind us. He'd quietly offered his condolences when he'd met us at the cemetery, and I appreciated his support. I'd also texted my brother and Brandon to let them know I was back in the living realm and okay. Logan demanded I return home as soon as possible, of course, but I refused, telling him I had to do something first.

He'd assume I meant Connor, but I wouldn't correct him or elaborate. The last person we needed in the cemetery right now was my brother. He wouldn't let Cathy exist. He wouldn't even let her speak. He'd sweep into her hidey hole and kill her before anyone had a chance to interrogate the killer.

My magic brushed along familiar death energy.

"There," I whispered and stopped walking.

Connor stilled beside me, his magic following mine until he settled on the same vibrations. He sucked in a breath and his body vibrated. His eyes shuttered and when he opened them again, he had to blink a few times before the black in the iris faded back to his regular brown colour.

I squeezed his hand. "We can do this with—"

"Don't you dare suggest I let you two leave me behind," he growled. "First off. I'm never leaving you alone again. And second, this bitch is as big a villain in both our stories. She will face the full wrath of us standing together."

Jacobs cleared his throat. "Are we still planning to arrest her, because the way you just said that..."

Connor turned around and snarled.

Jacobs held up his hands in mock surrender. "Just checking. I'm fine with whatever. I just need to be on the same page. Kind of awkward to try to handcuff a suspect when my partner is ripping her to shreds."

Connor returned his attention to me and hesitated. "Are you sure you want her to go to jail?"

"As much as I would love to see you rend her soul from her flesh, I want to see her rot in prison. Our judicial system is the real Hell, and you can't convince me otherwise. Anything less is too good for her."

Connor nodded and squeezed my hand before letting go. He drew his firearm and nodded at Jacobs.

The two detectives moved ahead, and without being asked, I hung back and let them take the lead. I pulled my magic around me, ready to lash out if needed, and followed as Connor used his magic to track Cathy. We headed toward a small mausoleum with the statue of an angel standing on top.

Connor and Jacobs yelled out their scripted warnings to Cathy before Connor kicked down the door. They rushed inside and a woman screamed.

Music to my ears.

I waited outside, relishing in Cathy's protests while the moon bathed my skin and Connor's magic danced around mine.

"Lark?" Connor called out.

I stepped into the mausoleum and stared down at the petite woman with brown hair as she lay face-down on the ground with her wrists handcuffed behind her back. She probably had enough blood on her to indict her on Maria, Mason, and Mom's murders.

Jacobs stood over her while Connor had distanced himself. His whole body vibrated with fury. He squatted to examine a large black duffel bag. I didn't need to walk over and look inside to know its contents. His grandmother's bones were in that bag—a jumbled mess with no effort to respect the dead.

"You truly are a monster," I said to Cathy.

She twisted on the ground to look up at me, her brown eyes full of fury. "You?"

"Yes, me. Did you think you could steal barghest bones and kill a necromancer's mother and somehow get away with it?"

"You can't prove anything."

"You're literally covered in blood. A few DNA swabs will pretty much cover it. Besides, you weren't able to destroy my mother's soul, were you?"

Cathy jerked away; a deep frown etched in her expression.

"Oh, you didn't know that, did you? One raising and I'll have witness testimony."

Cathy looked away from me, choosing to face the other way and stare at Jacobs' shoes.

"Tell me why you did it. Why my mother?" I asked.

Cathy laughed and shook her head.

Without warning, I thrust my magic inside Cathy and gripped her soul with my power. Cathy thrashed on the ground. I pulled on her soul, letting it writhe and try to escape my steely hold. I could rip her soul from her body. It would be so easy. I could probably crush it in my hands.

"Lark." Connor was suddenly at my side. His hand running down my back as if to soothe me like a wild cat. "You wanted her to live."

I blinked and leaned into his touch. He moved to stand behind me, wrapping his arms around my torso to pull me into the heat and strength of his body. His breath fanned my ear and tickled my neck as he spoke. "If you want to do this, then I'll support you. But you made it clear you wanted her to suffer."

I squeezed my eyes shut and pulled my magic back.

Cathy shuddered on the ground. A low keening escaped her mouth, and she started shaking.

"You'll take care of it?" I whispered. I still wanted to know why. I wanted to throttle the truth from

Cathy, but I didn't trust my ability to stop. I'd snap her neck like a twig and then I'd never get answers.

"Of course," Connor said with absolute certainty.

I nodded, gently pulled away from his embrace, and walked out of the crypt.

CHAPTER THIRTY-TWO

Connor hadn't wanted to leave me to take Cathy to the precinct. He'd hovered over me like a mother hen and kept checking me for injuries even though no physical altercations occurred when we confronted Cathy. When I told him Cathy's arrest was what I wanted, he'd switched into cop mode, dropped me off at my apartment building, and took Cathy in.

According to Connor's texts, Cathy confessed to killing Mom, Mason, Maria, and Lily in less than thirty minutes of being interviewed. She kept stammering and begging Connor to protect her from me.

Little did she know, she needed to be protected from Connor as well.

Apparently, Cathy had always been obsessed with Mason and something snapped four years ago when Lily revealed her unplanned pregnancy during their girls' night. Cathy had pretended to go to sleep early, but instead, snuck out of her place, leaving an unsuspecting Lily alone in her apartment while she stole Mason's car. Cathy then drove to Lily and Mason's meeting spot and started her career as a killer.

Mom's death left me hollow and numb. With my job, death constantly surrounded me, but that didn't help with coping. Knowing Mom's soul was free and safely in the veil did.

Part of me wanted to break into the precinct, hunt Cathy down, beat her up, scream at her, something... anything. And the other part knew I wasn't really a fighter. Not that kind anyway. And I certainly wasn't a police officer. I didn't need to confront Cathy any more than I already had. I had all the closure I'd get.

So after I walked out of the creepy mausoleum, I didn't participate in the interrogation or booking process. Instead, I came home to Logan and Brandon. We hugged and cried and hugged some more.

It still felt anticlimactic as fuck, but it was also exactly what I needed to heal.

Logan on the other hand...

Cathy might not make it to trial, though I hoped she would. I wanted her to rot away in prison, not die a swift death at my brother's hands. She didn't deserve a quiet, quick death.

Currently, Brandon, Logan and I binged some reality television show where contestants lost money if they slept together. We'd been watching the show for days. We were all in our makeshift pajamas of sweatpants and T-shirts, surrounded with snacks, and huddled together on the couch in the dark.

Someone knocked on the door. Logan and Brandon turned to me. We all knew who stood on the other side of the door, even though I was the only one capable of sensing his death energy.

Scooting out from under the blanket, I leaned over to plant kisses on both their cheeks.

"Tell Connor we said hi," Logan glanced up quickly before returning his attention to the screen.

I left them to their TV drama and made my way through the apartment.

Connor's magic seeped through the seams around the door and curled around me. I flipped the deadbolt, unlatched the safety chain, and opened the door.

His gaze flashed when it settled on me, and he scooped me into his arms. He buried his face into the crook of my neck and inhaled deeply. He'd showered before coming over, the scents of his shampoo and soap still clinging to his skin, his thick black hair slightly damp.

I'd missed him.

God, I'd missed him so much.

I wrapped my arms around him, pulling closer so my body pressed flush to his. Along with soap and shampoo, he still smelled faintly of cologne and metal.

Familiar.

Safe.

Mine.

"It's time to go home," he growled into my neck.

"I am home," I protested.

He shook his head, his nose brushing my ear. "Home with me, Lark. Our home."

He pulled back, his gaze flicking over my face. He'd give me space if I asked. He'd give me time.

I wanted none of those things.

"I'd have to pack some clothes," I said. "Grab some things."

His heated gaze scanned my outfit and messy bun.

"I think I prefer this look to the all-leather one."

"Including the heels?"

"Maybe pack those," he said, his expression turning thoughtful.

I hesitated and glanced over my shoulder. As much as I was grieving, I wasn't the only person in pain.

"I'm taking you across town, Lark, not the country," he said. "You can see them tomorrow and you don't need to pack a bag."

I started to protest.

"I don't really plan for either of us to wear much."

I snorted, but my body had already responded to his words, heating up with wild anticipation.

"I don't want to spend another night without you," he said. "Come home with me."

I wanted Connor. I wanted everything he offered.

Pain came in so many different forms. Losing Dad and never knowing his fate until recently hurt, still did, though time had helped. Nothing would top the sharp pain and emptiness created by Mom's death, and the guilt I felt for being the reason why Cathy targeted her. Even now, my eyes prickled and threatened to release more tears. When I had curled up on the dungeon floor, not knowing if I'd see Logan or Brandon ever again...that had hurt, too. The thought still made my heart ache. I loved the boys so much.

And then there was Connor.

The separation while I was trapped in the veil, and more recently, the time apart while he followed through with his promise to me, made one thing crystal clear in my otherwise chaotic mind.

Connor was mine.

I didn't just want him. I craved him. I needed him. He'd quickly become my world and while the intensity of my feelings scared me, I wouldn't run from them. I meant what I said when I'd first returned from the veil.

Connor frowned and reached out gently and tipped my chin, forcing me to look up. "What's wrong?"

"I love you," I said.

His expression changed. His gaze darkened. His body language told me how much my words affected him.

"You're in so much trouble," he said.

"Is that so?"

He nodded. "I was willing to let the first time you

told me slide because you'd just escaped the veil, but now there's no going back."

"I've already lost my heart. How much worse could it get?"

A slow smile spread across his face, and he reached out to gather me in his arms again. "You may have lost yours, but you've gained mine."

"And that's why I'm in trouble?"

He kissed me as his way of answering. From the flick of his tongue, I knew I was going to be in a lot of trouble indeed.

And I'd enjoy every minute of it.

CHAPTER
THIRTY-THREE

The door snicked shut behind me, leaving me alone with Connor in his bedroom. His death magic flowed over my shoulders and waist to wrap around me. The seductive taste of his power sparked every nerve in my body, and I slowly turned toward him.

His gaze had darkened with need and death magic continued to radiate from his body in one delicious wave after another. He stood still as if waiting for me to reach some sort of decision.

But I had already chosen Connor a long time ago.

It took me a few years to realize it, of course. But I never claimed to be the smart one in the family.

He pulled me toward him with his magic and I closed my eyes, relishing the feel of his power sinking into my skin to merge with my own. Warmth flooded my body and Connor replaced his magic with his arms, holding me close. His lips brushed mine, and I tilted my head up to kiss him back.

He groaned and brought one of his hands up to thread his fingers through my hair and grip the back of my head. He angled his mouth and deepened the kiss, plunging in his tongue to tangle with my own. I moaned into his mouth, and he swallowed the sound. His magic throbbed inside me, a beacon of his need.

We stumbled toward the bed, Connor ripping my shirt from my body, and he growled with appreciation when he discovered I hadn't bothered with a bra. He tugged my sweatpants down and they pooled at my feet, leaving me in only a pair of cheap cotton underwear.

I stepped out of my pants and worked at the buckle of his belt. The task should've been simple, but Connor moved his mouth from mine to explore my jaw, neck, and shoulder. He palmed my breast with his free hand, squeezing as he teased the sensitive skin along my neck with his mouth.

Finally managing to pull his belt free, I flung it across the room and ran my fingers through Connor's silky hair.

Without warning, he scooped me up and threw me on the bed. I squealed as I landed in an extra soft duvet that billowed around me. Connor was already on me, kissing me, caressing me. He smiled against my skin and worked his way down my body while I gripped his head like some sort of life preserver.

Laying down between my legs, he slipped his fingers under my panties and slid his hands around to grab my ass and pull me forward. His mouth clamped onto me, through my underwear, and I gasped. His hot breath along with the contact sent heat pooling low in my belly.

He pulled my underwear off, leaving me exposed for a second before his mouth was back on me. His hands kneaded my butt and kept me in place as pleasure consumed my body. The ache between my legs bloomed, spreading more heat. A moan slipped from my lips as Connor's power pulsed along my skin, claiming, and demanding.

Release came fast and hard.

I cried out as more pleasure rippled through me. Connor watched me as I writhed under his control, need dancing in his gaze. I was still riding his face, the aftershocks of the orgasm rippling through me. He pressed his thumb down on my clit and stars danced in my eyesight.

"I...I..." I was going to say I couldn't take any more, but we'd both know that was a lie. If I uttered the words though, Connor would stop, and I didn't want that. Not only could I take more, but I wanted more. Craved more.

"Yes, you can," he said, somehow reading my mind. He nipped the inside of my thighs, dragging his teeth along the sensitive skin. I arched into the soft duvet as his magic continued to surround me. "You can take everything I give you."

"I think you might be the death of me."

"That explains why you taste like heaven." He looked up at me, his head still between my legs, his gaze feral, his hair mussed from where I'd pulled and yanked while in the throes of an orgasm. He was the most beautiful thing I'd ever seen, and I'd never tire of seeing him like this—open and fueled by need.

He quickly stood and threw off the rest of his clothes, his gaze remaining locked on my throbbing body. He inhaled deeply. "Your smell is intoxicating."

"What do I smell like?"

"Like you're mine," he growled, reaching for my thighs as they continued to shake from my release. He spread them wide, pulled me forward and thrust inside me. I cried out at the fullness. My skin buzzed with sensation.

"You are definitely going to kill me," I panted.

He shook his head, kneading my skin. "I merely want to make you mine."

"I'm already yours, Connor."

"Good." He released my legs and leaned over me. I threaded my hands through his hair and pulled him down for a kiss. He tasted like me, like sin and desire. He kissed me back before moving his mouth along my jaw toward my neck. He liked to kiss me there, like he could taste my pulse, like he needed to be close to the beat of my heart.

Charged with another wave of growing pleasure, I needed more. Pressing my hands to Connor's hard chest and pushing off the bed with my legs, I rolled us over. He let me, not putting up a fight. Instead, his dark gaze flashed with power as he reached up to wrap his large hands around my waist. He leaned up and took one of my nipples into his mouth and a sense of déjà vu washed over me. I'd imagined us like this plenty of times.

"Yes, like that," I moaned and rocked against him.

He gripped my waist and lifted me from his body before spearing me on his large shaft. Pleasure swept through my body.

"Fucking ride me, Lark," he said, voice rasping along my sensitive skin.

Arching into the sensation, I drop my head back and moved while Connor continued to tease my breasts with his tongue and thrust his hips up to meet mine.

My heart beat a million times. The sensations overwhelmed me.

Pleasure and power built in my body as his magic sunk inside, wrapping itself around my own. I raked my nails down his chest. All I could do was hold on as I shattered in ecstasy, my back arching, my breasts jutting out and bouncing with each thrust, my body clamping around his. Connor broke me apart only to fuse me back together again with him as the glue.

"You're mine," he growled. He flipped me over and

withdrew long enough to roll me onto my stomach and pull my hips back so my ass was in the air. He gripped my hips again and slammed inside me, deeper this time. His magic flared. His movements became jerky. Connor roared my name and thrust one last time.

We stayed like that for a moment, silence descending over us as Connor pulsed inside me.

With a grunt, he wrapped his arms around my waist and rolled us onto our sides. Secure, safe, and warm, he held me to him, grounding me so I wouldn't somehow float off to the stars. His fingers caressed the sensitive skin of my stomach while my body quivered in the aftermath of our pleasure.

"Are we bonded now?" I whispered. "That certainly felt like something."

Connor chuckled behind me and planted a kiss on my neck. He continued to strum my skin with his fingers. "No. We don't need sex or ceremony to complete the bond, you just have to pull my magic into yours and accept it."

"Pretty sure I just took in a lot of stuff and accepted it."

Connor squeezed my hip with his hand. His chest rumbled against my back. "That's not quite the same thing. Accepting the bond can't be accidental, nor can it occur just from playing with my magic. You don't have to do it, though, Lark. I'm content taking you any way you're willing to give. There's no rush, either. No pressure or high stakes."

That was where he was wrong. There were high stakes. If I'd learned anything over these past few weeks, it was that the future wasn't guaranteed. I didn't want to miss another second of being with Connor.

I reached out with my magic and gripped his. He stilled behind me. Without saying another word, because words weren't needed in this moment, I drew his magic inside me. This time, I pulled it all the way in, right down to the well of power that lurked deep inside me. Connor trembled. His hand gripping my hip tightened.

I shoved his power into my magical well and slammed the door shut, locking it inside.

"Is that how it's—" I couldn't finish my question. Power exploded between us. Our magic flared, entwining together like the prettiest braid I'd ever seen. I'd thought Connor had shattered me before with intense orgasms, but those were nothing like this—like the joining of two intense powers. White filled my vision and blinded me as I splintered into a million pieces, only to be rebuilt all over again, but this time with Connor. There was no place where I ended and he began. We were now one, fused together at a metaphysical level.

Somehow, I regained my vision and feeling in my limbs. I still lay on my side, with Connor behind me. He still held me, but now an awareness of him stirred inside me.

"Lark..." Connor started. He must've been at a loss

for words though, because instead of finishing whatever he'd originally planned to say, he turned me around and his mouth crashed down on mine.

"Ugh, could you not," an unfamiliar male voice spoke. "This is really awkward."

I squeaked, and Connor flew back. We turned toward the bedroom door in unison, to find an unfamiliar drab dressed all in black standing at the end of the bed with a gun in his hand.

CHAPTER
THIRTY-FOUR

Before either of us could react, before I could reach out with my magic and pull the assassin's soul from his body, my brother stepped out of the shadows. Metal flashed as he struck with his dagger, hitting the vagus nerve, carotid artery and jugular with precision. The one stab wound alone was fatal—preventing autonomic functions like breathing, while also severing a large vein and a high-pressure artery. The assassin made a gurgling sound and lashed out, attempting to spin around and attack at the same time. Logan caught his arm and struck again, hitting the brachial artery, the blood vessel responsible for delivering blood to the arm.

Blood spurted out and the assassin crumpled to the ground with a grunt. His gun clattered to the floor.

I bolted from the bed, pulling the bedsheet with me, to stand over the twitching body.

"Please tell me you haven't been lurking in the corner all night." Connor walked over to join us, the moonlight from outside streaming into the room to illuminate the muscles of his chest. He apparently didn't give a fuck about walking around naked, not that he should. He was magnificent. But Connor wasn't even concerned about my brother wielding a knife so close to his junk.

"Of course not," Logan snapped. He squatted down to clean his dagger on the assassin's clothes. "I just got here."

We hadn't heard him enter Connor's home.

"Normally, I'd demand to know how you got into my house," Connor said. "But I'm assuming you used your abilities."

Logan shook his head and scowled at the assassin on the floor. "I didn't need to. This guy left the door open after he picked the lock. Apparently, you two were too distracted to notice."

Connor swore and something dark flashed across his expression. If I were a betting person, I'd lay down a wad of cash that he'd increase his home's security system after this.

The assassin stopped twitching on the ground by our feet. His open eyes stared at the ceiling unfocused. They'd start to cloud over in a couple of hours.

Connor reached over, snatched his boxer briefs from the floor and pulled them on. He turned his gaze to me, taking in what had to be impressive bedhead, and my sheet for an outfit. Heat flashed in his gaze and the corners of his lips quirked up. The bond between us tightened and I felt his...amusement.

I squinted at him, and he had the nerve to wink back.

Logan straightened and sheathed his weapons. He settled his serious gaze on me. "They're coming for you."

"Who?" I asked.

Connor stiffened.

"The vampires."

I stared at my twin brother as my mind reeled and tried to process the information. The vampires were coming for me? Because Gregor knew about my powers? "And they sent a drab assassin?"

"They couldn't risk sending a vampire, could they?" Connor asked.

Logan narrowed his eyes, but Connor was right. If Gregor knew I could control vampires, he wouldn't risk sending one that I could command.

I frowned at my brother. "How did you know about the assassin?"

"They sent one to the apartment, too," he said without emotion. His own assassin mask had wiped away his more amiable expressions.

Shock jolted my body. "What? How's Brandon? Where's Brandon?" Oh god. No. He better be okay.

"He's fine," Logan said, his expression softening for

a brief second. "I didn't kill the assassin sent to our apartment right away. I questioned him."

"Questioned?" I raised an eyebrow.

"Tortured." Logan shrugged as if he admitted to eating tacos without me. "As soon as I realized the vampires were behind the attack, I came here. I needed to know you were safe."

My phone vibrated on the side table. I exchanged a glance with Connor. He pressed his lips together and his gaze flashed. Not sure what was going on in his head, but I wouldn't be surprised to discover he planned to throw me in a locked padded vault until the danger passed.

That was so not going to happen.

The phone stopped making sounds, but the three of us remained frozen in our positions over the dead assassin.

The phone vibrated again.

I cursed and marched over to the bedside table. Gregor's name popped up on the display. "It's him."

I reached for the phone and accepted the call. Hitting the speaker phone button, I lay the device on top of the bed and stepped back, waiting for Gregor to speak.

"Ms. Morgan, how are you this evening?" Gregor asked.

Seriously?

"I can assume from my loss of connection with the

two men I sent your way, you are alive and well?" he continued.

At least he didn't pretend he hadn't sent assassins to kill me. "It will take more than two drabs to kill me, Gregor."

"Apparently," he said. "I'll remember that for the future. I didn't have high hopes on their success rate."

"Then why send them?" I asked, though I already knew the answer. He wanted to test me. He threw minimal effort into the attack and if it failed, he could better gauge my abilities and if it was successful, I'd no longer be an issue.

"I wanted to get your attention," Gregor said.

Apparently, he wasn't above spewing a little bullshit.

Connor snarled, his upper lip curling up to reveal his teeth.

"You really shouldn't have gone to all that trouble," I replied. "A simple call like this would've sufficed."

Logan moved closer to the bed, his expression still an impassive mask.

"But then how could I impress upon you the importance of meeting with me?" Gregor crooned into the phone as if discussing a lunch date, not the demise of his two assassins and attempted murder.

"You can't go," Logan hissed.

I reached forward and tapped the mute button before turning to my brother. "I fucking know that, but if I don't go, he'll keep sending assassins, and one day, he'll manage to either hurt me or someone I care for."

Logan snarled.

"I'm not saying I'll meet with him, but I should get as much information from him as possible right now so at least we have something to work with."

Logan's expression flattened again, and his gaze turned cold.

Connor watched our exchange, vibrating with anger. His eyes darkened as each second passed, his skin paled, adopting a grayish tone near his eyes.

I clenched my teeth and unmuted my call with the Master Vampire of Victoria. "Where would you like to meet?"

"Goldstream park, one hour after midnight."

Seriously? One hour after midnight? Could he not just say 1:00am? "Would it be too much to ask for assurances with regard to my safety and overall health?"

"It would."

"Then explain why the fuck I would willingly meet with you?"

"Oh, that's easy..." Gregor said. "I have Brandon."

CHAPTER THIRTY-FIVE

Mom drilled five essential rules to necromancy into my thick skull at a young age.

1. Never use your own blood
2. Never meet the Lord of the Veil
3. Never run into a barghest
4. Never reveal your lineage
5. Never take more than you need

I'd already made a mess of the first four, and frankly, I'd break number five, too, if it meant saving Brandon. I'll break all the fucking rules to save him. To save my family. And I wouldn't stop there.

I'd destroy the world to protect Brandon and Logan and their happiness. I glanced over at Connor who stood by my side, holding my hand. He caught me looking and squeezed it, offering a small smile before returning his focus to scan the area.

I'd have to amend my list, now.

Detective Connor Kang had worked his way into my life and into my heart. I'd destroy the world for him, too, and seeing how he already slaughtered my abductor and currently stood with me in a battle against the vampires, a battle that even if we survived might lead to outing him, I figured he probably felt the same.

"You're thinking too hard," Connor said, without looking over again.

"No, I'm not," I answered. "Merely reflecting. There is nothing difficult about my decisions or thoughts."

He lifted a dark brow and the corners of his lips quirked up. "You'll have to explain that to me after this is over."

He spoke with such certainty, and I appreciated his confidence. Not that I planned to fail—I planned to make Gregor and his goons pay for taking Brandon—but it was still reassuring to know Connor was with me, not just physically, but mentally and emotionally.

My heart raced as I surveyed the large clearing in the forest in front of me. Tall evergreen trees towered over us, their branches reaching toward the night sky as if trying to capture the moon.

A branch snapped in the distance, somewhere in the shadows of the trees surrounding the clearing. I pulled my magic toward me, coating Logan and Connor with my power like a shield.

Connor shivered, but Logan just scowled. He'd barely said a word since Gregor's announcement on the phone and it took everything I had to convince him not to go off on a one-man mission. I didn't doubt my twin's ability to assassinate drabs and glamies alike. He could easily slip in and out of the Master Vampire's compound, but he wouldn't get Brandon out alive. He couldn't take on the entire compound without risking his boyfriend's life. We had a better chance trying to use Gregor's arrogance against him.

Luckily, once Logan managed to shake the darkness shrouding his features, he agreed. We made a plan and now we had to hope it would be enough.

"You should surrender," Gregor said, stepping from the cloak of darkness. The edge of the forest was about a hundred feet away. The moonlight hit Gregor's face, illuminating his chiselled Italian features. He wore one of his expensive business suits and looked as though he'd just walked into an important board meeting instead of a rural clearing in the middle of a forest.

A number of vampires stepped out of the forest behind him, including his right-hand man Esmonde and his most trusted guards, Antonia and Pierre. There had to be at least twenty of them and more probably lurked in the shadows of the trees.

Estelle had joined the vampires as well, stepping

off to the side to lean against a tree and fold her arms over her chest. She wore tapered slacks, heels, and a white blouse with a ruffled collar that she'd tucked into her pants. Based on her outfit alone, she wouldn't be joining the fight if one broke out. And based on her pursed lips and cold expression, she wasn't happy to be here.

"Should I take it as a good sign none of them look ready to fight?" I whispered to Connor.

"No," he said. "Vampires will gladly slaughter anyone in any attire."

"Lovely."

Gregor continued moving forward with his retinue behind him. My magic brushed along them, drawn to their power and energy. They were all strong vampires. Would I be able to control them all?

We were severely outnumbered.

The last vampire to exit the forest dragged Brandon with him. Logan stiffened beside me, and I reached out with my free hand to grab his arm. He snarled and his body trembled under my hand.

"Stick to the plan. As soon as things turn to shit, you grab Brandon and get the fuck out," I said.

He squinted at his boyfriend, probably calculating how many people he had to kill to get to him. "It was a mistake coming here."

"The mistake would be you trying to infiltrate the Master Vampire of Victoria's stronghold to save Brandon," I said.

"I would just kill every single fucker in the building," he snarled.

Maybe he would do exactly that. Maybe he'd go during the day, use his unique form of magic to slip past all the locked doors, slaughter every human guard in the way, and get Brandon out. Despite my trust in Logan's abilities, though, I also found it unlikely Gregor would leave himself and his captured bait vulnerable to any attack, and Connor had agreed.

It didn't matter now, anyway. We were here.

Branches snapped and the presence of life pinged along my magical awareness. I straightened and scanned the clearing. Drabs stepped out of the forest. They wore jeans or jogging pants and simple T-shirts, and while their outfits all varied, each drab held a knife, the metal catching and reflecting the moonlight.

"As I said," Gregor's voice interrupted my thoughts. "You should surrender."

We were surrounded.

With people my magic couldn't control. Good thing I didn't need to control drabs to rip out their souls.

Realization hit me.

Gregor didn't know what I did to the men in the alley.

My gaze flicked to Pierre. He gave nothing away, but Gregor bringing a number of drabs to a glamy fight told me Pierre hadn't shared how I killed Stanley, if he told the master vampire about the incident in the alley with Denise at all.

A wolf's cry sounded in the distance. Another wolf answered its call.

I froze.

Did Gregor command the local wolf pack, too?

"I made a call. It's Jacobs. He didn't want to miss out on all the fun," Connor whispered, squeezing my hand. "We're not alone."

Relief swept through me, and I pooled my magic, coating the clearing. "Give us Brandon."

"Why would I do that?" Gregor asked.

"Did we not meet to broker some sort of deal?"

Gregor twisted his lips up in a nasty smile. "We met so I could exterminate you like the pest you are."

"Rude."

The wolf calls grew louder as the pack closed in on the clearing.

"You have a lot of friends," Gregor said, nodding at the trees. "It won't be enough. You'll be left all alone."

I shot a glance at Estelle. I'd told her once what my biggest fear was and although this truth was something Gregor could've easily figured out, his choice of words proved Estelle had violated my trust. I shouldn't have been surprised, and I wasn't. I never expected her to choose me over Gregor, but it still hurt.

Estelle grimaced and looked away.

"You'll be left alone," Gregor repeated. "And then you'll die alone."

"You seem to be under a misconception."

Gregor frowned. "What do you mean?"

"You think you've already won this fight."

"I have you surrounded by vampires and drabs."

"And that won't be nearly enough to save you."

Gregor snarled and barked out a command at the drabs. The men ran toward us. I reached out with my magic, curled it around their weak souls and ripped. The first wave of humans crumpled to the ground.

Gregor jerked back; his eyes widened. But after a blink of an eye and before I could pull my magic back to send it into the next wave or the nearest vampires, he spat another command and the vampires were on the move.

They came from all directions, and fast. I couldn't focus on them to wrap my magic around their minds.

The werewolves crashed through the forest, flanking the vampires, and slamming into the first wave.

Logan had already slipped away, dematerializing into a wisp of a spirit to flit through the battle. I pulled my magic toward me and slammed it into the nearest vampire. He staggered and his gaze snapped to me.

"Protect me," I commanded.

He snapped straight and spun around, slamming his knife into another vampire. Before he could do anymore damage, one of his own cut him down. My magic snapped back and slapped my brain.

I grunted and stepped back. My hand flew to my forehead as my mind reeled.

More vampires crept past the battle between their comrades and the wolves. My magic curled out, and I braced for the attack.

Logan rematerialized behind Gregor's group and cut down the vampire guarding his boyfriend. Brandon sagged, falling to the ground. Logan caught him and flung his arm around his shoulder to hoist him back to his feet. His gaze cut to the forest, but he hesitated.

Logan's gaze found mine across the battlefield, the cries and bloodshed.

"Go," I whispered, knowing he'd feel my words more than he'd hear them. "We're here for him."

Another vampire reached me. I slammed my power into him and wrapped it around his soul, just as I had for the other guy.

"Protect me," I ordered.

The vampire whirled around and crouched, but before he or I could react, another vampire lunged toward me, fangs flashing in the moonlight.

A large dark shape slammed into the vampire, throwing him off course. In barghest form, Connor clamped his mouth on the vampire's neck and shook, flinging the vampire's body across the clearing.

A number of vampires stopped in their tracks.

"What the fuck is that?" one of them hissed.

Connor rose his snout to the sky and growled, a

deep vibrating sound that shook the ground beneath my feet. The werewolves joined him.

And the battle resumed.

I reached out to any vampire that got close and took control, but they stopped approaching. More drabs flooded the clearing, their knives flashing and their shouts drowning out the snarls.

Logan pulled Brandon away from the massacre and toward the woods. He couldn't change into his spirit form. He would never leave Brandon.

Esmonde exchanged a look with Gregor and turned away from the fight to go after my brother and his boyfriend.

"No!" I started running. I didn't think about the knife-wielding drabs, or blood-thirsty vampires. I didn't think about what I ran toward. I took a deep breath and continued to charge through the heated battle. My power surged in my veins, the air thick with the scent of blood and the power of death. The werewolves and vampires snarled around me, pitted against one another.

My brother and Brandon were somewhere on the other side of the chaos and I had to get to them.

A vampire stood in my way, crouching low, ready to attack. Connor barrelled into him, clamping onto his skin with his strong jaws, his teeth piercing flesh and bone. He tore the vampire apart, barely breaking stride. His blood-matted black fur absorbed the silvery bands of moonlight as he raced along beside me, taking down any vampire or drab who dared to cross my path. He snatched another vampire by the neck and with a powerful shake of his head, he snapped the creature's spine before letting it fall to the ground, lifeless. Blood splattered the side of my face, my arms, and my legs.

Connor showed no mercy.

I sprinted forward, my lungs caught in my throat. With Connor running alongside me, we leapt over fallen bodies and dodged attacks,

The werewolves were strong, but the vampires were just as skilled and had the advantage of speed. I raised my hands and drew more power to me, sucking it from the vampires to slow them down.

Finally, a break in the throng allowed me to catch sight of Brandon and Logan.

And Esmonde.

He was right there.

I wouldn't make it.

I was going to be too late.

Panic drove through my chest like a dagger made of ice.

No.

No I wouldn't, couldn't, let anything happen to them.

My heartbeat pounding in my ears with each thud of my feet striking the ground.

I sent my magic spiraling forward, past Gregor and struck Esmonde. He grunted but kept moving toward Logan. It wasn't enough. I clawed at his powerful mental defences, scratching the wall he put up, screaming my rage.

He was too powerful.

I drew more and more power. Something wet and warm slid down my face as I closed the distance. I reached deep inside me, tapped the bottom of the well of my power and unleashed everything I had. Esmonde snarled.

But his mental block remained.

I slowed, my energy waning as the last dregs of power trickled out. "Logan, watch out."

I was tapped. I'd drained all my power and I had nothing left. Weakness threatened to buckle my legs and I staggered to the side. My vision wavered. I became light-headed.

My brother glanced over his shoulder and threw Brandon to the ground to meet Esmonde's attack.

But the vampire didn't strike at my twin.

He went for Brandon.

"No!" I screeched.

Silky smooth, alluring power brushed along my awareness. Familiar, tantalizing, Connor's. He offered me his power. Without hesitation, I grabbed his magic and struck. Forming a spear of power, I drove the remaining droplets of my magic with Connor's and rammed it into Esmonde. His wall shattered. Seconds from striking, he buckled over Brandon.

Stillness settled over the clearing. Time slowed. I saw everything so clearly. Logan was already moving toward the vampire, but if I hadn't struck, he would've been too late to save Brandon. Connor had a vampire in his mouth and shook him side to side, shredding his skin before ripping his limbs from his body. The werewolves were having a field day behind me, ripping apart inexperienced vampires and drabs alike. Estelle had remained to the side of the clearing, but she'd dropped her casual pose and had her back pressed to the tree. She wore a horrified expression.

And Gregor stood mere feet away from me with an expressionless mask. He clutched a dagger and moved toward me.

I had a chance to defend myself.

Connor growled a thunderous warning, but he was too far away.

Instead of defending myself, I gripped Esmonde's soul and wrenched it from his body with the last of my magic.

The vampire crumpled to the grass without a sound, no longer a threat to Brandon. He was worth more than my life. I took a deep breath and turned to meet my fate at the end of Gregor's dagger.

Connor cried out, a deafening howl puncturing the night and drowning out the clash of the battle behind me. My heart wept for what could have been, for the loss of something just started.

But Gregor's strike never landed.

The master vampire grunted, his eyes widening. In

slow motion, we both looked down at the top of the knife protruding from his chest.

Gregor staggered to the side. He dropped the knife and looked up at me. "I should've killed you when I had the chance."

"You should've left me alone," I said. "I was never a threat to you until you took Brandon."

He coughed, blood coating his lips, and fell to the ground. Standing behind him, with an impassive face, was Pierre.

I didn't know what to say to him, so instead, I looked down at my feet where Gregor lay. He looked up at the night sky briefly before turning his head toward the treeline. "*Chouchou.*"

Estelle screamed and ran forward, into the fray. She didn't make it to his side in time, she never had a chance to say goodbye to Gregor. His gaze had already drifted off and his body stilled.

The Master Vampire of Victoria was dead.

CHAPTER THIRTY-SIX

As soon as Gregor's soul left his body, the fighting stopped. The vampires sensed the broken bond with their master and the command to fight slipped away. With Estelle sobbing over Gregor's body, I stepped to the side and turned to face the clearing.

So much blood.

Death curled around me, and although I'd tapped my reserves, I felt my magic building back up inside me. I hadn't lost it, merely depleted it to the point I'd left myself vulnerable to die at the hands of the master vampire.

Connor stalked toward me, naked and covered in blood spatter. He must've changed back to his human form at some point, but he kept the feral expression. He didn't slow down when he reached me. Instead, his hand grabbed the front of my shirt, and he hauled me into the heat of his body while his mouth crashed down on mine. I held onto him, kissing him back and searing my name on his soul as the bond wrapped around us.

Someone cleared their throat. I slowly drew away from Connor, already missing the warmth his presence provided. Turning in his arms, I surveyed the aftermath of the supernatural battle.

A few werewolves lay limp on the ground, but their chests continued to move. I hoped for their sake, the rumours about werewolf healing were true.

The vampires had suffered catastrophic losses.

And the drabs...

I felt sorry for them. They'd either been magically coerced through blood bonds or misled. Maybe they were even promised to be turned if they fought well. It didn't matter what was said to them in the end because they were all dead. And no one was crying over their bodies.

"Vampires of Victoria," Pierre called out. "You serve a new master now, and I command you to return home. Clean up. Tend to your wounds. We will meet tomorrow night."

I gaped at Pierre. "You killed Gregor."

He nodded, keeping his gaze focused on the vampires as he tracked their movement from the clearing.

"To become the master vampire."

He shook his head. "For you."

"Wh...why?"

Pierre stepped in close, the breeze teasing the ends of his hair. "Because we both know he was never my real master."

I froze. Ice shimmied down my spine. I opened my mouth, then shut it again. "I wasn't controlling you."

"I know."

"Then why?" Connor snarled. His arms tightened around me in anticipation of the vampire's answer.

Pierre didn't answer him right away. His gaze scanned the clearing and surveyed the losses. The surviving vampires had all left the clearing by now, leaving only the werewolves, Estelle, Brandon, Logan, Connor, myself, and a whole lot of dead bodies.

My brother held Brandon to him as he sobbed. His whole body shaking. If I could resurrect Gregor—which I didn't think was possible—I would, just to kill him again, more slowly this time, to make him pay for the pain and trauma he put Brandon through.

Pierre finally turned his hazel honey gaze to me. "I will always protect you."

Connor growled.

"Relax, big boy. I know she's yours. I can see the strength of the bond between you."

Estelle chose that moment to stagger to her feet, distracting Connor from whatever snappy response he'd planned to say. We all turned to her.

What would she say? What would she do?

Part of me expected her to come running at me with a knife.

Instead, she stopped a few feet away and wiped at the tears streaming down her face. "We will never be friends again," Estelle said. "But maybe one day, I'll no longer think of you as an enemy."

Not likely. I saw the pain in her gaze and knew she'd never forgive me, even though I'd acted in self-defence, and all of this could've been avoided if Gregor hadn't sought to destroy me or use Brandon to do it.

Pierre turned to the former human servant. "If you need someone to blame, Estelle, it should be Gregor. He brought this on himself. If you're too deep in your grief to see that, then place the blame on me."

Estelle stiffened, and her expression closed off. She slowly turned to face Pierre. "What now?"

"You will always have a place in our home, should you wish it."

"I wish to be free," she said.

"Then I release you from your ties," Pierre said without hesitation. "Go free, and know we wish you well."

She jerked her head up and down before turning to leave. She hesitated by Gregor's body, stopping briefly to look down at his already decomposing corpse. "*Je serai la tienne pour tojours.*"

I will be yours forever.

My chest constricted. If it was a choice between me and Gregor living, I was always going to choose me. And if it was a choice between my family and Gregor, there was no choice to even contemplate. Yet, I hadn't hated Gregor until he took Brandon. The master vampire had healed Mom's blood disease and exponentially improved her quality of life. He'd also warned me of Mom's looming death, giving me time to rush to her apartment to say goodbye. And Estelle had loved him. This was such an unnecessary loss of life, and though I now despised Gregor for abducting and hurting Brandon and causing this shit show of a battle, my heart still ached for Estelle, her loss, and for what could have been if Gregor hadn't reached for more control.

I knew in my heart I'd never see Estelle again, and that even if she stayed, I'd lost her friendship. But she'd remained loyal to Gregor to the end.

That must be why she stopped returning my texts and calls. She knew what Gregor planned and kept quiet.

I'd lost her friendship long ago. If we were even friends to begin with.

And that hurt. I didn't have a lot of friends.

I glanced at Logan and Brandon and the pain in my heart eased.

Fuck that, I didn't need any more than what I had, because what I had was fucking awesome. I pulled free from Connor's arms to run over to the boys. They must've heard the very unladylike grunting and uncoordinated running because they both looked up at my approach. Without a word, they opened their arms so I could fly right into them for a three-way hug.

"You scared the shit out of me," I whispered, squeezing them. "You both fucking did."

Brandon dropped his head to the side so his forehead pressed into my temple. "I'm not going anywhere, Sparky."

"You better fucking not," Logan growled. "I didn't spend all that fucking money on an engagement ring just to have you get offed by bloodsuckers."

Brandon pulled back, eyes wide and full of unshed tears. "Re...really?"

"Of course, really." Logan sounded so mad when he had to talk about his feelings.

I stepped back with a big smile. Logan had never discussed his plans to propose to Brandon. He didn't need to. I already knew this man was the end game for my brother. And honestly, standing in a random clearing, in the middle of the forest, on the edge of a battlefield on blood-soaked soil...it just screamed Logan's proposal aesthetic.

I would do everything I could to ensure he had no part in the actual wedding planning.

"Will you marry me?" Logan asked, his voice dropping lower.

"Of course," Brandon said.

As much as I loved my brother and my soon to be brother-in-law, I had no wish to watch them tongue tussle three inches from my face. I pulled free from the embrace and turned to find Connor waiting for me, still naked and covered with blood. Pierre had left, slipping away without a goodbye at some point during my three-way hug. In his place beside Connor, another familiar person waited.

Jacobs.

And he was also naked and covered in blood.

I quickly averted my eyes and held my hand out as if it would somehow censor the image of his junk. "Is any of that blood yours, Jacobs?"

"Nope." He grinned and his gaze sparkled with amusement. "Didn't strike you for the shy type."

Heat flooded my face. "I'm not shy, but I also don't make a habit of walking around naked."

Connor coughed. It sounded distinctly like he was trying to cover a laugh.

I narrowed my eyes at him before turning my attention back to Jacobs. To Jacobs' face. "At least not in public," I amended.

Connor and Jacobs laughed, and suddenly it was as though we were all clothed and chatting by the edge of a crime scene like usual.

"Thank you for coming," I said.

"Of course." The humour faded from Jacobs' expression. He jerked his thumb in Connor's direction. "This one might not be a werewolf, but he's come to my aid countless of times. He's my brother. He's pack. And you're his mate."

I started to object but shut my mouth. Really, at this point I'd merely be arguing semantics.

"You're his mate," Jacobs repeated, his eyes narrowing. "And whether you like it or not, Morgan, you're part of the pack, now, too. We never leave anyone behind."

My eyes tingled, but I refused to cry. "We should probably have a barbeque then, so I can meet everyone."

"Probably," Jacobs said. "I'd like that."

I glanced at the trees surrounding the clearing, still expecting more vampires and drabs to launch themselves from the shadows at any point. "Will this make things difficult between the pack and the vampires?"

Jacobs shook his head. "No. In fact, it might make things better. The new master vampire seems much more agreeable. And from what I hear, he has a soft spot for you and anyone you consider your friend."

Connor growled.

Jacobs glanced at his partner and smirked. "It's not like that, bro."

"It better fucking not be," he said.

"What happens now?" I asked, trying to change the subject.

They frowned at me in unison. Their synchronized expressions were almost comical.

I waved at the dead bodies and then pointed at us. "Technically, we're all a bunch of murderers."

"What happens now?" Jacobs stepped forward.

"You're going to let Kang take you home and let me and the werewolves handle this. The vampires have also promised to assist with disposal."

"Oh." I straightened. I liked the sound of that.

Connor held his hand out. "Let's go home."

EPILOGUE

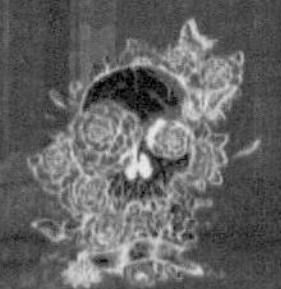

The air in the room hung heavy with magic. Powerful wards and enchantments marked every surface. A loud buzzer sounded and a door at the end of the room on the other side of the glass from me opened. Prisoners wearing gray jumpsuits shuffled into the small space of the new glamy correctional facility. A petite woman with brown hair approached the seat across from me and hesitated. Cathy looked over her shoulder at the guard, and he shrugged.

She could walk away and return to her mundane life in a glamy jail, or she could entertain this meeting and have a little change in the monotony of her life. Technically a drab, Cathy would've been housed in one of Victoria's other facilities, but due to the supernatural aspect of her murders and affinity for using spells, she was placed in this maximum-security prison with some of British Columbia's most dangerous glamies.

Thick, bulletproof glass separated the inmates from visitors like me. Intricate sigils etched into the glass shimmered under the fluorescent lights, but otherwise, nothing about this space indicated the jail was made for glamies.

The other inmates who'd walked in with Cathy had already taken their seats. They all looked so normal and drab until I saw their eyes. Danger and malice danced in their gazes. One of the women scowled at me, flashing her teeth.

I smiled in response and lifted my hand to give her a little finger wave. I was a badass necromancer who could rip her soul from her body. I might not be infallible, but I wasn't a pushover either.

Cathy sat down and picked up the receiver. "H-hello."

She killed Mom and destroyed the souls of two women and the supposed love of her life, yet she still greeted me with timid uncertainty. I wanted to rake my talons down her face.

"How did you know about the barghest bones?" I asked, not bothering with pleasantries. I didn't owe this bitch any.

Cathy hesitated, her gaze cutting to the people on each side of her. "Anyone with an internet connection and enough persistence to wade through the crap on the internet can find what they need." She paused, a frown tugging at her lips. "But that's not what you came here to ask."

"I need to know why," I said. I shouldn't have to elaborate. She killed Mom when we barely knew each other and had only interacted at a client-necromancer level.

Cathy pursed her thin lips together and looked over her shoulder again.

Maybe I should've let Connor kill her. Hell, Logan might still find a way to get to her.

"I already told you why," Cathy finally said.

"You rambled off a lot of nonsense on the phone, but I didn't realize you'd go after my mom. What the fuck did I do to you to deserve that?"

"You helped the cops."

"Of course, I helped the cops. You're a murdering psycho. Did you think about going after the cops, too? Or the crime scene technicians? Why did you single me out? Why my mom? Why her? She'd done nothing to you." I choked on the last words. I'd gone to a therapy session already, but it did little to help the gaping hole in my chest that spasmed each time I thought of Mom.

"If you hadn't told Mason I killed Lily, none of this would've happened," she spat.

I opened my mouth and then shut it again, my mind reeling. "What are you talking about? We didn't realize you were behind things until after you killed Mason."

Cathy narrowed her eyes. "You can stop lying. That vampire told me everything."

A shiver ran down my body as if someone dumped a massive bucket of ice water over me. Cathy didn't need to elaborate or specify which vampire. Hell, she didn't even need to explain why the vampire did what he did, though I doubted Cathy understood Gregor's motivations for lying.

I did.

Gregor had somehow figured out Cathy's connection to my police case—easy enough to accomplish if he had me followed. He took advantage of Cathy's unstable mind to set me up into accepting a lifetime of servitude to save my mother.

I knew he'd make some sort of play to indenture me. I never expected he'd go that far and Mom paid the price.

If Gregor wasn't already dead, I would kill him. Even now, I considered finding a way to resurrect a dead vampire from dust for the sole purpose of murdering him myself.

"The vampire lied," I whispered. Setting the record straight wouldn't change anything. I certainly wouldn't bring Mom back.

"I wanted a family, and you destroyed it."

"No, Cathy." I shook my head. "You destroyed it. You killed that poor woman, Lily, not once, but twice and had her soul destroyed the second time. You did the same to Maria. Then you killed the object of your affection, and you also tortured a barghest with your actions. There were so many opportunities down this road of murdering mayhem for you to stop, for you to veer off the path of destruction, but instead you kept going. You put your head down and decided to double down and push through like a bulldozer and now you're facing the consequences of your own actions."

Cathy leaned back in her chair and draped her free arm over her stomach. "What do you want? An apology?"

"No." I frowned. That was unreasonable. I didn't really have a reason for coming. Not really. Hunting Cathy down and having the police arrest her had been therapeutic in a way, but I still dreamed of ramming my elbow into her face, of shredding her weak human body with my talons.

I squeezed my eyes shut. I'd wanted confirmation that I'd made the right decision to let the Canadian legal system handle the punishment.

The lack of closure was telling.

"I made a mistake."

Cathy snorted and jerked out of her seat. She probably thought I meant I'd made a mistake coming here to visit her. That wasn't it.

I'd made a mistake in sparing her life.

Numb, yet still so full of anger, I pushed away from the glass and stood. A shadowy outline of a spirit appeared in the corner of the room. Logan had snuck in with me after all, and now he waited for me to leave so he could finish what I couldn't start.

I nodded at him and walked away.

Part of me should feel guilty. Heck, a small part of me actually did, but the rest of me felt calm sweep away the numbness as I made my way past the security checks and out of the prison. With each step, the anger dissipated.

I stepped out into the damp early spring air and took a deep breath. Cleansing. I loved springtime on the island. The cherry blossoms would be out soon, and the birds were already flittering about, hailing the summer months to come. The winter had been mild, but I'd spent a majority of the time on leave, hibernating at Connor's place.

Our place.

I'd officially moved in last month, though I hadn't spent a night out of Connor's bed since he brought me home after the confrontation with Gregor. And if either of us had anything to say about it, I never would again. We hadn't discussed marriage and I doubt we would any time soon. We were bonded in a way so complete and consuming, a legal document really felt like a technicality at this point.

Besides, this spring was all about the boys.

After my leave from work ran dry, I'd returned part-time, slowly increasing my hours. Denise kept texting me funny gifs and I wasn't sure who was more excited for me to return to work full time next week, me or her. Though I was looking forward to carrying a challenging workload again, I was also a little nervous, too. And I'd certainly miss meeting Brandon on his lunch breaks to discuss wedding plans. He and my brother were planning a small wedding this spring.

No one ever appeared on my doorstep asking about Cooper or Stanley—the two men I'd killed in an alley to save Denise. Connor had dug a little into their history and they'd apparently belonged to a no-name anti-vampire vigilante group. Based on Stanley and Cooper's comments, and the group's known activity, they could've been responsible for my paternal grandfather's disappearance. We'd never know for sure. My concern was future interactions and the possible threat they posed to my safety, even though I no longer raised vampires for Gregor. Connor had shared the information with Pierre and the new master vampire had sent me a text to let me know the group would no longer pose a threat and that all evidence supported Denise's statement that she wasn't involved. I decided not to look into or think about that message too much.

In addition to assuring me of my relative safety from vigilante groups, Pierre had also reached out to check in with me. Apparently, I wasn't so subtle in my dislike of the prejudiced hiring policies of policing agencies, and he had decided to take it up as one of his new projects. Maybe I'd see change before I retired. But it was nice to know the vampires were on my side. So far, I'd experienced no retaliation for my involvement in Gregor's death and Pierre assured me I never would. He also confirmed that whatever Levi told Gregor about the vampires from the Book of the Dead, died with Gregor that night. The master vampire hadn't trusted anyone inside his inner circle with the information.

As for the werewolves, they had only suffered minor losses in the fight, and after they healed from their wounds, they'd brokered peace with the vampires. My family was fine, Denise was fine, the werewolves were fine, and the vampires were fine. No one had heard from Estelle, but rumour had it, she'd returned to France. I realized she may have been a friend, or friendly, but her loyalty had always been to Gregor, and I understood that. I didn't fault her for her pain and loss. I hoped she found peace wherever she ended up.

I took another deep breath and turned toward the man waiting by the car.

Connor smiled at me and opened the passenger door. "About fucking time, Morgan."

Lark Morgan's
Rules to Necromancy

1. ~~Never use your own blood~~

2. Never meet the Lord of the Veil

3. Never run into a barghest

4. Never reveal your lineage

5. Never take more than you need

CHARACTERS

Alice Zheng: Lily's Mother

Bernice "Bernie" Olsen: Maggie's previous owner

Brandon Callahan: Logan's boyfriend

Connor Kang: Detective with the Victoria Police Department

Cooper: One of two men associated with Denise

Denise Ray: Lark's friend, co-worker, and fellow necromancer

Estelle Beaumont: French. Gregor's human servant

Felix Colburn: James Miller's attorney

Frances Sharrock: Connor Kang's maternal grandmother

Gregor Fissore: Italian. Master vampire of Victoria

Harper Morgan: Lark and Logan's mom

Hudson Harrison: Client

James Miller: Mason's father

Jane Kang: Connor Kang's sister

Officer Rodriguez: VicPD officer

Oliver Jacobs: Detective with the Victoria Police Department

Leviathan: Lord of the Veil

Lily Zheng: Murder victim. Chinese name: Zheng Mei Hua

Logan Morgan: Assassin, Lark's twin brother

Lark Morgan: Necromancer

Maggie: So much more than just a cat

Maria Espinoza: Mason Miller's fiancée

Mason Miller: Lily's boyfriend

Pierre Deveau: First baby vampire Lark rose for Gregor

Rebecca Miller: Mason's mother

Rose Harrison: Deceased. Witch. Previously possessed the
Book of the Dead

Spiral: Popular club downtown

Stanley: One of two men associated with Denise

Steve: Barista...and an awful human being

Tony Zheng: Lily's father

ACKNOWLEDGMENTS

There are so many people to thank for the creation of a book, and I always worry that I'll forget to mention someone. To anyone who's ever picked up any of my books and divested your time to immerse yourself in the world(s) I've created...thank you.

I'd like to thank my friend Megan for checking my French and offering suggestions to ensure I wasn't butchering the language. Luckily, you don't have to hear me pronounce any of the phrases found in this trilogy (your welcome).

Thank you Nicole, Wendy and Karen for beta reading. Your feedback is invaluable and I can't thank you enough for offering all the critiques that made this book stronger.

I'd like to thank my ARC team who are just as (if not more) excited for my books to release as I am, and spend their valuable time with my stories.

Also a big thank you to Lara Parker for editing, Book Nook Nuts for proof reading, Tricia Beninato for the gorgeous cover and Kalynne_Art for the stunning character art.

And to my friends, family and readers who continue to support me and offer words of encouragement, thank you.

Barghest Mating Guide

Warning:
Do not try to apply Mendelian genetics or any other pattern of inheritance to this.
Magic makes anything possible.

B = Barghest
D = Drab
N = Necromancer
R = Reaper

Male B + female B = B babies

Male B + female N = N & R babies

Male N + female B = B babies

Male N + female N = N & D babies

Male N + female D = N & D babies

Male B + female D = no babies

Male D + female B = B babies

Male D + female N = N & D babies

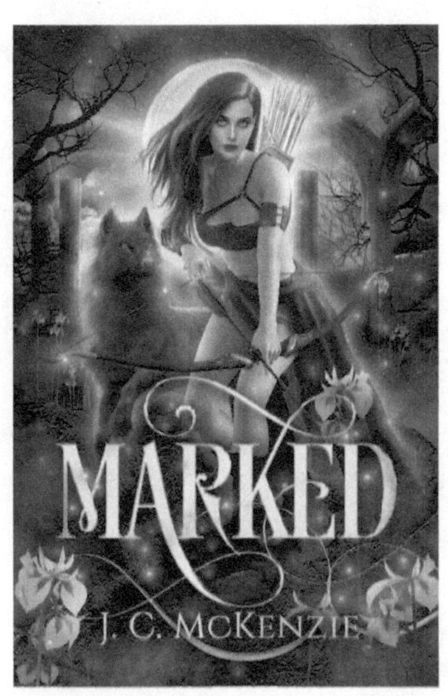

I might be marked, but I'm not dead yet...

As the last guardian of forbidden woodland creatures, I thought my biggest challenge in life was protecting mystical animals from greedy poachers. And it was...until I got saddled with the most arrogant recruit.

Ace isn't just arrogant, though. He's talented and beautiful and just happens to be the man I loved once upon a time.

Honestly, that's bad enough.

But then a well-known immortal turns up dead, killed with the same poison used on my loyal familiar, and I have to work with the man I despise to prove I'm not part of a heinous plot to overthrow our immortal leaders. As events chaotically unfold, a number of things become abundantly clear--a merciless killer is on the loose, Ace isn't who or what he claims to be, and I've been marked.

Don't miss this addictive dystopian contemporary fantasy with fae and fighting by international bestselling author, J. C. McKenzie.

Purchase book today!

http://www.books2read.com/cotiMARKED

About the Author

J. C. McKenzie is a book loving, gumboot-wearing, unapologetic science geek. She predominantly writes urban fantasy and post-apocalyptic dystopian fantasy with strong romantic elements. When she's not spinning tales, she's in the classroom sharing her passion for science and mathematics while secretly warping the young, impressionable minds of our future to carry out her evil plans for world domination. She lives in the Pacific Northwest with her family.

Visit her at jcmckenzie.ca

facebook.com/j.c.mckenzie.author

x.com/JC_McKenzie

instagram.com/j.c.mckenzie

tiktok.com/@jcmckenzie6

bookbub.com/authors/j-c-mckenzie

www.ingramcontent.com/pod-product-compliance
Lightning Source LLC
Chambersburg PA
CBHW020529020726
47494CB00006B/1687

* 9 7 8 1 9 9 0 1 4 3 2 8 1 *